Reign of the Dead

Reign of the Dead

Len Barnhart

iUniverse Star
New York   Lincoln   Shanghai

Reign of the Dead
Visit the website at: http://www.reignofthedead.com
Email: staff@reignofthedead.com

iUniverse Star
an iUniverse, Inc. imprint

For information address:
iUniverse, Inc.
2021 Pine Lake Road, Suite 100
Lincoln, NE 68512
www.iuniverse.com

If you liked this book you will also like its sequel:
Apocalypse End: Reign of the Dead
Coming Spring of 2005 *Reign of the Dead: Outbreak*

ISBN: 0-595-29721-8

Printed in the United States of America

CONTENTS

Acknowledgements

A very special thanks goes to Carol who gave me inspiration and believed in my ability to complete a novel. Without her I would not have attempted such an undertaking. I am better with you than I could ever be without you. You complete me. You are my greatest love and my soulmate.

LEN BARNHART

REIGN of the DEAD

PREFACE

I was very young when the great Death Plague nearly extinguished humans from the earth, but I remember those times with much clarity and distress. I remember the horror and grief, the sickness of heart, and the sorrow, especially the fear. The fear I felt and the fear others expressed through their actions or words.

I also remember the heroes, the ones who selflessly gave their lives so that others could survive. It is to them that I owe my life, and the lives of my sons and daughters, for they would not exist if I had perished. Their bravery will always be remembered. Not only by myself, but also by everyone whose lives they touched. For in the early days, we were without direction and they came to show the way.

This account is dedicated to those courageous few, to their long-lasting memory, so that they may never be forgotten.

PART ONE

GAIA'S REVENGE
THE AWAKENING

CHAPTER 1

The alarm clock broke the silence in the mountain cabin. Jim Workman fumbled in the pre-dawn darkness and found it on the stand next to the bed. He put an end to the unpleasant racket and then lit the kerosene lamp beside it.

It was five o'clock Sunday morning, the final day of his three-week stay. His sabbatical had gone by far too quickly but he had savored each day, a relaxing departure from his fast-paced other life. If he'd had his own way, the simple cabin nestled in the foothills of the beautiful Blue Ridge Mountains would be his permanent residence. But of course "real life" made that impossible, at least for the time being.

Jim was the owner of a large construction company; he had little time for anything except keeping the ever-growing enterprise pointed in the right direction. Each year he yearned for the simpler things, and each year his expanding endeavors demanded more of his precious time. Three weeks of seclusion this year was stretching the boundaries.

There was only one person in the world that knew where his retreat was, his secretary Rita, and she had strict orders to notify him only in an emergency. Even Sheila, his ex-wife didn't know exactly where the cabin was. She was part of the reason he needed this retreat and the last person he wanted to deal with while trying to clear his muddled thoughts, particularly since the divorce hearings had consumed nearly nine months of his life.

Jim dressed then went to the kitchen and lit another lamp. The small cabin didn't have the convenience of electrical power or running water but it was perfect for his yearly getaway. He was after all, what he liked to think of as self-reliant, able to take care of himself no matter what confronted him.

A fresh-water stream and fully stocked lake kept him fed. An abundance of wildlife flourished in the surrounding National Park. The four thousand acres of mountain wilderness was a buffer between him and those who would intrude upon his temporary heaven.

Jim stared at his reflection in the mirror on the kitchen wall. His hair was dirty and uncombed. There are some advantages to modern conveniences after all, he thought, scratching at the three-week growth of beard. Even so, his love of this kind of life was beginning to outweigh his drive to be successful.

Jim filled the basin with cold water from a galvanized pail and began cleaning himself up for the trip back to civilized humanity. With each swipe of the razor, more and more of the survivalist disappeared, exposing a handsome man of forty, the Jim Workman who was a survivalist in the so-called civilized world of business and commerce.

Jim carried two duffel bags out to his truck and tossed them in the back, then went to the task of rounding up his weapons. He'd brought only two with him on this vacation, a .44 magnum for personal defense, and a 30.06, his weapon of choice for deer hunting, though rifle season was still two months away. Convinced he had forgotten nothing, he blew out the lamps and left the cabin, ready to take on the world once more.

The sun was rising. It peeked over the deep purple mountains to the east in splinters of orange and yellow that sent spikes of light through the fluffy clouds and reflected back toward the ground like thin, white spotlights. Jim placed the .44 in the glove compartment and then watched until the ruler of the day topped the mountain and burned the layers of fog away from its uppermost peaks, into nothingness. The sounds of the mountain wilderness filled the woods with soft breezes and bird song. In the distance a large buck chewed at the sweet grass beneath his feet. They were old adversaries. Jim had hunted the same old boy for several seasons but had never been able to get a clean bead. Always a step ahead, the twelve-pointer would disappear into the thick underbrush before he could squeeze off a shot. Since then he had resigned to the fact that the deer had become part of the landscape, and earned his right of passage. The sight pleased his eyes.

Jim drove away, leaving behind his mountain man lifestyle. His retreat would be forgotten—wiped away for another year replaced with deadlines, bottom lines and the bottom dollar.

The town of Warren was a forty-minute drive from the cabin down a long and winding country road. The deep blue mountains, a testament to the history and grandeur of the Shenandoah Valley, faded further behind as he drove toward town. He would refuel there and get some much-needed coffee. His supply had dwindled to nothing two days ago. If there was one vice he had acquired from his busy life, it was an addiction to caffeine. After the fill-up he would drive back to Manassas and resume his busy lifestyle in the suburbs of Washington, D.C. All in all, it would be a two-hour drive.

Some music would make the trip a bit more bearable, but if he could find one of those happy-voiced morning guys it could lighten his mood. There was one in particular that made him laugh. It was Sunday though, and that guy would still be home in bed. Some music would be just fine, maybe some classic rock.

Jim scanned the dial as he drove, his finger pressing the presets from left to right searching his favorite stations. A light static filled the speakers on some. An irritating whistle sliced through the morning calm from others. Discouraged, he turned the radio off and continued down the road in silence.

Jim paused at a malfunctioning stoplight when he entered the town of Warren. Something was wrong. He took notice of the sprawling shopping center to his right. The sign warning truck drivers that overnight parking was prohibited was slightly askew. Storefront windows were dark, gapping holes lined with jagged broken glass. The tattered remnants of "The Biggest Sale of the Year" advertisement in one of the store windows fluttered in the morning breeze. Trash blew around the parking lot, small tornadoes of rubbish. The smell of rotted flesh tainted the morning air. It looked like a war had decimated the town.

Scores of people milled about the ravaged strip-mall. Some stood on the covered walk in front of the shattered windows, others walked aimlessly around the parking lot, their expressions trance-like.

When they began to take notice of Jim, his first thought was that they might be looters, like the ones he'd seen during the L.A. riots, except that these people didn't have that scurrying, roach-like fervor of looters. These people were different. There was no hurried rush to gather what they could steal and flee. They didn't even seem interested.

Tattered and bloody, they turned their blank stares on him and staggered in his direction with an almost concerted effort. They all looked as though they had been the victims of varying degrees of unspeakable violence. The faces of the three who were closest to his truck, a teenage boy and two older women, were a dead, bluish-gray. The boy's arm dangled grotesquely from his shoulder, as though attached by a thread of sinew. One of the women was missing an ear. Repulsed by the strange sight Jim instinctively pressed hard on the gas and sped away.

As he drove through town, he saw more of the same. Three weeks ago he had passed through on the way to his cabin and all had been normal. Had war broken out while he'd been communing with nature? Possibly, but an inner voice told him to keep moving.

Other than Jim's truck, there were no other moving vehicles, and from what he could see, no policemen to keep the strange looters at bay. If it had gotten so bad that the local authorities couldn't handle the situation, why wasn't the National Guard brought in to help? Some of those people were injured. Yet he knew not to stop to help. Their appearance was...unnatural. The Town of Warren reeked of death.

Jim reached over and pulled the .44 from the glove compartment and fumbled to strap the belt around his waist as he drove. He still needed to get fuel from somewhere; the tank was nearly empty. Like it or not, he would have to leave the safety of the truck.

It wasn't long before Jim spotted a service mart, one with gas pumps and a small convenience store. He drove in and came to a stop by the pumps. His hope of gassing up and getting away diminished when he saw the state of ruin. The large glass entry doors had been smashed and from his location at the pumps he saw that the store had been emptied of its contents.

Jim scanned the immediate area and cautiously stepped out of the truck. At this point his only option was to see if there was power to get the needed fuel.

He grabbed the nozzle from its resting place and inserted it into the tank. He flipped the lever several times to no avail. The power was off and the pumps were dead. Disappointed, he replaced the nozzle and guardedly approached the darkened store, glass crunching beneath his boots with each step.

Upon entering the wrecked store, it was obvious that he would have to look elsewhere for what he needed. The strange people he had encountered earlier were probably looters after all. The only items left were cleaning supplies and non-edibles. Food, cigarettes—anything of value—was gone.

The confusion of the moment made him feel unsure of his own sanity. His stabbing blue eyes stared blankly through the store's broken window as he fought for clarity. What should he do next?

He had noticed a pay phone on the wall outside.

Jim stepped through the smashed doors, careful not to cut himself on the jagged edges of protruding glass. The immediate area was still devoid of anyone but himself, and for the moment he felt safe as he dropped two quarters into the phone's coin slot.

The usual dial tone was replaced by a clicking noise that repeated several times before it fell silent. Jim placed the phone back on its cradle. When he did the coins were returned, and he tried again. This time a faint, rhythmic whine emitted from the earpiece accompanied by short bursts of electrical pink noise. Jim dropped the useless device and let it swing from the twisted steel cable.

As he turned to walk away, a cold hand gripped his shoulder like a steel claw. Jim spun around to see a man about his height, but that was where the similarity ended. A large hole the size of a tennis ball in his left cheek exposed yellowed teeth that snapped at him like a junkyard dog ready to bite. His dark blue shirt, ripped and covered in dried blood, had a label over the breast pocket that said BURKETT'S AUTO PARTS. His head was tilted at an awkward angle. The man groaned, as though his head was too heavy to hold erect. His eyes were covered with a milky film and he emanated the putrid odor of a dead carcass that had lain too long in the hot sun.

Jim's extensive military training and lightening reflexes served him now as he quickly got his arms between himself and the bloody apparition, pushing him away. The man stumbled back, regained his balance, and then lurched forward again. With all the strength he could muster, Jim threw an uppercut that landed under the stranger's chin. The force of the blow sent him flying backward. He hit the ground ten feet away, teeth still gnashing and grinding, though now his lower jaw was disturbingly out of alignment with the rest of his face.

New movement caught his attention and Jim spun to meet it. More people, as strange and grotesque as the parts-store clerk, approached from behind the store. There were two men and a woman. One man moved with his arms outstretched in front of him like the Frankenstein monster in the old movies. The woman's face was mangled beyond recognition. All three moaned as though in pain.

Jim stepped back and withdrew his gun from its holster. "Stop right there!" He yelled.

The rabble continued to advance toward him and the parts-store clerk got to his feet, joining the fray.

Jim wondered if he should shoot. The whole scene was beginning to give him a disoriented, surreal feeling. He was beginning to doubt the reality of the situation. He decided that discretion was indeed the better part of valor and made a dash for the truck, jumping in and locking the doors. He was reaching for the keys when he heard the sound of another vehicle. He looked over his shoulder in time to see a black pickup with metal bars on its windows race into the parking lot. It squealed to a halt and two men with rifles jumped out. Three of the repulsive figures were immediately dispatched with a bullet through the head. The parts clerk had advanced to Jim's truck and was banging bloody hands against the windshield.

Jim watched in stunned disbelief as the driver of the black truck, a blond mustachioed man about six feet tall, moved to the front of the truck, leaned over the hood, took aim and fired. Chunks of bone, hair, and gray matter sounded like rain as they splattered over the window of Jim's truck.

The shooter's partner, a tattooed, wiry-looking biker-type with a shaved head, took a rag from his pocket and wiped the blood from the window. "You okay?" he shouted, peering inside. He turned without waiting for a response and walked over to one of the bodies.

The other shooter straightened from his position over the hood. "You can get out now!" he called to Jim and then joined the bald man looking at the bodies.

Jim wondered whether he might be their next victim. It didn't seem likely that they would come to his aid only to shoot him afterward.

He got out of his truck and stepped over the slain clerk. With the .44 still in his hand, he walked over to the two men.

"Don't know him," the man with the shaved head said, looking at the corpse at his feet.

"Me neither," the blond said, sounding relieved.

Jim shook his head, trying to clear his thoughts. "What's happening here? What the hell is wrong with these people?"

"I'm Mick," the blond said, extending his hand politely. "This here's Chuck." he nodded toward the biker-type. "We're out on patrol, searching for survivors."

"Survivors? Survivors of what?" Jim reached out and shook Mick's hand. The small niceties of civility made the situation seem all the more surreal.

Jim was alarmed and wondered if this was all a bad dream. Perhaps he was still asleep in the cabin. He felt as though he had awakened in the middle of an episode of the Twilight Zone. Like the Twilighters, he was totally in the dark about what was going on. At least these guys seemed well acquainted with this strange New World he suddenly found himself in.

Chuck cocked his head at Jim. "Where the hell have you been, man? On a desert island or something?"

"In a manner of speaking. For the last three weeks, I've been on a mountain top, at my hunting cabin."

Chuck gave Jim a toothy grin as he walked to the black truck, returning his pistol to its holster as he went. "Well, shit. Don't that beat all? I'll bet you're just fuckin' trippin' out about now."

"You could say that," Jim said, looking back at the bodies littering the ground. Aside from being shot in the head, they all had various other injuries. One was missing the left arm from the elbow down. Through a tear in his pants just above the knee, Jim saw that a large chunk of flesh had been ripped out on the other man. The woman showed no other signs of injury except for her previously disfigured face, which had virtually disintegrated into a mass of putrid flesh and gray matter, with no resemblance to a face.

"Would one of you please explain what the hell is going on here?" Jim demanded.

"Not now! We gotta go!" Chuck said, pointing. Mick and Jim turned toward the shopping center Jim had passed earlier. Slowly making their way toward the three of them were at least one hundred of the same kind of people Mick and Chuck had just slain.

"What the hell is going on here?" Jim asked, horrified.

"No time now," Mick said. "I'll explain on the way. You come on with us. Your truck's not safe."

Jim stood frozen, eyes fixed on the approaching army.

"Let's go! Now!" Mick barked, grabbing Jim by the arm.

Jim snapped out of his stupor. The mob's moans and screams were like nothing he had heard before. Their eerie wail rose to a feverish pitch as they inched and stumbled their way closer.

The three men piled into the black truck. Mick started the engine and drove out of the parking lot toward the approaching army. He turned sharply at the intersection, just ahead of the mob, and drove north through town.

For the moment they were safe.

CHAPTER 2

Amanda awoke with a blood-curdling scream, gasping for air and shaking profusely. Another nightmare had jolted her from what little sleep she'd been able to get. Her life had become a nightmarish game of survival, worse than anything she could possibly imagine. She struggled for clear consciousness from her nocturnal terror, only to embrace the more terrible one, the one that was real.

She relaxed her grip on the hunting rifle that lay across her lap and leaned it against the wall. It was 7:45 in the morning. She'd gotten a whole hour of sleep, if it could be called sleep. What little sleep she'd been able to get was constantly interrupted by nightmares of her husband's death. She had come to fear sleep almost as much as the horror of the waking world.

Amanda and William had married three years before and their life had been a happy one for the most part. She was a reporter for a local newspaper and he owned his own surveying firm. They met at the local courthouse by chance one day when they were both searching county records. That life now seemed a far away and distant memory. She found it hard to remember William's face. The face in her dreams was the dead, yearning physiognomy he had now become, not the man she had loved.

The only way to visualize him now was to connect to a specific memory. Only then could she remember him as he had been in life. It was an increasingly difficult task in her deteriorating state of mind.

Amanda strained to see in the darkened room. Will had boarded over all the windows and doors before he died. She was safe for now, but food and water were running low.

Today was the day. She would have to get out now before it was too late. The heavy, plodding footsteps continued on the porch. All day, and even through the night, the sounds invaded Amanda's mind as the devils relentlessly pawed at the smallest crack and crevice in an attempt to gain entry.

They wouldn't go away as long as she was there. Of that she was sure, and more and more of them arrived each day. Before long she would be hopelessly outnumbered. She would die of starvation; or worse, at the hands of the evil-smelling monsters outside.

Amanda stood and stiffly walked to the kitchen. Several cans of vegetables were all that was left to sustain her. She held one in her hand and grimaced at the thought of another cold meal. But instead of eating its contents, she crammed it, and the others that remained, into an old backpack she'd found in the basement.

Amanda was thirty-one. She'd been beautiful before everything had fallen to pieces. Now her long black hair was a tangle of knots and her startling emerald eyes were bloodshot from lack of sleep. She hadn't had a real bath in some time and she felt she was teetering on the edge of a breakdown.

She wondered how everything had gotten out of hand so quickly but deep down, she knew the answer. She was as guilty as the rest of the poor fools. Most people were unable to destroy what they'd perceived to be family or friends. Then there were the authorities that attempted to rationalize the situation to the point of absurdity. Oh, there was plenty of blame to go around. In spite of the facts, people had reacted with emotion.

She had been beside Will when he died. She knew what to expect. Eventually the news reports were allowed to admit the truth, "*Anyone who's bitten by an infected person will positively die and return as one of them.*" Even though dead, the body would incredibly revive to kill.

There were many theories on what was happening. At first, television and radio stations reported varied waves of violence, cause unknown. The first such occurrences were limited to the eastern seaboard of the United States but had quickly spread to the rest of the country and then worldwide. It spread so fast people were unable, or unwilling, to believe what they were told; bodies of the recent dead were returning to life, attacking the living, and eating their victims.

"Eating their victims." That phrase stuck in Amanda's mind. It haunted her as she slept. What was happening couldn't possibly be true. That denial was one of the reasons things were as they were.

Will had been attacked by one of them. He'd been bitten a week ago, when they'd gone to town to pick up the needed supplies to tough it out for the week or two it would take for this bizarre epidemic to be brought under control. They hadn't realized how far things had gone.

The whole town was in a panic. A throng of people in the grocery store was unruly to the point of rioting. She urged Will to get the barest essentials and leave. They decided to go for canned goods that would sustain them if the power should fail.

As they rounded the corner of the canned goods isle, the scene before them was a total free-for-all. There was barely room to get by and people were pushing and shouting. "To hell with this!" Will had shouted, and pulled her away from the mob. "Let's get out of here. These people have lost control!"

Those words had barely escaped his lips when two women arguing over a large can of ravioli fell, screaming, scratching and pulling hair, against the shelves directly in front of them. This caused an ensuing turmoil of pushing, shoving, and the grabbing of anything and everything the unruly mob could get their hands on.

It was such a frenzied riot that no one noticed the ambling, shuffling vision of horror in their midst. No one, that is, except Will. The thing reached out for a four-year-old girl who was screaming in fright as her mother rolled on the floor, a death grip on a can of pasta. Will moved so fast that even Amanda didn't know what had happened until it was too late.

He leaped over the brawl at his feet and swept the screaming toddler out of harm's way like a cartoon super hero. The ghoul, lacking the discerning taste of the fighting women, was perfectly content to take a large chunk of Will's forearm in lieu of the other tender little morsel.

Will kept his head as he always did. He set the child down a safe distance away and then picked up the can the women had dropped and bashed the thing's head in.

His condition deteriorated rapidly. The hospitals were overrun with wounded and doctors were without a cure for the creature's infectious bites. It was believed that a strange new virus was responsible for the plague of flesh-eaters. Amanda didn't believe that. Perhaps it was a throwback to her Southern Baptist upbringing. Though not a religious person, she believed this was a curse from the bowels of hell. No mere virus could do this.

Will's wound was bandaged, antibiotics administered, and he was sent home without further treatment. In spite of the antibiotics, the infection spread. His fever rose to one hundred and six degrees and stayed there. The sickness eventually sent him into convulsions, hallucinations, and finally a coma. He was dead in less than three days.

Amanda was now faced with a terrible duty. He would surely revive as one of the undead, returning not as the husband who loved her, but as a soul-less, uncaring monster with only one goal, one need. Driven by some otherworldly instinct, he would attack and kill her without remorse.

She could've prevented the evil transformation by destroying the brain with a blow to the head, or with a bullet. She struggled with that dilemma for several minutes but in the end she couldn't bring herself to do it. She dragged his body to the front porch, where he eventually revived. He was there now, clawing, and scratching at the front door. His red hair hung in matted bangs over his glazed eyes as he moaned horrible wails through the door to her.

Others began arriving shortly after. There were at least eight or ten of them trying to get inside. She should have spared him this fate when she had the chance. Instead, she let him be damned, doomed him to live a tortured, cursed existence.

Thinking back on it, Amanda felt the overwhelming grief return. All her efforts to hold herself together dissolved into a rush of unshed tears. Her shoulders shook violently with repressed sobs and ended in hiccups as she finally surrendered to it.

She dropped to the kitchen floor and wrapped her arms tightly around herself in a brief respite of insanity. She rocked back and forth in her own embrace, wailing, "Damn you, Will! Damn you!" She screamed until she was hoarse. "I can't do this alone. I can't do this!"

She sobbed brokenly, her torrent of rage and grief pouring out for nearly twenty minutes. Finally, collapsing in complete exhaustion, she lay with her face against the cold linoleum, gasping jagged breaths like an infant who had finally cried itself out.

She slept without dreaming.

Amanda awoke with a start as her dead husband banged endlessly at the front door. The breakdown was cathartic; she awoke with a new resolve. Will was gone, that life was gone. Nothing survived of it. Nothing, that is except for her, and she was going to be damned if she'd let those things get her now.

Today *must* be the day. She had to leave before it was too late.

Amanda's backpack was filled with the necessary items needed for a short trip on foot. Unfortunately, that was how she would have to make her escape because Will still had the car keys in his pocket. She had forgotten about them when she dragged him onto the porch. It was an incredibly stupid thing to do but she had been uncharacteristically negligent the past week on more than one occasion. She had also made up her mind about something else; She would do Will the courtesy of ending his miserable existence when she left. She doubted she would get the keys even then. There were the other walking dead things to think about and she didn't have many shells for the gun. It was best to be ready.

Amanda put the backpack and rifle by the front door. Every door and window had been boarded up by Will before he got too sick to do so, every door, except the one in the front of the house. That was the one he endlessly banged and clawed at for entry. Somehow he knew it was the weakest part of her defense. Something subconscious still remained of his memory, though nothing of Will himself remained. But the creature that occupied his body knew.

If she was to get out, she needed to draw them away from that door. She had thought about leaving through one of the boarded-up windows a few days before but when she tried, several creatures heard the noise and crowded around before she got the first board off.

At least the ghouls were slow and awkward. If she could just get out of the house, she could outrun them.

An idea formed. Maybe she couldn't leave through the window but perhaps she could use it to draw them to that side of the house, away from the door. Then she could unlock the door and safely make her escape.

Amanda went to the kitchen and found Will's heavy carpenter's hammer he had used to board up the house. She forced the claws under the first board and pulled with all her might. The nail made a creaking noise but didn't budge. Will had done a good job of nailing them in tight.

She tried again, this time placing her foot against the wall for more leverage. The board broke free and caused her to stumble backward.

After several tries, a lot of sweat, and an undignified bruise on her right hip, she managed to get three of the boards off before the first creature ambled around the corner.

The window was waist high from the ground. This could be a very dangerous predicament if her plan failed. The creatures had an easy way to get to her.

"God help me," she prayed, knowing she had to work fast.

The first creature was a small chubby boy named Todd Ross. She had seen him many times before the plague, riding his bike in the neighborhood. Pity for him welled up inside her. He was never very popular with the other kids and now this was to be the poor child's fate.

The small pale-faced boy tried to reach her through the window but he was too short to effectively be a threat. Amanda leaned out and used one of the boards she had removed to push him to a safe distance. Three more creatures stumbled their way around the corner toward their mindless equivalent of lunch. One of them was the boy's equally chubby but now mutilated mother, Beth Ross. A large portion of her throat had been ripped away.

Amanda's fear and revulsion at the sight of her mutilated former neighbors caused a moment of sheer panic. She jerked backward and tried to pull herself back inside the window but her jacket caught on a nail. Three more appeared, bringing the total to seven who had spotted her. The first group was less than ten feet away.

Amanda struggled to free herself. As panic rose in her throat, it became difficult to draw breath. "God help me!" she cried as she thrashed and jerked against the window frame.

She yanked on her jacket and the fabric tore free. At that precise moment, there was a heavy cold thump on the back of her head that felt like a slab of raw meat had grabbed her hair. She had been watching the Rosses with such intensity she missed one of the ghouls coming from the opposite direction.

Amanda reeled backward into her dining room, her long black hair ripping painfully out of her scalp as she fell. She cried out in agony, shock, and fear.

The ghoul attempted to climb in through the small opening, Amanda's hair still clutched in its hand. The window wouldn't hold long, not with some of the boards missing.

Amanda jumped up and ran to the front door and peered through the peephole. Only Will remained but he was slowly moving to the side of the house with the others.

The ominous sound of boards splintering away from the window frame quickened Amanda's pulse. She turned and saw that the creature had broken through the window and was halfway into the room. It screamed out as it fought to enter completely. Amanda's adrenaline rushed as she hurriedly unlocked the door, grabbed the pack and gun, and ran outside.

She didn't stop until she had covered more than half the distance to the road at the end of the driveway. She turned then, dropped the back-pack, and raised the loaded gun. She took aim at Will, who had turned her way.

"Come on, damn it! A little closer," she whispered as she focused down the barrel. She put the sight on his forehead.

She dropped her aim for one last look. She needed to convince herself that this was not Will, that there was no part of him left.

Will's dead eyes stared blankly at her as he moaned pitifully. The sight assured her that there was nothing of him left in the walking specter. Will, or rather who Will used to be, was dead. This thing was not Will. It didn't really even look like him anymore. Like a dead body lying in a coffin rarely resembled their former living selves, the creature lacked Will's soul and what made him who he was.

"Do it! You have to do it," she told herself.

He was twenty feet away now. Amanda squeezed the trigger. The gun kicked surprisingly hard against her shoulder as the shot rang out.

Will's head snapped back. He paused for a second, then continued his march toward her, his groaning more urgent, his pace a little faster.

Amanda lowered the gun. The kick had caused her to graze the side of his head. She quickly took aim again. This time she would be ready for the kick. After careful aim, she pulled the trigger. "Click".

Her heart skipped a beat. She pulled the trigger again. Again there was the soft, metallic click of the hammer striking the empty chamber. Her heart felt as though it would pound its way out of her chest. Blood rushed in her ears.

Will was getting too close and now the others followed. She grabbed the backpack and took a few steps back, cursing herself for not remembering that she had to reload after each shot.

When she felt that she was far enough away, she dropped the pack and pulled back the bolt on the rifle. The spent cartridge popped out and she shoved another in the chamber. Again she took aim and pulled the trigger.

The shot fired and the butt slammed against her shoulder again.

This time Will dropped and remained motionless on the ground.

"I did it!" she cried softly. "Goddamn you, I did it!"

A tear slid down her cheek but she had already mourned Will. There was no time for regrets now; the others were getting too close. They were too close to get the keys from Will's pocket. She had to run.

Amanda turned toward the road and raced away. She would go to town. There was nowhere else to go.

CHAPTER 3

Mick drove through town dodging cars that had been abandoned along the way. Several burned-out buildings still smoldered. Everywhere Jim looked there were groups of the disfigured walking dead, some alone, others in large groups. Mick had explained the mind-boggling situation but the proof was there to see. Somehow mankind, in its infinite wisdom, had really screwed up this time.

A virus, Jim thought, that's what Mick had explained, was the most widely accepted theory. Mankind would now pay because a government—probably ours—had created the ultimate virus and then carelessly or perhaps not so carelessly, loosed it on the world. Our worst fears had finally been realized. It was common knowledge that world governments were inventing super bugs that could wipe out populations while leaving buildings and everything else intact but this was different. This, Jim thought, came straight from hell.

"Where are we going?" he asked Mick, looking out the window to the river below.

"To the last operational safe station in the county. Almost there," Mick said, "Just across this first bridge. The shelter is situated on a strip of land between the north and south fork of the river. There's only one-way in from either direction, and that's across a bridge. Easy to defend, at least until those things learn to swim."

Jim looked out the window at the bridge that spanned the north fork of the Shenandoah River. The bridge was old and showed signs of disintegration. Built in the 1940s and in dire need of replacement, town leaders had spent the better part of the last fifteen years arguing who should pick up the tab for repairs as both bridges continued to fall into a further state of neglect. A moot point now since the whole human race seemed to be in a state of serious disintegration. Man, striving to be the master of his own fate, continued to bring destruction upon himself.

"All of the other stations are gone, and the people who were in them…"

Jim looked past Chuck to Mick, who didn't finish what he was going to say, but Jim now knew the fate of those who came into contact with the walking dead. They were gone, too, their bodies still walking around, feeding on the living.

Mick turned into the parking lot of the rescue station. The building was a large concrete structure about two hundred feet wide and at least that deep. Two metal bay doors on the front right side contained a small window in each, about one foot by six inches with a small metal door to the left of them. Armed guards were posted at various positions around the building.

A guard stationed at the edge of the parking lot spoke into a walkie-talkie as the truck approached and came to a stop in front of the shelter. Jon Henry, the man in charge of security, stood by the smaller door. He was the only known surviving member of the Warren Police Department. Grossly overweight, his jowls flapped as he spoke into a hand-held radio.

The three men stepped out of the truck. Mick reached into the back and pulled out four cases the size of shoeboxes and put them on the hood. He waved Jon over.

Jon stuck the radio on his belt and huffed and puffed his way over to the truck.

"Told you I'd get them," Mick said, pulling the lid off one case and retrieving a pistol and silencer. "Give these to whoever is on duty and tell them to use them. I'm tired of having more of those things show up every time we have to fire off a shot."

Jon took the pistol from Mick and attached the silencer He took aim at a tree and fired off an imaginary shot. Through pursed lips, he made the sound of a gun with a silencer—"Poof."

"This should help," he said happily. "But you never know. The sons of bitches may have pretty good hearing."

Mick frowned at this remark and Jon put the pistol back in its case. He looked at Jim curiously. "Where'd ya get the newbie?"

"Hanging out at the Seven-Eleven," Chuck laughed. "You know that coffee is addictive. He was sitting in his truck, cornered by a few of our hungry friends."

"He'd been in the boonies for a few weeks. Didn't even know this shit was happening," Mick added

"You're a lucky mother fucker," Jon said gruffly, picking up the cases containing the guns. "Not many are surviving out there right now. Welcome to the Warren County Hilton. It's good to have you on our side."

Jim watched Jon walk to the nearest guard and give him his new weapon. Mick and Chuck gathered their guns and headed for the building.

"The lucky ones are probably already dead," Jim muttered, as he followed Mick and Chuck inside.

They entered the building through the small metal door. Inside, a large room was filled with people, some lying on blankets, others engaged in conversation. With no windows to give natural light, the room was dim with kerosene lamps.

The strong stench of sweat, kerosene fumes, and filth burned Jim's eyes and he had to fight the urge to cover his nose. Mick and Chuck appeared unfazed by the smell as they squeezed their way through the crowd to an office area, Jim in tow.

The office was a mess. Two-way radio equipment was piled high on an old desk with a scratched surface. A small television graced a table in the corner and a stained and filthy mattress lay on the floor. The television was on but only the station's test pattern was currently being broadcast. Two chairs were in front of the desk. Jim sat in one of them.

"What was this place used for before this happened?" Jim asked, looking around the room. Knowledge is a person's most valuable weapon in a bad situation. This was a bad situation and he was virtually clueless.

"At one time it was a furniture warehouse but a few years back they turned it into a nightclub," Mick answered. "It even has a usable kitchen, gas powered."

"You really think it's safe here?" Jim asked. "Wouldn't it be safer on a mountain top, some place more remote, away from those things?"

"There *is* nowhere away from those things," Mick said, frowning. "Don't ask me how, but they always manage to find you. This will be fine for now. As long as we stay alert, we'll be fine."

Jim nodded as he scanned the room. "You told me what happened, but you've still not told me how this got so far out of hand. It seems to me that the situation should've been contained easily by the authorities."

Mick chuckled softly as he rubbed the bridge of his nose. He felt another headache coming on, maybe if he rubbed his temples it would stop. "You'd think wouldn't you? In less than a week, Washington D.C was a war zone. Survival instincts went ballistic. No one worked together—there was no unity. I'm telling you I saw my neighbors—people I had known for years become savages. Infected-uninfected, it didn't matter panic consumed them all. As food became scarce the ones that had none found it worth killing for, the ones they killed came back to kill. By the second week, businesses were closed, rioting routine, and death was everywhere. We lost the battle ourselves, but the war's not over…not yet."

Mick opened a desk drawer and pulled out a walkie-talkie. Clicking it on, he pushed the button and called for Jon to come to the office.

"Ten-four," Jon's answered. "Be there in just a sec."

"I heard New York went down in the first week," Mick continued, "Those crazy sons of bitches didn't stand a chance. Washington D.C is faring a bit better, but I'm not holding out for anything good outta there either. We do still get television broadcasts from time to time."

Chuck leaned against the wall. "Just one thing I wanna know." He blurted. "When do we get to go out and shoot them dumb bastards in the head, take *our* town back and win this war?"

"When we're ready," Mick said matter-of-factly, cutting off the walkie-talkie and setting it on the desk. "If we go out there unprepared, we'll get our asses bitten off."

"Shit, Mickey," Chuck said, a cigarette he was about to light flapping as he spoke "There's more and more of them every day. It'd better be soon." Chuck lit his smoke and pocketed a gold lighter with an eagle on it.

Mick's eyes narrowed at Chuck, who was always in too big a hurry for his own good. Chuck was fearless or, perhaps more accurately, fool-hardy when confronting those creatures. One day it would surely be his undoing.

"You're right," Mick said. "There are more and more of those damned things every day and less of us, but we can't risk it just yet."

Jon clipped his walkie-talkie to his belt as he walked into the office. "What do you need?"

"Here," Mick said, pushing the pile of radio equipment on the desk toward him. "Put these in the two trucks we use to look for survivors so that no one gets stuck out there without being able to call for help. I don't want a repeat of the other day. We lost two good men because we didn't know they were in trouble."

Jon picked up a box of blankets from the floor, dumped them out, and scooped the gear into it. "I'll have them in by this evening," he said, walking out.

Jim stood. "I'll need some gas for my truck. Where can I find some so I can be on my way?" he asked.

"On your way where?" Mick asked, surprise raising his eyebrows.

"Back to Manassas. I've got to get home."

Mick walked around his desk and faced Jim "You got family there?"

Jim had no family in Virginia. His parents were dead, his brother David lived in Montana, and who knew where his ex-wife was from one day to the next? At least David would be fairly safe in Montana with its miles of open country.

"No, but I have to—"

"Bullshit, man!" Mick shouted. "Haven't you heard what we've been telling you? The city's a mess! All cities are a mess—a thousand times worse off than here. You'd never make it in alive. Roads are blocked with abandoned cars and a motorcycle is the last thing you'd want to ride in there."

Mick went back to his desk and sat down. Neither man said anything for a few seconds, both trying to come up with more points to support their views.

"Look," Mick said finally, "we need help here trying to get those son of a bitches under control. I could use you. Most of the men here are too afraid to go out there and kill them, or they don't wanna leave their families. You try to get into the city and you'll just add to the enemies' number. Haven't you heard a thing I've been telling you? You'll be just one more dead bastard whose brains someone will eventually have to blow out."

Maybe he was right, Jim thought. It was bad here, even in a small town. Manassas was probably crawling with the dead. He'd be of no help there. Not now.

"Okay," he said, "but I'll be damned if I'll sit around here like a rabbit in a trap and wait for those things to show up. I want to be involved."

"You got it!" Mick smiled and rose to open a closet door. Jim peered in at the firearms filling the closet.

"Take your pick," Mick grinned, waving his hand like a game show host displaying prizes.

Jim picked out an AK-47 and some ammunition. "This will do. And some ammo for the forty-four." Spotting some in the bottom corner, he took a box and shut the closet door.

Mick held out his hand. "Welcome aboard," he said. "And good luck. You'll need it."

"That I will, Mick. We all will."

CHAPTER 4

The morning air was heavy and unusually humid for October. Amanda wiped away a trickle of sweat dripping into her eyes. It's gonna be a scorcher, she thought, passing the houses in the abandoned subdivision where she lived.

Amanda stuck her hand in her pocket and pulled out the shells she had left. There were four, five counting the one in the chamber. It was best to save them for when really needed.

She put the shells back in her pocket and straightened the pack on her back. It was heavy and uncomfortable but she had to have food and water. Her body ached and it was a chore just to walk. Lack of sleep didn't help but she couldn't stop. Several creatures had already spotted her and were following somewhere behind. She had run until they were out of sight, thankful the soulless monsters were slow and awkward. As long as there weren't too many she could run from them.

Amanda stopped and pulled the bottle of water from the backpack's outer pouch. She wanted to take greedy gulps of the refreshing fluid but she quelled the urge. She replaced the cap after one sip. Plenty of time, she thought, looking at the sun in the eastern sky. There was plenty of time before dark.

The last thing she wanted was to be outside after dark, when she couldn't see the monsters before they got too close. At least in daylight she could run but traveling at night was sure disaster. She wouldn't worry just yet. She'd find shelter before it came to that.

Amanda neared a Tutor-style home with its sprawling front yard. Mr. Jennings, a seventy-year-old, who had the best-kept yard in the neighborhood, owned it. Every day he'd plant and trim from morning until night. The yard was unkempt now, the shaggy grass turning brown. The front door, broken into several pieces, was scattered across the porch.

Amanda stopped and stared at the wrecked homestead. Mr. Jennings stood on the porch, staring down the road the way she'd seen him do many times before, waving to neighbors as they passed. There was a visible wound on his neck and the front of his shirt was covered in dried blood.

Amanda began walking, watching him, ready to run, but Mr. Jennings never moved. His wrinkled, discolored face turned a vacuous stare on her but he remained where he was. He was one of *them*. There was no mistaking that, not with half of his neck ripped away, but he merely stood and watched her.

She kept an eye on him until she rounded a turn in the road. She thought it very strange that he didn't pursue her. Each ghoul seemed to have a separate personality of sorts. Some were angry and alert; some were slow and trance-like, while others begged to have you. Mr. Jennings was a kind old man. Maybe some of that kindness was still buried deep in his subconscious.

The highway came into view and Amanda breathed a sigh of relief. Hopefully someone would drive by and pick her up. It was a four-mile walk to town from her house but the road was clear of danger as far as she could see. A sudden breeze gave her some relief from the humidity and she stopped to relish it for a moment. It was almost ten o'clock. Amanda dropped the pack and removed her jacket, stuffing it inside. It would be easier to run without the extra hindrance and it sure felt better without it in the rising heat. Throwing the cumbersome pack over her shoulder, she resumed her journey toward town.

Her growing feeling of security since reaching the highway turned to nervous tension when she came to the remains of a head-on collision fifty yards away. One car was overturned; the other had come to a stop by its side.

Amanda froze.

If there were fatalities, she might have company. It was hard to tell how long the cars had been there. She was still too far away to see much detail. She checked the rifle to make sure it was loaded and then slowly walked toward it.

The front of the upright car was crushed to the dashboard. Amanda saw blood on the webbed windshield. When she peered inside, gasoline fumes overwhelmed her but there was no one there. Relief washed over her. She wouldn't have to look into any glazed, emotionless eyes. When she had looked into Will's eyes, she saw no soul, no emotion. Maybe that's what they were, human bodies without their soul and spirit, she thought. Maybe they craved filling that emptiness inside, something only the living could do. In their splintered way of thinking they craved consumption of the spirit through the flesh. She shivered at the thought.

Amanda crept to the overturned car. The roof was almost flat against the dashboard. She got to her knees to look inside. She had to put her head almost to the ground in order to see anything. Amanda jerked away by reflex. The driver's forehead was a mess from impact with the steering wheel. His open eyes saw nothing. The injury to his head must have been severe enough to prevent him from resurrecting into a flesh-eating ghoul. Either that or the accident had just happened and the transformation was not yet complete. Amanda got to her feet. If the latter was the case, she did not want to be there when it happened.

The trek to town was mostly downhill, and that made the trip easier, but the threat of ghoulish encounters kept her ever vigilant. She had not communicated with anyone in well over a week. She had no idea what would greet her in town, or anywhere for that matter. Only God knew what lay ahead.

God and religion, now there's a topic, she thought. Recent events had changed her preconceived ideas of that, too. Who was this God that allowed such horror to rear its ugly head and claim the earth as its own? Not the one she had learned about as a little girl in Sunday School.

Amanda turned and looked at the wrecked cars behind her one last time. They were mere specks in the distance and she saw no visible movement from the lone occupant.

She felt remarkably calm for a moment. She listened to birds chirping in the roadside trees. It was heavenly music in her ears.

CHAPTER 5

Reverend R.T. Peterson sat in the front pew of the New Life Church. The National Guard had come and gone ten days before in the small village. They had evacuated everyone to protected locations around the county but he had hidden when they came to make a last search. There was no place more protected than the house of God, he thought, as they strode through the chapel calling for survivors to make themselves known so they could be taken to safety.

The church was empty now, a hollow shell that had no purpose without a flock. No one was left in the village to attend services except a few of the damned souls who were turned away from God's eternal peace to roam the Earth, unnatural shadows of what they once were.

The Reverend stood and walked to the pulpit from which he had preached every Sunday. He turned to observe the empty church. He was indeed alone.

I am cut off from God, he thought. Even the Almighty had turned His face away, leaving him to ruin. The final Day of Judgment was here, of that he was certain, but what was his place in it? Where was he to fit into God's plan? Peterson wrestled with that thought.

The stained-glass window behind the pulpit was shattered, broken by an angry member of the congregation who had lost his faith in God when the emergency began. The Reverend walked to it and looked out at the deserted neighborhood.

The windows were twelve feet from the ground and there was no danger of the undead getting through them. They were quite slow and not very agile and the preacher had witnessed only a small amount of reasoning power. There they were, he counted five, roaming aimlessly unsure of where to go, and unaware of their own identity.

A bottle of Jim Beam was on the pew next to where he had been sitting. He picked it up, twisting it in his hands as if to wring out a wet rag. He opened it for another drink, but found none left and threw it across the room. The bottle smashed against the wall, sending broken glass in every direction.

"Why hath thou forsaken me?" he cried out loud and then stretched out on the pew, crawling to it on all fours. The barricaded doors began to thunder with the efforts of several creatures to gain entrance. He turned onto his side and fell into a drunken sleep.

Six hours later the preacher awoke to silence. The banging had stopped. His head hurt from too much drink. That's why God had not delivered him from the horror of what was happening; there was no place in God's kingdom for a drunkard. He must've fallen short of God's glory.

The preacher went to the table where he had set the bread and wine for sacrament each week. He tugged and pulled at his tunic until the cloth ripped free from his chest and picked up the knife used to cut the bread.

"Forgive me," he said, bowing his head, "for I have sinned!" He began carving a cross in his chest with the knife. "I repent!" he shouted, falling to his knees. Blood dripped and formed a small puddle on the floor.

Robert Thomas Peterson had always been a flamboyant preacher. He was full of his own self-righteousness and quick to judge the actions of others. He had always dreamed of a large flock and an elegant new facility like those fancy TV preachers with diamond rings and Rolls Royce's. It never came to pass, though. Death and destruction is what he was called to evangelize, the coming day when God would deal with sinful man, the day when they would have to pay for their actions. He believed that Armageddon was now upon them. The world was full of sinners, so many sinners. He had warned them, oh how he warned them. But his prophecy had fallen upon sinfully deaf ears.

The preacher got to his feet. The bleeding had lessened and now the sign of the cross was on his chest, declaring his faith. His head throbbed and he found it hard to concentrate. Thirst from alcohol dehydration made it difficult for him to swallow. He went to the kitchen through a door hidden behind a scarlet velvet curtain. Another door in the kitchen went to the Special Event area of the church but it was boarded and nailed shut. The Event room had too many windows to safely fortify and wouldn't be safe.

Peterson snatched a bottle of codeine tablets from the table and fumbled with the childproof top. The lid gave way and he shook out two tablets into the palm of his shaking hand. The bottle was almost empty. The headaches were more frequent now, brought on by disturbing dreams he couldn't recall after awakening in a cold sweat. Soon he would be out of the helpful pills.

Popping them into his mouth, he drank feverishly from a milk jug filled with water, quenching his parched throat until he was satisfied. He gazed into the mirror on the wall beside the door and moved closer. Returning his stare was a pale, tired, unshaven face. The pockmarks were unusually deep today, almost casting shadows in themselves, a gift from his sinful parents.

Like his father, he'd had acute acne as a teen. He'd been too embarrassed to go out in public or attend school at times because of it. "It's their fault," he told his reflection. "All of my failures are their fault."

His father had been strict and beatings had been severe and plentiful. He was dead now. A heart attack had taken his life two years ago. An image of his father's grossly decayed body clawing at the lid of his coffin, yearning for food and unable to satisfy uncontrollable urges, made the preacher smile.

The smile faded when nightmarish memories began to flood his mind. His tortured childhood had haunted him even into adulthood. He brushed the mental images from his mind and turned away from the image in the mirror.

Peterson returned to the sanctuary where he stared at the empty room. It was such a tragedy to have a house of God with no one in it to hear his sermons. Well, he'd told them their sins would lead to death. They're probably burning in hell at this very moment, he thought, giggling softly.

"My flock has flown," he cried, walking to the podium. "Bring them back, Lord!"

His voice echoed throughout the room. The pounding on the doors began.

CHAPTER 6

EMERGENCY ASSISTANCE COMMISSION BLUEMONT, VIRGINIA

Dr. Cowen covered the man's face with a sheet and clamped straps around the wrists and feet. "He's dead," he told his assistant. "Nine-fourteen A.M."

"What is it that's killing these people?" General Britten asked, hating how helpless he felt.

"I don't have an answer," Cowen said, knowing full well it wouldn't satisfy the General.

"Why not?"

"I don't know. Nothing shows up. We can't isolate the cause. I'm sorry."

"I'm sorry, too," the General said hoarsely, then coughed. "The world is going to shit. They're multiplying too fast. We can't keep up. We're

losing the battle. We need to know how to stop this now or we're finished. They will win." He gave Dr. Cowen the research papers he'd been
reading and turned to leave.

"How's your arm?" Dr. Cowen asked before the General got to the
door.

General Britten turned to face the doctor, His once strong stare now
seemed weak and unsure. His face was pale from illness, and he sub-
consciously covered the injury with his hand. "It hurts like hell," he said
soberly. "The son of a bitch got me good this morning." he groaned,
rubbing the bandages. "Look, you've got to find an answer for what's
happening, son. The people up top won't last too much longer. When
they're gone and there's nothing but those goddamned zombies left, we
won't have anyplace to go. We can't stay down here forever." General
Britten left the room, slamming the door behind him.

Cowen glanced across the room to his assistant, Dr. Sharon Darney,
an expert in the field of virology. She stood by the intercom, stopwatch
in hand, watching the readout as the seconds ticked off.

"What now?" he asked.

Sharon looked up from the clock, her high cheekbones especially
noticeable in the laboratory light. "We start over. We keep trying until
we find something. There *is* a reason; we just haven't looked in the right
place."

They walked over to the examination table together and pulled the
sheet from the restrained corpse that had not yet re-animated.

"No blood flow to the brain," Dr. Cowen said, "no functioning
organs—hell, their body is at room temperature after re-activation, for
Christ sake! There's no way this thing should get up and walk." Cowen
rubbed his forehead in frustration.

"It has to be something in the human DNA structure," Sharon said.
"No other animal has been affected to the same end. The re-animated
dead only attack warm-blooded animals, though it seems humans are

their favorite, but no other animal gets sick with this virus, and only human bodies reactivate after death."

Dr. Cowen shook his head in bewilderment. "Nothing after weeks of solid study. We can't even find an organism that *might* be causing the problem." He threw the research papers on a table. "We haven't learned anything new."

The makeshift research facility was housed inside Mount Weather, near Bluemont, Virginia, a huge underground military complex designed as an evacuation stronghold for the President and his cabinet in case of nuclear war or other national emergencies. But since the end of the cold war the site had been used for little more than warehousing records and war games, though the Presidential suite remained intact.

The base was impregnable. Four entrances surrounded the mountain complex and two helicopter pads lowered to conceal the choppers after landing. A small airstrip was located on the south end of the property.

The base had remained top secret until the 1970s, when a plane crashed into the side of the mountain and word leaked out making its whereabouts common knowledge. Now six of Washington's best researchers and 120 extra troops were ordered to staff the impregnable site to find answers to the sudden plague.

Dr. Cowen's laboratory was originally intended to take aboveground readings of radiation fallout and other tests in case of a nuclear confrontation. The room was fairly large, with concrete floors and block walls. It wasn't the best setting for research in this particular field but there had been little time to set up properly.

"The eyes are open!" Sharon shrieked.

"How long?" Dr. Cowen asked, focusing on the cadaver's glazed and darting eyes.

"Ten minutes and fifteen seconds from death to re-animation," she said, looking at the notes clipped to the table and then at the stopwatch.

"That's two minutes longer than the last one."

"What's the meaning?" Sharon asked. She wondered why over the past week, each specimen took a little longer to revive.

"I don't know if there is one," Dr. Cowen said. "And I'm afraid we'll need more time than we have to find the answers."

The freshly-re-animated body of a man in his thirties strained at the straps that bound him. Various types of medical implements for autopsies or dissections were strewn on the table next to the creature.

Sharon stared thoughtfully down at him.

"They'll remain mobile for ten years, maybe more," Cowen said, as he drew blood from the creature. "The decomposition rate has slowed down drastically."

"Rigor mortis doesn't seem to be setting in at all," Sharon said.

"Oh it's there, but to a much lesser degree than normal. That's one reason they're so awkward and slow, I think. I imagine it's quite painful for them to simply take a step, and they do feel, you know. Watch this."

Dr. Cowen took the scalpel from the table and cut a deep incision into the creature's left arm. It reacted with a moan and a hiss.

"You see? He felt that. I'm not sure how intensely he felt it, but he felt it." He seemed to show some compassion for the creature as guilt crossed his face for slicing into it. Cowen threw the scalpel on the table and took the blood sample to the microscope. He deposited a small portion on a slide to examine it for anomalies. After peering through the scope for a minute, the little man raised his head and removed his glasses to rub his bloodshot eyes.

"Normal for a dead man's blood," he said, disappointed. He returned his glasses to his face. "Just as it was the last time I checked. And the time before that."

Sharon fell into a chair in front of a computer console. "I don't get it. If we didn't cause it, the Russians may be the ones. Has anyone heard? As though they'd tell us."

"They didn't do it. At least they say they didn't. They're being hit as hard with this as we are. As a matter of fact, no one's heard from

Moscow in two days. The satellites show about the same kind of chaos we're experiencing here."

Sharon picked up the glass of water next to her keyboard and took a drink. "Well, if we didn't do it, and they didn't do it, and it's not a virus, what else could it be?"

"Hmmm. Your guess is as good as mine. For all I know, it could be in the water."

Sharon choked on her water and shot him a frightening look.

"Just kidding," he smiled.

It was the first time in days she'd seen him smile.

The complex was quite damp in the deepest area. Droplets of water trickled from the ceiling in many areas, making the concrete floor slick in some places. As General Britten walked down the long hallway to his office, he thought it was akin to residing in a deep, well-appointed cavern.

After what seemed like an eternity, he arrived at his office. The room was dark except for a small light on his desk. He moved toward his favorite overstuffed chair and collapsed into it, kicking off his shoes without bothering to untie them.

The bite on his arm was on fire and that side of his body ached from shoulder to waist. He had been careless when one of the specimens in the lab had broken free and attacked Dr. Cowen. Unable to shoot for fear of hitting the doctor, he pulled the monster off but in the process it sank its teeth into his arm, tearing open the skin. Not a bad injury but bad enough. Any injury inflicted by one of those things was fatal.

The general loosened his tie. Destroying the brain of the creatures was what killed them. A body with a defunct brain would not rise. That was good to know. It helped with the decision he had made.

Without a second thought, General Britten took his revolver from its holster, put it to the roof of his mouth, and pulled the trigger.

CHAPTER 7

Ernie Bradley finished his peanut butter sandwich and entered Studio One at WFPR-FM radio station, where studio speakers emitted the Emergency Broadcast System warning tone.

He sat in the swivel chair and pulled himself close the microphone. After pulling the Emergency Broadcast tape from the machine, he switched to live send.

"This is Ernie Bradley. I have urgent news to report on the following rescue stations so please pay close attention."

The cheerful voice he used on his morning show was gone. There was no time for jokes and happy talk. This was a national emergency.

"County Hospital and the high school are no longer operational as safe havens. Do not attempt to go there for assistance. Instead, try to make your way to the Riverton Warehouse on Dock Street. Repeat. The Riverton Warehouse on Dock Street is the only rescue station still able to guarantee your safety."

Ernie wiped his forehead and took another drink of water from the Styrofoam cup on the console before continuing.

"Also, you are no longer allowed to occupy a private residence, no matter how secure or well stocked. The government has declared martial law and everyone must now go to the nearest rescue station. I will not be sending any more news from here. I am going to shut down. Remember, the old Riverton Warehouse is the only rescue station still operational. May God be with you. I'll see you there." His voice trailed off, and he shut down the microphone.

Ernie rose from the chair and went to the main lobby, where Felicia lay sleeping. The main power was off and a generator ran the station. It wasn't running at full capacity but it was the best he could do under the circumstances.

Ernie could hear the generator whining in the basement. It was attracting attention and before long they would be trapped. The building could not fend off a big crowd if they really wanted inside.

Felicia slept with a blanket pulled over her head like a child afraid of the dark. Ernie carefully pulled it away, trying not to alarm her in doing so.

"Hey, hey. Wake up," he said gently, nudging her shoulder.

Felicia's eyes flew open. "What time is it?" She asked as she sat upright.

"Ten o'clock. You've been asleep for hours."

"Did they come?"

"No." He dropped his head. "Nobody's been here."

One of the station's other disc jockeys was supposed to return at eight o'clock to relieve Ernie, who had already been on duty for more than twenty hours. Ernie guessed he was either dead or just not coming back. Under the circumstances, he couldn't blame him. At this point, even he was abandoning his post.

Felicia stood and rubbed the sleep from her eyes. It was hard for her to think after waking but fear and the premonitions quickly returned. "We have to leave! We have to leave right now! They're not coming; no one's coming to relieve you. It's not safe here."

"We're leaving," he said. "As soon as I get some things together, we're outta here so get ready."

The night before Felicia had pounded on the door in a panic and he had let her in. She was scared out of her mind and said things that didn't make sense to him. Felicia was a tall, slender blond with a knack for being hysterical one minute and perfectly calm the next. She had collapsed in an exhausted sleep on the couch minutes after arriving.

After gathering what he needed, Ernie returned to Felicia. "Let's go."

"Where are we going?" she asked.

"To the rescue station in Riverton. We'll get help there. Run straight to my car and get in. Be careful, though. There's a couple of them out there."

"No! No! That's wrong. Let's stay!"

"Shhh," Ernie said, putting an arm around her. "It'll be fine. Just do as I say. You were the one wanting to go just a minute ago."

Felicia nodded, her sense of foreboding calmed slightly. Ernie unlocked the door and opened it a crack. One of the dead things was fifty yards away. It turned toward the door when Ernie opened it. The creature began its arduous shuffle toward them.

"Now!" Ernie ordered. "Let's go!" He grabbed her hand and pulled her through the door.

Felicia struggled to keep up with him as he pulled her toward the car. She ran to the passenger side and jumped inside, locking the door as soon as it was shut. Ernie locked his door and put the key in the ignition. The motor turned over but it wouldn't start. He kept trying until the battery went dead.

"Shit!" he yelled, butting his head against the steering wheel. "Of all the fuckin' times!"

He couldn't believe his luck. A car was not the place to be stuck. They could get in by breaking the windows. The radio station wasn't the answer, either. None of the windows were reinforced. It wouldn't be long before the creatures realized they were inside and came crashing through.

The creatures approached them; a short, hideously mangled man whose entrails dangled from the open stomach cavity all the way to the ground was closest. They became entangled in his feet as he shuffled toward them, pulling farther out and dragging behind him in a ghastly display of gore.

Ernie grabbed a tire iron from the back seat and opened the door. "Stay here, Felicia. I'll take care of this one and try to start the car again."

Felicia was terrified. A familiar jolt ran through her body, almost like an adrenaline rush but much more intense. Intuition? An omen? A curse? She wasn't sure, but she'd had a similar feeling just before all hell broke loose. It had been so intense that she was unconscious for an hour. This particular feeling always meant doom.

"Ernie, let's just run!" Felicia cried.

Ernie slipped out of the car; tire iron raised like a baseball bat.

He swung the tire iron against the creature's head as though hitting a home run but the creature remained standing. It put its bloody hands on Ernie's throat and tried to bite him. Ernie managed to take another swing at the gruesome head. The force hit hard enough for the creature to lose its grip on Ernie's throat but then it grabbed his arm instead.

"Look out"! Felicia screamed, seeing two more ghouls who were attracted by the commotion.

Ernie didn't notice them or hear Felicia's warning so occupied was he with the monster he was fighting.

Felicia got out of the car. "Ernie, look out behind you!"

Ernie turned to see the others closing in. The monster he was fighting sunk his teeth deep into his forearm.

The sudden pain and the rush of hot liquid as a portion of his arm was ripped away made Ernie scream in terrified agony. Part of his arm hung from the ghoul's mouth. He was bleeding profusely. Shocked, he hesitated.

Smelling blood, the other two creatures quickly closed in on Ernie. When one bit him in the jugular, Ernie lost consciousness. He fell to the ground and the creatures covered him like buzzards at a fresh kill.

Felicia screamed and one of the demons turned toward her. Rooted to the spot in fascinated horror, it was difficult for her to tear her eyes away from the grotesque monsters gorging on human flesh. Two of them continued to feast on Ernie while the third slowly made its way toward her.

She ran up the drive away from the radio station. At the top of the hill next to the highway she dropped to her knees to catch her breath.

Her side ached. She could go no further. The highway ran east, out of town to Interstate 66 and from there; to Washington, D.C. Felicia focused all of her attention on the immediate area. One sound, one flicker of movement, and she would race away, pain or no pain.

The Riverton rescue station! But it was all the way on the other side of town, a three-mile walk, and she was afraid, very afraid. Without a weapon it would be a dangerous journey, not that she would have known how to use a weapon if she'd had one. She'd probably end up shooting herself.

After a few uneasy moments of rest, she staggered to her feet and looked around. From her position she could see the entire south end of town. There was no moving traffic but deserted cars were strewn here and there. In the distance she saw hordes of the walking dead milling around the shopping center and an adjacent apartment complex.

Felicia thought back to a few days before. She wondered where her mother and sister were. She had not seen them in four days. John, her mother's boyfriend, knew of a place far from everyone. They packed essentials to take with them on their journey to the refuge. "Enough for a month or so," John had said. "The authorities will have it under control by then."

How wrong he'd been! The emergency had only escalated. Felicia had been sent to a store for fresh flashlight batteries. There were still some stores open then—before the situation intensified, before the creature population had exploded.

She looked from store to store before finding the batteries. Upon returning home, the house was empty. Most of the supplies were still there but her family had vanished.

She couldn't understand how they could leave without her. There were no signs of a struggle, no blood. "They're not dead," she had told herself over and over. She would not accept that possibility.

Felicia lived a few blocks from the radio station and knew that they were still broadcasting. After a few frightful nights alone, and the realization that her family would not be returning, she headed there for help and safety. It had been a short-lived safe haven but at least she'd been able to sleep and decide what her next move was going to be.

Felicia began walking toward the south end of town. The dead were all around but if she stayed out of sight she might slip through and make it to the rescue station. It was that or a ten-mile walk around town to reach the same destination. The short trip was preferable.

Walking corpses wandered aimlessly this way and that. They bumped into things and each other. Some dragged items. A small boy with a pale blue complexion pulled a red wagon behind him. A Frankenstein bride carried a wedding dress close to her chest. If Felicia's predicament weren't so grave, she would have laughed.

Felicia quietly made her way to the intersection. She hid at times if a creature got too close. Now she stood out of sight at the corner of a 7-Eleven.

Peering around the corner, she saw several creatures close by. Then she saw it. Sunlight reflected off a metallic blue pickup parked in front of the fuel pump, as though someone had abandoned it in the midst of a fill-up. The truck gave her a sudden sensation of security. Creatures were near the truck, but maybe she could outrun them. If the truck had keys she would be home free. If it didn't—well, she didn't want to think about that.

Felicia bolted for the truck so fast she hit the driver's door, unable to stop her momentum. The force knocked her to the ground and the wind from her lungs. When she finally looked up it was into the barrel of a gun pointed at her from the other side of the blood-smeared driver's window.

Felicia screamed and for a second she thought her intuition had failed her.

"Jesus!" Amanda shouted. "I almost shot you for one of those things."

Though it was an unfamiliar face, it was a living one. Felicia's heart steadied.

The creatures heard the commotion and began stumbling toward the truck. Amanda turned the key and the engine roared to life.

"Get in!" she screamed to Felicia.

Jumping up, Felicia ran to the passenger door and scrambled inside. Amanda put the rifle between them and squealed out of the lot.

"We need to go to Riverton. There's a rescue station there," Felicia said.

Amanda nodded. "Let's just hope we have enough gas to make it."

CHAPTER 8

Jim watched Mick fumble with the wires to the radio base station. Chuck, who could never stay still for long, paced the office floor.

"If you need help, I know a little about those things," Jim offered. "We used them in the supervisor's trucks to keep in touch throughout the day."

"I think I've got it figured out now," Mick answered.

Jim nodded. "Where'd you get the equipment?"

"I sent Chuck and Jon to get it from the trucks over at the concrete plant. They use them in their fleets, too."

"Yeah! And we nearly got our asses bitten off doing it," Chuck grinned.

"Yeah, well, Jon could stand to have a little of his ass removed," Mick said. "Eating donuts all those years on the force have given him quite a load to carry."

Jim laughed. Jon did have a big ass. In fact, there wasn't anything small about him.

"Give me a hand putting the radio on the table over there," Mick told Jim. He held the wires away from the back of the radio so he wouldn't get them confused after sorting them out.

After Jim helped Mick set the radio on a table, Mick stood back and looked suspiciously at it, pulling thoughtfully on his blonde mustache and then rubbing the rough stubble on his chin.

"What's wrong?" Jim asked.

"This thing runs on one-ten current. How are we going to power it up? There's no electricity."

"Get a generator."

"Too noisy. It'll attract trouble?"

"They make some pretty quiet ones. Just stick it in the basement with an exhaust pipe to carry the fumes outside."

"Yeah, that might work." Mick looked at Chuck. "Why don't you and one of the off-duty guards sneak into town and grab one? Get the quietest one you can find…and be careful, damn it. Don't get foolish."

"Foolish? Me? I'm not foolish, I'm stupid," Chuck grinned, crossing his eyes and scratching the top of his baldhead.

Mick gave him a hard look and Chuck picked up his rifle and headed out the door.

"What a character," Mick said. "If he's not careful, he's gonna end up dead."

Chuck was gone no more than a few seconds when the test pattern on the battery-powered television switched to two men in a newsroom. One wore a disheveled suit and Mick recognized him as the local evening newsman. The other wore a military uniform. The reception wasn't very clear so Mick fumbled with the retractable antennae until it was watchable.

"Are we on? Are we sending?" the suited man asked, pressing the earpiece against his ear.

Jim and Mick sat down to watch, hoping for some good news but not really expecting any.

"I'm Dan Brenner and next to me is General George Custis. We are broadcasting from WRG in Washington, D.C."

The names of safe stations in the Washington, D.C. area began running across the bottom of the screen, giving viewers information on where to go for assistance.

"Please pay close attention to the following," Brenner said, noticeably shaken. "Only attempt to go to the rescue stations we are broadcasting live to you now. Do not attempt to go to any that are not listed. You would be walking into a hostile situation."

Brenner turned to the military man next to him. "General Custis, what is the situation in the Washington, D.C. area?"

"Grave. If you can get out of the city, I suggest you do so in an orderly fashion. If you cannot, get to the closest rescue station as soon as possible. A few days ago the situation went from what we thought to be under control to a national emergency-"

"What happened?" Brenner interrupted.

"Not having the necessary information we needed to deal with the problem, combined with a lack of cooperation from the general public to heed the warnings issued by the government." The General continued. "That's the main reason circumstances are what they are. All bodies of dead or infected persons must be handed over to specially equipped units or to the local police. Anyone not adhering to this will suffer the consequences."

"Consequences?" Brenner asked.

"Martial law is in effect in Washington, D.C. and the surrounding area. You *must* proceed to the nearest rescue station or leave the city. If you find a corpse, do not touch it. Contact the proper authorities and a disposal team will be dispatched. Attempts to remain in a private residence, or keeping the bodies of the dead, will be treated as a capitol crime, punishable by death. This is a very serious matter."

"My God," Jim said. "They've gone mad! What the hell are they thinking? They're just making it worse!"

Jim looked at Mick, who was still looking at the screen, mouth agape. "Lunacy! We've got to be prepared for more than fighting the dead. We may have to defend ourselves against the living as well."

"It looks like the authorities have enough to deal with in the cities," Jim said. "They won't have the time or resources to come to small towns like this and give us any trouble. At least not for awhile."

"But someone else may," Mick said. "People aren't acting very rationally right now. We don't know what to expect."

"You may be right. We should be ready for anything. Christ, just when you think the world couldn't possibly get any worse, it does."

Jim and Mick turned their attention back to the television.

"…They are not your friends. They are not your family," the general said, "They will not respond to you as such. You cannot reason with them. All dead bodies must be disposed of either by destroying the brain or separating it from the rest of the body. Cremation is also an accepted solution."

"And therein lies the problem?" Brenner asked.

"Yes, that's the reason it's gotten out of hand. People are reacting with emotion and that's allowed enemy numbers to increase dramatically. We are in a grave situation folks if we don't?"

The television flickered and then faded out, leaving a pinpoint of light in the center of the screen. Mick got up and smacked the side of the television. "Ah, shit, the batteries."

"You have anymore?"

"Yeah, but to tell you the truth, I've heard about all I wanna hear from those guys." Mick walked back to his chair and sat down, folding his hands in his lap. "We've gotta get better organized. We need search-and-destroy units and clean-up units. After we shoot the sons of bitches, we can't just let them lie there and rot. The town stinks bad enough as it is with those things walking around. Do you think you can organize it?"

"How many people do we have here that I can draw from?"

Mick laughed. "About one-hundred and thirty, but you'll have a hell of a time getting most of them to go out there."

Jim was surprised. "That's it, one hundred and thirty survivors? That's all that's left alive?"

"I'm sure there's more hiding out there somewhere. That'll also have to be part of our job, to get those people to safety. That may be the hardest part." Mick picked up his rifle and slung it over his shoulder. "Come on, Jim. I'll let Jon know you're going to be in charge of setting up the search teams."

Jim got his AK-47 and followed Mick into the large room filled with people. Jim scanned the room searching for prospective volunteers. Most of them were families, huddled together for solace. They looked like refugees, beaten and tired after the long journey to a new home. Jim doubted if he'd find many volunteers.

The two men stepped out onto the porch. The air was warm but a light breeze cooled the warm autumn air.

Jim studied the neighborhood. If not for the armed guards, he wouldn't have known anything was wrong. A few houses were in the front of the building but woods surrounded both sides. The North Fork of the Shenandoah River flowed sluggishly a hundred yards from the rear of the building. Mick was right. There was only one way in from town, one lane to defend, but that also meant one way out as well.

Mick called to Jon, who was walking around the corner of the building toward them. "I'm giving Jim the job of cleaning out the town and bringing in any stragglers. I need you to be his right-hand guy and give him any help he might need. Okay?"

Jon glanced to Jim as if making a quick check of character and then gave an approving nod to Mick. "Yeah, sure. I'll give him whatever he needs."

The three men turned at the sound of a gun with a silencer and saw a body fall to the ground. Two guards ran to retrieve it.

"That's the third kill we've had since your return this morning," Jon said. "Even with the silencers, they still continue to show up."

"There's a shit load of them in town now," Mick said. "They're everywhere. When we ran into Jim, droves of those things were walking down South Street. Keep using the silencers. If they don't know we're here, they won't show up. I'm hoping those were just roamers, going whichever way the wind takes them."

They watched as the corpse was carried to a dump truck in the lower end of the lot. One of them opened the dump gate, exposing a pile of bodies. It reminded Jim of old Holocaust footage, of Jewish bodies piled high for cremation by the Nazis.

A crackling voice on Jon's walkie-talkie broke Jim from his vision.

"Someone's coming, Jon." The voice proclaimed

"Well?" Jon asked. "What are they? People or zombies?"

"It's a truck, Jon. Not one of ours. Looks like two girls."

"Let them through."

The truck rounded the turn and pulled into the parking lot. It came to a stop in front of them.

"I'll be damned," Jim said. "That's my truck."

CHAPTER 9

Sharon Darney walked up the hall to the last checkpoint. The guard stepped into her path, blocking her progress.

She pulled the security badge from her blouse and displayed it before he had the chance to ask. "I need a breath of fresh air," she snapped. "I'm tired of breathing this recirculated stuff."

"Ten minutes," the guard said. "Don't make me come looking for you. I could really get in trouble for letting anyone go up top."

Massive doors slid open and sunlight and fresh mountain air filled Sharon's senses. "Imagine that," she told the guard, "the sun is still shining, the world is still turning. Life, such as it is, goes on. Who'da thunk?"

She walked to one of the stone benches by the flower garden and sat down. She snapped one of the flowers off, put it to her nose and inhaled its fragrance. It had been a while since she'd taken the time to literally stop and smell the flowers.

The flower didn't have the effect she thought it would. The little pleasures in life now took a back seat next to the desire to survive. It suddenly looked to Sharon as though mankind had been added the endangered species list.

She examined the manicured lawns encompassing a dozen or so buildings bristling with antennas and microwave relay systems. Not far from the installations entry gate was a control tower and one of the helicopter pads. The mountain's real secrets were not visible at ground level. Ten-foot high chain link fences with razor wire surrounded the complex and soldiers defended the perimeter.

"What are you doing up here, doctor?" a familiar voice asked from behind.

Sharon suppressed a shudder and she turned to see Gilbert Brownlow, the man in charge of the site. An entire shadow government was ensconced there, where every aspect of the country's leadership was duplicated. In the beginning this procedure had been created in case elected leaders were unexpectedly done away with. After the main center of the nation's defense was moved to Norad and the cold war ended, they never bothered to depose this little feudal kingdom. Apparently there was no end to what the country's leaders wasted millions of tax dollars on.

Brownlow represented the office of the President and expected to be addressed as such. When hell freezes over, Sharon thought. Hell may have ascended but it wasn't frozen yet.

"I needed a little sunlight, Gil, just to be sure it was still here."

Brownlow ignored her informal address. "You don't have time to enjoy the weather, doctor," he said sharply. "There will be time for that later. I don't want you to come back out here again, any of you. There's too much work to be done."

"Well, Gil," Sharon said, standing, "I hardly think you can afford to fire me this late in the game. In case it's slipped your mind, I'm a civilian researcher not one of your military vassals."

Sharon brushed past him, his mouth agape, and stormed back inside. She couldn't help but think of the place as a prison, the leadership a dictatorship. Those stationed here before the emergency had assumed the roles of the country's leaders in order to be ready should the real government break down. Now they had gotten much too comfortable with the anthropomorphism.

As she walked along the busy street of the underground city, she found it amazing that they had thought of everything; shops, apartments, cafeterias, a hospital, even a subterranean lake supplied by a fresh underground spring. Television monitors and cameras were placed at various positions so workers were never out of sight, always powered and ready for the next announcement.

When she came to the end of the street, she turned left toward the lab. She opened the door and found Dr. Cowen studying one of the medical monitors.

"Find anything?" she asked.

"Brain waves. Faint but there."

Sharon looked at the specimen still strapped on the table. Its head was covered with sensors to relay data to the monitor Dr. Cowen watched.

"Have you heard any news from the other facilities?" Sharon asked.

"Nothing. And Johnston and Mitchell have been transferred to Norad, so we now have two less heads working here."

"Don't they know it works better when we can confab with colleagues? Discuss our ideas and findings?"

"The big wigs in the Situation Room?" he asked, rolling his eyes. "Those idiots! They're too busy looking at those big screens and maps, figuring out how long it will take for us to be overrun to find an actual solution. I don't think they have a clue as to what this really means."

He stopped what he was doing and walked to the specimen. He tore the sensors from its head, tossing them to the floor. "There's nothing here! No answers to be found, no solution. This place is one big grave made just for us. We may never leave."

"It's going to be all right, Rich," Sharon said. "Look, we've all been working too hard with too little rest. Just take a deep breath. Have the others found anything?"

"Mr. *President* has those two working on finding a way to rid us of these creatures by looking for a virus to kill them, just what we need. It would probably end up killing everyone but those things and then we can all be one big happy family. I swear those two are useless. If

Brownlow makes a quick turn they're liable to get their noses broken they have them stuffed so far up his ass. I'm glad we don't have to share the same lab with them."

Rich put his hands on Sharon's shoulders and pulled her close. "We need to get out of here. Sharon. If we stay here, we'll end up like him." He tilted his head toward the creature.

"Where would we go?"

"I don't know yet. Somewhere where there are no people."

"We can't leave. We have to stay and try to find the answer to this. If we don't, who will?"

"There are no answers!" he shouted. "It's not for us to find."

"No!" she shouted back. "Not yet! There's got to be an answer. I have to stay. For now anyway."

CHAPTER 10

Amanda opened the truck door and stepped out, slinging the backpack over her shoulder. Felicia remained in her seat, studying the people, just to be sure. It looked safe to her. What's more, it felt safe. She savored the relief.

Felicia was familiar with the building. She had been there several times when it had been a nightclub. She had seen Foghat, a band from the seventies, and had gotten so drunk her boyfriend had to carry her to the car. He broke up with her after that. He gave her some lame excuse but she knew he was spooked by her gift, by her ability to know things before they happened. At work she sometimes overheard others whispering about her, things like "strange, freak, and weirdo." She had since learned to keep things to herself.

Jim walked over to the pretty, raven-haired woman standing by his truck. He patted the hood and rubbed the fender like one would a faithful dog.

"Didn't put any scratches on it, did you?" he said with a crooked smile.

"Excuse me?" Amanda said, not sure what he meant.

"This is my truck. You found it at the 7-Eleven, right?"

"Yes. We needed it to get here."

"I'm glad it could be of some help to someone. Are you both all right?"

"Yes."

"Good. Come on, we'll get you both settled in.

Amanda turned to Felicia and motioned her out.

Felicia opened the door and slid off the seat, dropping gently to the ground. Jim noted her ethereal beauty, her fairy-like quality. Her appearance was almost otherworldly, sprite-like.

"I'm Jim."

"I'm Amanda. And this is Felicia." She nodded toward her newfound friend.

"Now that we've been introduced, I'll show you inside."

Jim took them inside, passing Mick on the way. Mick looked the women over and gave an approving nod to Jim as they went by.

They threaded their way through the crowd and found a spot for them to rest and put their things. Amanda's nose wrinkled at the filthy condition of the room, but kept quiet her disgust. Jim noticed her displeasure and held two fingers over his nose. "I'm sorry, there's not much room. It doesn't have the comforts of home but it's all we've got right now."

"The comforts of home were not very comfortable when I left," Amanda said, dropping the backpack.

Jim gave an understanding nod. "If you need anything, let me know."

Amanda felt as though she'd found an ally.

Jim made his way back through the crowd, a slight smile tugging at the corners of his mouth. It had been awhile since he'd been attracted to anyone but he was certainly taken with Amanda. Even in her unkempt state she was beautiful. It had been hard to take his eyes from her striking beauty.

Mick combed his hair back with his fingers and the rubbed a week's growth of beard. His damp shirt was stuck to his skin. More of the dead would be showing up soon. Jim's truck will attract them to their location, some because they saw it, others because they'd heard it.

He looked around once more to make sure the guards were at their posts and walked toward the door. As he approached, Mayor Stan Woodson, a scrawny man in his fifties, sauntered out and raised his hand in front of Mick to stop him.

"This place is a pig sty!" Woodson snapped, pushing his hand against Mick's chest. "I can't deal with the filth in there! I DEMAND a room for myself and my family."

Mick angrily brushed the mayor's hand from his chest, as though removing a repugnant bug from the front of his shirt. "You'll have to deal with what you've got. Just like everyone else."

"I'm the mayor! I should have a decent place to stay!"

Mick grabbed the mayor's shirtfront and slammed him against the wall. "Yeah, you're the mayor, you son of a bitch! If you had acted earlier, we could've saved more people. The only thing you were concerned with was saving your own ass. In my opinion, you cost thousands their lives!"

"We didn't have the facts!"

"You didn't have the guts! You were afraid of being incorrect. That might lose some votes. If the accommodations here aren't to your liking, I suggest you go on into town and get a room at The Inn. I hear they have a few vacancies, you sniveling bastard!"

Mick pulled the mayor close to him, their faces inches apart. "Stay away from me, you hear? You have no authority here. None!" Disgusted, Mick shoved him into the wall once more before releasing him.

The mayor straightened his collar. "We'll see about that." He gave Mick an indignant look and stomped back inside without another word.

Mick stood by the door, his fists still clenched, trying to cool his rage. Stan Woodson was going to be trouble. He'd have to keep an eye on him.

*   *   *

Amanda slid down the wall she was leaning against. It had been weeks since she had really slept and what little strength remained was quickly disappearing. She was nearly overcome with fatigue.

She noticed two blankets lying close by and since no one seemed to be using them, she spread them out to lie on. "There's enough room for you to lay down, too," she told Felicia, who was scanning the room.

"I can't sleep yet. Maybe in a while."

"Well, I can. Actually, it's hard not to," Amanda yawned.

"Ya'll just get here?"

Amanda looked at the slightly stooped old man with a long white beard leaning on a cane.

"Yes."

"How's it look in town?"

"Pretty bad."

"When I got here a week ago, some people out dere was still tryin' to go about business as usual."

"It's a dead town now," Amanda said. "Nothing but the dead."

"Yup, I figured."

The old man began to walk away, then turned and leaned heavily on his cane. "There's an old saying," he said, a rueful grin pulling at the corners of his mouth. "There's only two things you can count on; dyin' and payin' taxes. Now, I'm athinkin', most of the tax collectors are dead and I'm not so sure 'bout the dyin' part either."

CHAPTER 11

Chuck and Duane surveyed the immediate area of the hardware store from the safety of the shielded truck. The store had been hit pretty hard by looters and those reinforcing their homes.

The undead were everywhere. Thirty or so roved the parking lot. Some noticed the truck and began their unearthly march toward it, their sunken, discolored faces devoid of any expression.

"No way!" Duane said. "I'm not risking it. If they want the generator that bad, they can come in here and wade through these sons of bitches themselves!"

Chuck analyzed the situation. There were too many; they would never make it to the door. However, one of Chuck's favorite sports was rattling Duane's cage and he couldn't resist this prime opportunity for some fun.

Duane was thirty-five and still single, never held a job and shunned responsibility, but he would volunteer to help as long as the chore was more thrilling than difficult. He was quick witted and held a certain amount of trivial knowledge. He was trustworthy, and generally fun to be around. Chuck had known him for several years.

A ghoulish man with one eye dangling and a knife buried in his chest reached the truck and began beating on Duane's door. Duane crouched back in fear.

"Okay," Chuck said, "you take that one out and haul ass inside as fast as you can. I'll be right behind you."

"Are you fuckin' nuts? No way!" Duane said, eyes wide.

"Come on! It'll be easy. We can out run them." Chuck barely suppressed a grin. His eyes darted from Duane to the hardware store to Duane again.

"You're kidding, right? You're just kidding?" It began to dawn on Duane that Chuck was deliberately trying to get a rise out of him.

Chuck put the truck in reverse and backed away from the hungry hoard. "Of course I was! I'm in no hurry to become dinner for those ugly stiffs."

The truck careened down Royal Avenue, the main thoroughfare. Ghouls lined the street on both sides. If one happened to stray in front of the vehicle, Chuck quickly ran it down. Bloated from the heat, a few of the creatures exploded on contact. Body parts and blood splattered the hood and windshield.

"Hey, I know where we might find a generator!" Chuck said. "And there may only be a few of those ugly bastards around."

"Where?" Duane asked, happy at the prospect of having fewer monsters to deal with.

"Munson's Rental Depot. I doubt if many people would've thought of cleaning the place out. It's more secluded than the hardware store."

"Yeah, you're right. They have a shit load of them there. But only if it's safe! Okay?"

Chuck knew Duane was afraid but that was okay. If he was afraid he wouldn't get careless and Chuck wouldn't have to baby-sit. It was going to be tough enough.

The Rental Depot was on the eastern edge of town and close to the railroad station. Chuck whipped into the parking lot only to be met by three creatures. The truck sparked a renewed purpose in them and they surrounded the vehicle as quickly as their limited mobility permitted.

Chuck opened his door and hit the nearest creature, sending it staggering backward. Duane's side was clear and he nervously jumped out. Drawing a revolver from his holster he promptly blew the brains of another into a spray of blood and gray matter.

Chuck pulled his machete from its sheath and with one fell swoop, sliced the head off the monster he was still dealing with. The head hit the ground with a hollow thud and rolled, the eyes still searching for prey, the mouth still snapping and slobbering.

The third fiend ambled toward Duane, its arms outstretched like Frankenstein. Chuck snuck up from behind and sunk the machete deep into its skull. The ghoul dropped like a rock. Chuck wiped the blade on the creature's shirt and returned it to the sheath, then checked the area for more. A few roamed about in the distance but appeared uninterested or unaware of their presence.

"No problem" Chuck said confidently, lighting a cigarette. He took a deep drag. "We'll get in, get the generator and we'll get out. No problem-o."

Chuck grabbed the tool bag from the truck and ran to the front door. "You stay there for now," he ordered. "Keep an eye out for more trouble."

Revolver ready, Duane scanned the area. The distant ghouls continued to show no interest. One was preoccupied with a small radio and Duane strained to see if it was one of the undead. The manner in which it lumbered about convinced him that it was. He wondered what the mindless monster found so intriguing about the radio. They couldn't comprehend such things as music; nonetheless, it juggled it between its hands and cocked its head in interest.

Chuck picked up a large rock and smashed the thick safety glass out of the front door. He fumbled with the lock until he was able to turn the floor bolt and cautiously entered the large, dim room, propping the door open with the rock.

Various power tools and other items cluttered the floor. A large rat scurried out from under a canvas tool bag and ran between Chuck's legs. He stumbled backward over a riding mower and to his surprise, fell into a gas-powered generator. It was a large one and probably quite noisy from the look of it. Not quite what Mick had asked him to find but he was all out of ideas where to find another.

Chuck gripped the wrap-around handles and heaved with all his might and dragged it as best he could across the concrete floor. After a few minutes, he released his grip to catch his breath. He was just about to get Duane when he saw something shiny in the shadows. COVINGTON POWER SILENT was written across the top-mounted gas tank in bright red letters. He could carry this one.

"Looks like this'll fit the bill," he said, hoisting the generator onto his shoulders.

Shots sounded from outside and Chuck danced through the maze of scrambled tools on the floor, balancing the load on his shoulders.

When he got to the door, he saw Duane crouched beside the truck, holding his left ankle and spewing obscenities.

"What the hell happened?" Chuck asked.

"Son of a bitchin' mother fucker bit me!"

"What bit you?" Chuck scanned the area. Only the three they had disposed of when they arrived were close.

"That!" Duane cried, pointing to the severed head a few feet away. It now had a large hole in the back of the skull.

"What the fuck?" Chuck frowned "How the hell could that thing bite you, damn it? It can't walk."

"I kicked it. The son of a bitch was still alive!"

Chuck's jaw dropped. "Jesus H. Christ! How stupid can you be?"

"Pretty fuckin' stupid I guess. I didn't know I could still get bit by just a fuckin' head! Christ, this is fucked up!"

Chuck examined the bite. It had barely broken the skin but that wouldn't change Duane's fate. Chuck put the generator on the ground and without warning he smashed his fist into his Duane's right temple. Duane crumpled to the ground, unconscious.

Chuck ran to the back of the pickup and got a torch from the tool-box. Pulling the machete from its sheath as he returned to his fallen comrade, he brought it down hard just above the wound. The infected appendage separated cleanly on the first blow, blood gushing and spurt-ing from the stump. Chuck lit the torch and cauterized the hideous wound until the bleeding stopped. The smell of burnt human flesh made him gag and he fought hard not to vomit as he completed his gruesome task. In the last couple of weeks he had seen the procedure performed several times in an attempt to stop the infection before it spread away from the initial wound, but he'd never stuck around long enough to see if the method was ever successful. At least Duane would have a chance.

Several creatures had now noticed them and began closing in. More came from the open doors of nearby houses and buildings. Chuck guessed there were nearly forty within a short walking distance.

He grabbed Duane and dragged him to the truck, stuffing his limp body into the cab before retrieving the generator. One creature was almost close enough to reach him. Chuck kicked it in the mid-section, knocking it off its feet, before driving away.

Duane had been motionless since the blow to the head and Chuck hoped he hadn't killed him with his remedy. One way or the other, it didn't matter much. Dead was dead.

CHAPTER 12

The echoing retort of gunfire sounded again from outside. Jim picked up the AK-47 and ran to the door. Several guards were scurrying about, most to positions in the outer perimeter next to the road leading into town.

"We need more firepower!" Mick yelled from his position on the road where he watched a horde of undead crossing the bridge over the south fork of the river. Some were nearly halfway across on their trek toward the rescue station.

Jim Workman, like any good lieutenant, ran to the road with the others to join six armed men. He pulled the cartridge from his weapon. Full metal jacket, he thought, studying the ammunition. Piercing power. I should be able to kill these bastards through a brick wall with this.

He slammed the cartridge back and took his position next to Jon and Mick.

The undead were still one hundred and fifty yards from where the survivors made their stand. Jon gave the order to wait. "I wanna make every round count," he said, looking at Jim, "Aim for the head." He said, slowly.

Jim nodded. Kill the brain and you kill the monster. Body shots did no good. It was basic post plague knowledge.

"Get ready!" Jon shouted over the ghoul's rising shrieks.

The advancing army of horrid, living dead was now one hundred yards away. Moans and screams rose as they approached with mounting excitement. Jim looked at Jon.

"Like sharks," Jon said, "they're building into a feeding frenzy."

The creatures drew closer.

Jim raised his weapon.

"Take 'em down!" Jon ordered.

Gunfire exploded and the first line collapsed quickly, causing others to stumble and fall over their bodies. More fell but the others kept up their mission unfazed by the slaughter around them.

Jim was reminded of a scene from a Revolutionary War movie where formations of soldiers marched toward the enemy. Line after line fell, hoping some would be left for hand-to-hand combat. Only this army didn't return fire.

The explosion of gunfire continued until every last creature lay still. A massive pile of bodies cluttered the bridge. Vultures circled above, waiting for an opportunity to feast.

"It's gonna be rotten," Mick told Jon. He lowered his rifle. "Get the dump truck up here and have someone clean this up. Take them over to the quarry and burn them."

*   *   *

Chuck's truck came to a screeching halt when he reached the bridge. "Holy shit!" he shrieked, seeing the massacre before him.

Duane was still unconscious on the seat beside him. He had to get him back to the shelter before he woke to the pain and shock of what had happened. Chuck was not prepared to explain why he'd chopped off Duane's foot. What if it didn't help? The only thing Chuck had accomplished then was to cause even more pain.

He could see Mick and the others on the other side of the bridge. He picked up the walkie-talkie and extended the antennae. "Mick, this is Chuck. Come in."

"Yeah, Chuck, go ahead."

"Duane's been hurt. I had to cut his foot off. I can't get the truck across the bridge. Send someone over to help carry him. Hurry!"

"Ah, shit," Mick said. "Ten-four. Be right there."

Mick put the radio back on his belt. "Jim, I need your help. Follow me."

Jim nodded and followed Mick across the bridge, stepping over the rancid smelling corpses.

"What happened?" Mick asked when they reached the truck. He looked at Duane.

"He was bitten. I had to try to stop the infection."

Mick quickly examined the burnt and oozing stump, wincing at the thought of having to perform such a grisly task. "Damn. Let's get him back. The Doc can keep him under for a while." He reached inside the truck and pulled Duane out of the vehicle. Jim quickly moved in to help. Each man lifted one of Duane's legs, carrying him in a firemen's chair back to the rescue station. Chuck grabbed the generator from the back and hoisted it onto his shoulder.

Once the three men cleared the bridge, a dump truck backed up to the pile of bodies and several masked and gloved guards began to load the dead.

Mick and Jim carried Duane through the crowded room and into the makeshift infirmary, where several wounded lay on small cots. Some were bandaged from injuries inflicted by the marauding dead. One was covered with a bloodstained sheet.

Dr. Brine, a general practitioner now retired, leaned against his cane. "What do we have here?" he asked wearily.

"Bitten. Chuck had to cut off his foot. Can you keep him asleep for a while?" Mick asked.

"I've never seen it help," the doctor said, "amputation I mean, but we'll give him every chance."

Mick and Jim put Duane on an empty cot and covered him. Dr. Brine held up a needle and squeezed the air from the dose. "It spreads too quickly," he said, giving Duane a shot. "Amputation of the infected area doesn't work."

"What happened there?" Jim asked, pointing to the covered body.

"She died this morning. I gave her an injection of sulfuric acid through the eye socket, into her brain, so she couldn't get back up and hurt someone. It eats up the brain, keeps them from rising again. It beats the hell out of sawing off their heads. I'm too damned old for that kind of work."

"We need to get that dead body out of here, Doc," Mick said. "If the damned zombies don't get us, the filthy conditions will. Let Jon know it's here. Mick turned to Jim. "Come with me."

Jim followed him to the basement. At the bottom of the steps, Mick lit a kerosene lamp. The basement was as large as the space above and had only one metal door for an exit. They walked to the western wall, facing the woods and river. Mick put his hand on the wall about waist level and patted it lightly.

"We can knock a hole here for an exhaust on the generator and run a extension cord through the floor to the radio in the office." Mick removed his hand from the wall and turned to Jim. "I'm worried. I want to have a meeting with everyone tomorrow morning. Supplies are running low and the traffic coming across that bridge is leading them right to us. We'll end up with all of them in our laps if we're not careful."

CHAPTER 13

The preacher awoke to the sound of breaking glass. The Event Room, he thought. They've broken in.

He continued to lay in the pew, listening as tables were upset and windows smashed. He had guessed right; they would eventually break the windows in that room and climb inside. That's why he'd boarded the door leading from the event room to the kitchen so thoroughly. He was confident that they couldn't get through it.

Morning sunlight radiated through the stained glass. He had survived another night. He could stay at the church until it was all finally over if need be. There was enough food to last quite a while. The old hand pump in the kitchen would still pump water from the well.

He glanced at his watch. 9:45. He sat up and rubbed his weary eyes. His stomach growled painfully. He had not eaten at all the day before, and only once the day before that. Food must be rationed since he didn't know how long he might be a prisoner. He was sure, though, that God would give him the answer before he starved.

The preacher went to the kitchen. The commotion in the Event Room was much louder there. He had to be careful not to make too much noise; he didn't want to aggravate the intruders behind the door. If they tried hard enough there was always the chance they could break through.

R.T. Peterson opened the pantry door. The shelves were still filled with the canned goods bought for the church picnic that never happened. It was to have been last week but recent events put it on permanent hold. There was enough to eat for a month, maybe more. Rationed properly he could possibly double that time.

He chose a can of baked beans and opened it as quietly as possible, picking up the jug of water on the table he went back to the sanctuary and sat down to have his meal. As he ate he thought about his situation. He was safe for now; God had seen to that. He was being protected, hidden away from His wrath. Why else was he still alive?

"God will protect me!" he shouted, slamming the can of beans down on the pew.

He jumped from his seat and ran to the kitchen. "Do you hear me?" he screamed through the barricaded door to the Event Room. "You can't have me! The Lord has work for me to do. DO...YOU...HEAR...ME?"

The creatures in the Event Room began pounding on the door and the preacher slowly backed away, falling into a chair beside the table.

"I am chosen. I AM chosen," he said, and then wept.

CHAPTER 14

Amanda knelt where Felicia lay sleeping. She breathed evenly, her sleep undisturbed despite the fact that at sometime during the night she had acquired a bedmate. A small fair-haired child lay curled tightly against Felicia, Felicia's arm draped protectively over her. The sight tugged unexpectedly at Amanda's heartstrings. She brushed a wisp of silky white-blonde hair from the little girl's face.

The unfamiliar touch set off an internal alarm. The child gasped and her eyes sprang open in terror. The sudden reaction startled Amanda but equally as startling was the child's wraith-like countenance. She was, without a doubt, the most hauntingly beautiful child Amanda had ever laid eyes upon. Her striking blue eyes were positively mesmerizing.

The sudden movement of the child stirring against her brought Felicia to a state of semi-wakefulness. Her arms automatically closed comfortingly about the small girl as she tried to clear the mental cobwebs and assess the possible threat as quickly as her mind would allow.

"What's wrong?"

"Nothing" Amanda assured her. "It seems that you have another new friend. It's breakfast time. If you sleepy-heads want something to eat, you'd better get up."

Felicia lowered the blanket and sat up against the wall. The little girl mimicked her actions exactly, looking around the room.

"What's your name, sweetheart?" Felicia asked.

The girl looked up at Felicia without a word and Felicia felt that familiar tingle begin to buzz beneath her skin. The girl reached her hand up to stroke Felicia's face and her touch gave off an almost electrical shock. Felicia likened it to touching a tongue to a battery to check the charge.

A quietly profound moment passed between them as Felicia returned the gesture. A deep, inexplicable bonding of souls had taken place. Felicia knew that this was a life-altering event. Her survival of this harrowing ordeal was somehow pre-ordained to bring her to this place, to this child.

Amanda witnessed the amazing exchange that passed between them. It was strangely unsettling, as though there were volumes of unspoken dialog passing between two fairy-people. The hairs rose on the back of Amanda's neck as she watched this silent communiqué.

          *   *   *

People stood in line to receive their ration of food for breakfast. Most of them were still shell-shocked by the unfathomable turn of events in their once mundane lives. They eagerly wolfed down their meager portions with no heed to civilized etiquette, reminding Felicia of the ghastly feeding frenzy she had witnessed while on the run. They crammed their mouths, blank expressions on their faces, almost in a trance themselves.

"What are they having?" Felicia asked, wishing away the disturbing vision.

"It looks like oatmeal," Amanda said.

"I hate oatmeal. My mother wore me out on it when I was a kid. How about you, Isabelle?" she asked her new charge. "Want some oatmeal?"

The little girl responded with a less than enthusiastic look as she wrinkled her nose in distaste.

"Well," Amanda smiled ruefully, "it looks like the special of the day and the only thing on the menu."

Felicia's thoughts went back to her mother and her family. They were not here so they must have made it to safety somewhere else, maybe in the mountains of West Virginia. She didn't want to think of the possibility of them being dead. Death was no longer eternal peace; it was now the dwelling place of demons.

Felicia and Isabelle followed Amanda to the long line of people waiting for nourishment. A small portion of plain oatmeal was spooned out to each person. Most ate theirs without the benefit of utensils, scooping up their share with two fingers, wiping every last morsel from the plate. The three girls waited patiently for theirs.

"Do you know her?" Amanda asked, nodding toward Isabelle.

"In a manner of speaking. We are both what my Grammy used to call old souls, though I've never set eyes on her before this morning. We know each other on a much deeper level."

"Then how do you know her name is Isabelle?"

"Because it was Grammy's name," Felicia replied as though that was simply all there was to it.

Amanda wrinkled her brow, bewildered by her unique and strange new friend.

When Duane began thrashing about and hallucinating, talking to people only he could see Dr. Brine gave him another shot of morphine. Duane's face was pale, with dark circles under his eyes. The infection was taking its toll.

Mick walked in and stood by Dr. Brine's side. "How's he doing, Doc?"

"Not too good. He's not gonna make it."

"How long does he have?"

Dr. Brine put his hand on Duane's forehead. "Today, maybe. He's burnin' up. There's nothin' I can do except kill the pain and make him comfortable. The disease those things carry is nothin' I've ever seen before. An answer may never be found. Hell, we can't even cure a damned cold so I don't think we'll be findin' an easy answer for this any time soon."

Duane suddenly reached out and grabbed Mick by the arm, startling him. "I need a glass of water. I'm so thirsty."

Mick nodded to Dr. Brine, who held a cup of tepid water to Duane's parched lips. Mick wanted to try to comfort Duane but he was overcome by the futility of the situation. Seeing people he had come to know die a slow and painful death gave him a terrible sinking feeling in his gut. He couldn't stand to witness it for too long.

"Hang in there, Dewey," was all he could muster before going back to the office.

Jim, Chuck, and Jon were waiting for him when he entered the office. As the chief at the fire department he was used to meetings with the volunteers but he was out of his element in this situation. Who wouldn't be in this waking nightmare? Extinguishing a fire was different than eradicating an army of the walking dead.

"You're late." Chuck joked. "Ten minutes late." His jokes were a way to push his true feelings away. He couldn't help but feel guilty about Duane. One by one his friends were being eradicated. Until now, he had felt the two of them to be invincible. The sudden turn of events had altered his way of thinking.

"Sorry to inconvenience you, Chuck."

"I'm gonna have to ask for a raise," Chuck said, trying to lighten the mood

"Fine. I'll double your present salary. And put that damned cigarette out. It bothers me," Mick grumped, swatting at the smoke-filled air.

Chuck frowned and crushed the cigarette out on the sole of his shoe.

"We have problems." Mick said, as he sat behind the desk. "If we don't do something, we're liable to be overrun. I need some ideas from you on how to make it safer here."

"Well for one thing," Jon said, "every time the trucks come back, some of those things follow. We're gonna have to start coming back to the shelter by going out Route 66 and coming in from that direction. That way the ghouls won't see the traffic coming from town and follow."

"That's a good idea, Mick said. "I've thought about that myself but is Sixty-Six clear of obstructions? Can we get through?"

"Yeah, it's clear, in that area anyway. I was out there yesterday."

"Okay. From now on, everyone comes back to the shelter via Sixty-Six. Pass it on to whoever needs to know. All of the grocery stores in town are about cleaned out. We have to find somewhere else to get rations."

All of the large grocery chains were empty and the small mom and pop stores wouldn't have the volume needed, even if they hadn't been pillaged. Mick recognized this early on as a problem.

"Schools!" Jim said, suddenly realizing where an abundance of food could be found. "The schools in town will have enough food to feed a thousand kids for a week. Properly rationed, it should be enough to take care of us for months."

"Yeah, good thinking, Jim. The schools will be well stocked. When this started there were only a few days until the new school year was to begin. It'll be hard to get in and get the provisions before being outnumbered by zombies but it's the only place left in the area to get what we need."

"There's one more thing," Jim said in a troubled tone. "We were almost surrounded yesterday by a horde coming from town. We can't let ourselves get caged in without an escape. Finding a solution needs to have priority over anything else."

"No, we can't. Any suggestions?" Mick asked.

"The school has plenty of buses." Jim chimed in again. "Why not get a few and pull them along side of the door in the basement? We can evacuate everyone to them in case of an emergency and move to a new location."

Mick nodded his approval. We can also use them to get the food from the schools. I don't think a truck will haul enough. We won't be able to go back to each school more than once to get what we need. The bastards will flock to wherever we are in town and stay for a while. You have to get everything, and get it quick." "

CHAPTER 15

Sharon studied the creature lying on the examination table, the arms, legs, and head firmly strapped. It was dressed in blue jeans and a T-shirt with a tear on the right shoulder exposing a bite size wound that signified the cause of death.

The creature was much calmer than it had been when it first revived. It had almost grown accustomed to their presence now and this puzzled her. They had at least some slight ability to learn new behavior. She wondered if it was released from its bindings if it would still feel the urge to attack. She almost felt sorry for the bewildered thing. They didn't seem to know the evil they were doing. Some unknown force resurrected them from the dead while some dark instinct drove them to crave warm flesh.

Dr. Cowen came in carrying a research logbook. Tossing the book on a desk with a resounding thud, he turned to Sharon.

"What is it, Rich?" Sharon asked, seeing something horrible on his face.

"Washington has been evacuated. They're overrun with the plague. The brass are considering dropping bombs on all of the big cities."

Sharon felt as though someone had just delivered a roundhouse karate kick to her chest. The wind was effectively sucked right out of her lungs.

"Oh my God! They can't do that! They can't be serious!"

"Oh, really?" Dr. Cowen sneered. "This is the all-knowing government. They can, and they are."

"If they do that, there will be nothing left to save. We may as well pack up our research here and just settle in for the duration."

"A lot of people would have to okay such a move. Let's just hope someone has enough sense to kill the bomb idea."

He picked up the logbook. "I've got some news. A brain-dead patient in Charlottesville died last week but didn't resurrect. He stayed dead."

"That means we were right in our assumption which area of the brain is affected by the phenomenon."

"Yes," he said. "It gives us a starting point to focus on. He didn't come back because that part of the brain was inoperative. The rest of his brain controlling lower functions, heartbeat, breathing, and so on were fine. But it still doesn't mean we'll find out anything except where it starts. We may yet hit dead ends."

"True, but at least that's something," Sharon said hopefully.

Dr. Cowen went to the refrigerator under an air circulation duct against the wall. It was an ancient Frigidaire about five feet high, circa 1950, with a rounded top and had been in the complex since the early sixties. He pulled the handle and the door swung open. Inside were various blood samples from the walking dead with biohazard labels and the date the sample was drawn.

He grabbed a Diet Coke from the bottom shelf and cracked the tab. He drank half the can before lowering it and studying the container.

"You want a drink?" he asked, holding the can at arm's length.

"No. I don't care for soft drinks. Too sweet."

"Okay, but this may be your last chance unless we can train these re-animates to work in a factory," he said.

Sharon didn't like sodas and she sure wasn't going to drink any that were kept that close to blood samples from those things.

Dr. Cowen finished the rest of his drink with another big chug, crushed the aluminum can and tossed it in a nearby trashcan. With a burp and a wink he retrieved his notes from the table and settled himself in front of the computer the way a hen settles herself onto her nest. "I'm going to input this new information into the program and see what answers it has for me, if any."

"I'm going to have lunch," Sharon said, turning for the door. "You want to come along before you do that?"

"No, I'll go later," he said, already typing away. "You go ahead."

Sharon stepped out of the lab into the short hallway that led to the main corridor of the complex. Resembling a street more than a corridor, it was a paved roadway with buildings on both sides. There was a mass transit system to transport personnel from one end of the installation to the other. Lights were mounted in the ceiling to give a daytime appearance to the subterranean city. To keep everyone in sync with the outside world the lights were dimmed in the evening.

When Sharon pushed through the double glass doors of the cafeteria it was twelve o'clock and the room was fairly full. She pulled a tray from the stack at the beginning of the buffet, pulled a knife and fork from a canister, then slid down the track in front of the unappetizing display of food. Choosing ham and applesauce from the selection of available items she found a seat at an empty table and began to eat.

"May I sit here?" Gilbert Brownlow held a tray of food and stared down at her. He always had a way of sneaking up on Sharon when she least expected it.

"Why not?" she said. Perhaps his presence would completely kill her appetite and she would be spared the tasteless fare.

He seated himself across from her and unfolded a napkin on his lap. "Any new discoveries?" he asked, taking a forkful of instant mashed potatoes with powdered gravy.

"Only one," she said, playing with her food so as not to make eye contact. "But it's really nothing to be excited about just yet."

"You don't like me, do you, doctor?"

"I object to the way you and your kind have handled this situation." She looked him in the eye. "I think the government has done as much as anyone to deepen our dilemma."

"We are doing what we must to save mankind," he said in an even tone. "Sometimes you have to sacrifice a few to save the multitude."

"Yeah, right, Mr. Spock. Live long and prosper by dropping atom bombs? That's your idea of saving us?"

"They congregate in the cities. It's our best chance to kill them in large numbers. That will only be done as a last resort. It's really up to you and *your* kind to give us other options."

"The dead will only last about ten years or so before decomposition destroys the body, making them immobile. It will take a lot longer than that for the earth to repair itself from *your* grand plan."

"Nevertheless, we will do what we feel we must."

Sharon stood abruptly and picked up her tray. "You always do, which is probably why we have this problem to begin with." She turned on her heel and walked away.

She slammed her tray on an old cart piled high with discarded trays and exited the cafeteria. She walked down the street until she came to the lake. The size of a football field it was very impressive. Fake shrubs and trees were planted all around the lake giving it the appearance of a finely kept park.

Sharon sat on a wooden bench and peered across the water. The lake was not only meant to be one of the water sources but also a calming, moral booster. She stretched out on the bench and closed her eyes.

CHAPTER 16

"The world is an evil place," the voice said. "Do you understand that its destruction is at hand?"

Reverend Peterson stared at the sphere of the earth passing by in a cloud of smoke until it was only a twinkle in the dark void. Darkness engulfed him and a chill penetrated his soul as he floated.

"The sins of man have piled high; even to heaven, and shall now be cast in the lake of fire."

Flames rose all around him but did not burn and soon faded in the direction the earth had gone. Once again he was alone in the dark void.

"Every man's sword shall be lifted against his brother and my angels shall destroy those opposing me. And there shall be a plague with which I shall smite all of the evil ones. Their flesh shall rot while they are still on their feet. Their eyes shall rot in their sockets; their tongues shall rot in their mouths. And in that great day panic shall fall upon man. Eaten up will be the flesh of those who refused to see the signs, eaten up while they stand on their feet."

The darkness lifted and he saw a great throne, and God was seated on the throne. To His right was a smaller throne and the reverend saw himself seated there.

"You shall lead the way for a new earth. As my staff, you will dissolve the wicked. You will begin your quest when you receive the sign."

The voice faded and the preacher's eyes opened to the cathedral ceiling of the sanctuary. In the Event Room the dead continued their relentless attack on the barricaded door.

The preacher stood with a newfound strength. To him it was more than a dream. He had indeed found favor with God. Judgment day was here and he had been deemed worthy and worthy of the position he deserved. God had told him this in the dream. He was not the useless, sinful loser his father had pounded into him as a young child.

He shivered and gritted his teeth whenever the bitter memories of his childhood came to mind. He always did his best to push it away into the furthermost corner of his mind. Out of sight, out of touch, as if it never was.

Again the vision of his father in the coffin, clawing at the lid came to mind. The uncontrollable urge unfulfilled. Judged and sentenced. Thou shalt not judge, unless thy be judged. A fitting end to an old fool, he thought.

The preacher stretched, and then put one hand on the lower part of his back. It was sore and that made it difficult to move for a while after waking. A pew was not an easy place to sleep and it took some time for the pain to diminish each day. He stepped up to the pulpit and stared out of the broken window to the lawn. More of the dead had come since he'd last checked. Their numbers grew every day and they now numbered more than the population of the small village before the plague.

He wondered where they were coming from, why there were so many. It could be that they are coming in from all the surrounding rural and mountain regions but why to this place? Could it be that they have a purpose there as well?

It had been almost four weeks. He had been cut off from the world outside for two of them. How long would Armageddon last? How many of the wicked had been destroyed so far? He wanted to know what was left of a corrupt world and how much longer he would have to stay locked away.

Reverend Peterson went to the kitchen and opened the cabinet under the sink to retrieve the small battery-operated radio. Water had leaked from the drainpipe onto the radio. He set it on the table and then went back to the cabinet to retrieve a toolkit. He didn't notice the open latch and its contents clattered to the floor; the pounding on the door intensified. He plucked a screwdriver from the floor, grabbed the radio, and ran back to the sanctuary to do the job.

Quickly he removed the six screws holding the cover in place. With a towel he dried the inside as best he could until he was confident it was dry enough and replaced the cover. Static buzzed from the speaker as he scanned the FM dial. He moved the dial from left to right until the entire spectrum had been covered but there was only static. He switched to AM before giving up. A human voice, finally he had found life, faint but there. A man was saying, "*...to be considered extremely dangerous and must not be contacted. No one should make any kind of attempt to enter the city of Chicago or any of its suburbs. The United States military are engaging the armies of the dead, and you will be notified when it is safe to return.*"

The preacher listened intently to the man's words. Mankind was fighting a losing battle. How could they win? You can't beat God. He turned his attention back to the radio.

"*The city of Los Angeles has been declared off limits to any trespassers. Anyone found entering the city will be shot on sight, no questions asked. The same is said to be true for Miami, Dallas, Philadelphia, New York, Atlanta, and Washington DC. Please do not attempt to go to any of these locations. The cities are all very dangerous. Any attempt to go to any densely populated areas is suicide.*"

Brother against brother, he thought. The Prophecy was coming true. Soon all of the wicked will be crushed and the righteous would rule.

A crash and the sound of metal and wood hitting the floor came from the kitchen, taking his attention from the radio. The preacher jumped from his seat and ran to the door. One of the boards across the door had been torn away and one of the locks had been forced off. The nails in the frame were backing out as the door vibrated. The noise created by the tools falling and the sound of the radio had agitated them into trying harder to enter.

He pushed against the door in a futile attempt to keep the intruders out. More nails popped out. The door was going to collapse. The preacher ran back to the sanctuary and waited. In a few minutes, the door burst open and the twisted figures staggered through.

The preacher made his way to the pulpit and the broken window. The walking corpses surrounded him, slowly forming a tight circle. The preacher looked out of the window to the lawn below. One creature stood below. He had no choice but to risk it.

He landed on top of the thing and it fell under his weight. It had broken his fall but squirmed beneath him, uninjured. The preacher quickly rolled away from the ghoul and got to his feet. More of them were coming from all directions.

This must be the sign, he thought, It was why there were so many of the creatures in the small community—to force him to leave the secluded church. God had plans for him elsewhere. The Preacher became bloated with his own self-importance.

Confidently but carefully he walked away to begin the quest ahead of him. God would show him the way.

CHAPTER 17

The three trucks used for rescue and supply runs were parked in front of the shelter. Jon lay on the seat of Jim's truck, working under the dash as Jim and Chuck watched. Bars had been welded over the windows of each truck, including Jim's.

Mick walked up to the three men. "Are all of the radios installed and working Jon?"

"Yeah, everything's finished," Jon answered, sliding out from under the dash. "All of the radios work. The base station is also up and going. We're ready to go."

"Good. Does everybody know what to do?"

"We know." Jim said. "And we'll be careful, don't worry. No one's gonna take any unnecessary chances."

"In and out, okay? No unnecessary risks," Mick said, staring deliberately at Chuck.

Chuck shrugged and went to one of the trucks and strapped on his usual arsenal of weapons. Jim checked his and got in his truck with Jon, who rode shotgun. Chuck motioned to George Henry, a short stocky man of few words who had proven to be cool under fire. He had just been relieved of guard duty and joined Chuck for the ride.

"Come in, Ghoul Buster One. Do you copy?" Chuck spoke into the mic in Jim's truck.

Jim rolled his eyes and picked up the mic to reply. Chuck's carefree attitude didn't bother Jim nearly as much as it bothered Mick. It might be Chuck's way of retaining his sanity through each day.

"Ten-four, loud and clear. You follow, I'll lead."

The two trucks drove out of the parking lot and into town. Disfigured fiends roamed the streets and yards as the trucks made their way to the school board office where the buses were kept. Jim did his best to miss them as they clumsily made attempts to reach for the moving vehicles. Chuck steered toward the creatures, bumping as many as he could just enough to send them flying through the air in a comical display of flailing arms and legs.

"Hey, knock it off, Chuck!" Jon radioed. "You'll have those things lying all over the road. We have to drive back through here."

Chuck shrugged.

Rows of school buses lined the parking lot around the stuccoes building. They pulled in beside a few parked in the rear, out of sight. Jim grabbed a tool bag from the seat and headed for the nearest bus. The rest took positions around the lot and secured the area.

Jim crawled under the dash of the school bus and disconnected the proper wires to start it without keys. Fifteen feet away, half the distance to the back of the bus, a pair of gray, molding hands grasped onto the back of a seat and a partially devoured face appeared.

As it moved quietly up the isle, Jim was unaware of the approaching danger. Nearing its prey, the realization of gratification caused the creature to drool and moan, awkwardly shuffling its feet as it's pace quickened.

Secure in the knowledge that his crack team was guarding the perimeter, Jim didn't hear the shuffling corpse until he felt a tugging on his jeans. He tried to pull his leg away but the creature held tight, lowering its head for a bite. Its mouth opened and closed on Jim's pants leg, tearing out a portion of the well worn, thinning fabric.

Jim used his other leg to deliver a devastating blow to the creature's forehead. It flew backward and landed in the isle and lay still. Jim had killed the creature with a single kick. Jon heard the disturbance and moved with surprising quickness to Jim's aid.

"You okay?"

Jim pulled the pant leg up to his knee and examined the area. "Yeah, I think so. It got my Levi's, nothing else."

Jon saw the corpse lying motionless in the isle and realized Jim had killed it without the use of a gun or a club. "Son of a...You're one lucky bastard!"

Jim nodded and went back to the work at hand.

Jon pulled the body out of the bus by its feet, its head bouncing off each step.

"All done?" Jon asked, coming into the bus and wiping his hands on his shirt.

"Yeah. Tell the others to come on in. Let's get the hell out of here."

Jon left to gather the rest of the party and Jim stared at the monster lying on the asphalt. I was lucky, he thought. All of my life I've been careful and thought things through, yet this thing managed to sneak up on me. I could have just as easily been bandaging a wound now, headed for the dead myself. In the future I will have to be even more cautious.

Once the crew was gathered, it was decided that Jim would drive the bus to the school to collect the food. Jon would lead the way in Jim's truck, and Chuck and George would follow.

"All right, listen," Jon said. "I'll drive up next to the door of the school cafeteria and you back the bus in close. We'll load the food through the rear door, and then we'll flank each side of the bus with the trucks. Two stand guard and two load. If you back the bus close enough to the door, they won't be able to get in there."

"Assuming the bus will start," Jim said. "It's been sitting quite a while."

"You awake, Chuck? That sound okay with you?" Jon said.

"Aye-aye, Captain," Chuck said, snapping to attention and saluting, military style.

"Jesus," Jon exclaimed, returning to Jim's truck.

Jon pulled up beside the cafeteria door and hurried to pick the lock. Jim backed the bus in and stopped a few feet away to give Jon room to work. Chuck drove the other truck and positioned it on the opposite side.

The walking dead were sparse around the school. Jim hurried to the back of the bus and opened the rear door.

"Got it!" Jon shouted, swinging the school doors open. A door on the right side of the hallway said CAFETERIA.

Jim backed the rear of the bus against the entrance. When he felt it bump against the brick exterior of the building, he closed the front door and walked down the isle to the rear emergency exit and into the school.

They carefully walked down the hall, weapons drawn, to the cafeteria door. Jim peered into the room through the door's small window. "Looks clear. I don't think any are in there."

"You sure?"

"Yeah, but I can't see into the kitchen from here. There could be some in there."

Jim pulled the walkie-talkie from his belt. "Chuck, how's it going out there?"

"Looks pretty good. There's a few headed for us but I'm not gonna shoot till I have to. Don't worry if you hear shots. I'll let you know if there's real trouble."

"Ten-four," Jim said, returning the radio to his belt. "You ready?"

"I'm hungry," Jon said, swinging the door open with a kick. They entered the room; weapons aimed like two FBI agents on a drug bust.

"So far so good," Jim said, dashing across the room to the kitchen door.

The kitchen door was solid, with no window to see inside. They could easily be met by hungry hordes waiting on the other side. Jim counted down from three with his fingers and they burst in. The door flew open and the men stood ready, their weapons poised to fire at any movement.

The kitchen was empty but a horrible stench filled the room. It was the smell of rotting corpses, the smell of death.

Jon blew a sigh of relief when they realized the odor emanated from the freezers that had been off since the power went out. He pointed to a closed door on the opposite end of the room. "That must be the pantry."

Jim pushed a large four-wheeled cart to the pantry door. He thrust the door open and stepped back. Shelves of canned food filled the pantry. Canisters of flour and sugar rested on the floor.

"Jackpot!" Jim said happily. "Let's get to work."

They made trip after trip to the bus until the pantry was empty. Every so often, a shot rang out as the men outside dispensed of the walking dead.

The last cart was wheeled to the bus and Jon handed the goods to Jim, who was inside the bus. "It's getting pretty thick out here," Chuck said over the walkie-talkie. "Let's hurry it up."

The gunfire was more frequent now. Jim saw many more moving in. The situation was becoming very dangerous.

As Jon set the last can inside the back door of the bus, he flinched and a shocked look crossed his usually calm countenance. "Awww, fuck!" he bellowed, disappearing from Jim's sight.

Jim heard his agonized scream and jumped into action. Kicking the empty cart out of the way, he hurdled himself through the door.

Jon thrashed on the ground under the bus, trying desperately to fight off two foul demons that had gotten beneath the bus and were now climbing Jon's body in a feeding frenzy. They had managed to pull him under the bus by his feet.

Jim grabbed Jon's hands and tried to pull him out but couldn't because of the added weight of the two ghouls. As Jon screamed, Jim took the .44 from its holster put a bullet into the brains of each creature and pulled Jon out from beneath the bus.

Jon was choking on his own blood. The monsters had ripped a large chunk of flesh from his throat and he was bleeding to death in short order. Chuck, who had come to their aid, looked in through a crack between the bus and the wall of the school. Shots continued from the guard still plucking away at the advancing dead. Jim held Jon in his arms, keeping his head high to ease the choking.

"You've gotta kill me," Jon gurgled, "Please! Don't let me go through—" He coughed again, unable to finish.

Jim looked up at Chuck, who nodded and then turned away, unable to watch any longer. It would be cruel to let Jon suffer the agonizing effects of the creature's bites and then allow his body to be used by whatever it was that occupied it after death. Jim tried hard to suppress his exploding emotions as he readied himself for what had to be done.

"Close your eyes," Jim's voice trembled.

Jon closed his eyes and Jim laid him to the ground, aiming the .44 at his head. He hesitated a moment. "God have mercy," he said and pulled the trigger.

CHAPTER 18

The evening had turned cool and storm clouds were moving in from the south. It had been quiet that day; no shots had been fired.

Felicia leaned against the wall and closed her eyes, enjoying the cool breeze as it blew through her hair. It wasn't easy to take her mind off of the horror that had overwhelmed her. The vacation she had taken at the beach in the spring was an enjoyable memory and flooded her mind with remembrance. Visions of long strolls by the ocean with her lover and moonlight dances swam before her inner eye, purple and orange sunsets and seagulls. She remembered how the call of the seagulls mixed with the roar of the ocean had soothed and calmed her.

"I'm sorry, Miss, but you have to go inside."

The voice startled Felicia. She opened her eyes and her quiet world of beauty disappeared, replaced by a hollow-eyed black man holding a gun by his side.

"I'm sorry but you can't stay out here," he repeated.

"It's okay," a man said from behind.

Felicia turned to see Mick's twinkling blue eyes.

"I'll take it from here," Mick said. The black man nodded and walked away.

Mick rocked back and forth on his heals, hands clasped behind his back, not sure what to say next. He was shy with girls and could never think of anything witty to say. "Looks like a storms brewing," he said finally, cursing himself for not being able to think of anything except the weather.

"A storm has been hovering over us for weeks," Felicia said, looking up to the dark clouds. "When will it go away? When will it all stop?"

"I don't know," Mick said. "Maybe when it's accomplished its goal."

Felicia saw for the first time how strong yet gentle his face was. "What do you mean?"

Mick watched the approaching storm and gathered his thoughts. "Some people have said that the earth itself is the reason we have so many new diseases, that we've messed this planet up pretty good and it's fighting back, trying to rid its body of our pollution. The only problem is that we keep curing the cure. Maybe this is a last-ditch effort to save itself, get rid of most of us and start over. The theory has a name but I can't think of it."

"It's called Gaia's Revenge. Do you really believe that?"

"It sounds as good as anything I've heard so far. The truth is, nobody knows for sure. I doubt if anyone ever will."

Felicia walked to the edge of the porch and lowered her head. She couldn't get her family off her mind. She hadn't seen or heard from them in several weeks and her concern for their safety gnawed at her. A lone tear rolled down her cheek. She was afraid and alone, except for the silent ghost-child who seemed to have adopted her. That, at least, was a comfort to her.

"You okay?" Mick asked, putting a hand on her shoulder. "Is there anything I can do?"

Felicia turned and put her head on his chest and let the tears come. "I'm alone," she sobbed. "I've lost everyone I care for."

Mick held her tightly. "It'll be okay. I'll see that you're kept safe. Don't worry."

Felicia cried until some of the pain eased and then wiped her eyes. "I'm sorry," she said. "I'm sure you don't have the time for this."

"No, it's fine. Come see me anytime you feel the need to talk."

"The bus is coming!" one of the guards yelled, interrupting their moment.

Mick gave Felicia's hand a final squeeze and let go. "Go on inside now. I'll come see how you're doing in a bit."

Felicia turned to go inside but that old foreboding tingle suddenly crept up her spine. Mick watched her stop and waver. He reached out a hand to steady her. "You okay?" he asked. When she didn't reply he turned her gently by her shoulders, shocked at her glazed and grim countenance. "Felicia! What's wrong?"

She trembled beneath his hands and looked right through him. Her eyes closed and Mick thought she was going to fall into a faint but she stood stone-like before him. "Felicia, please!" he pleaded. "Say something!"

Felicia opened her eyes. "Oh, Mick, no!"

Jim brought the bus to a stop, pulled the lever to open the doors, and stepped out. Mick and Jon had been friends. He didn't relish the idea of being the one to bring such bad news.

Mick turned toward the bus when Jim stepped out "Where's Jon?" he asked.

Felicia stood at Mick's elbow, her hand against the small of his back.

"He didn't make it, Mick. I'm sorry."

Mick stood silently for a several seconds. Felicia's touch seemed to steady him. He drew a deep breath. "Jesus, what happened?"

"Some got by us. He got tore up pretty bad. I brought him back Mick. He's in the bus."

Mick moved to the rear of the bus and reached to open the door but Jim put a hand on the door, holding it shut. "Are you sure you wanna see him?"

"Yes, I'm sure."

Inside, Mick stared at Jon's bloody, mangled body then turned away. "You shot him?"

"He asked me to. He was dying."

"It's what I would've done," Mick said, then hesitated in brief silence. "I want him burned separate from the rest. I'll see to it myself."

"Did he have any family?" Jim asked

"No. They're all gone-with the rest. I was the only real friend he had left here. I've known him most of my life. He was a good man—a good friend."

Jim helped Mick move Jon's body onto the truck that would take him to the burn area. He walked over to Chuck to give Mick some privacy.

Felicia turned to follow Jim but Mick reached out and pulled her gently toward him. She slipped her arm around his waist, aware of the grief building inside of him.

The sky grew darker. Soon the trees bent from the force of a northern wind that gusted with strength. Jim watched as Mick stood over his fallen friend. The approaching storm and distant flashes of lightening completed a portrait of despair and darkness.

Mick and Felicia clung to one another in the howling wind, a portent of the real storm they all knew was coming. They resembled a painting, a moment of anguish and hope suspended in time.

CHAPTER 19

Reverend Peterson sat by the side of the road wondering what to do next. The church was miles behind him, its doors broken down, its sanctity violated by roving demons in search of human victims. There had been no traffic in the two hours he had been walking. Occasionally he'd had a run-in with a few creatures but they were easy to outrun. Town was still a day's walk and it was getting dark. He needed to find a place to spend the night.

He knew of a remote school a mile or so ahead that had been used to treat troubled teens. Rich and famous parents sent their kids there at the first sign of trouble. It was an easy way of getting them out of their hair instead of doing the job they were supposed to do, which was parenting their children. The place was probably abandoned by now. It would be a good place to hole up.

The preacher continued his journey. There weren't many houses in the area so there weren't any creatures milling about. During his uneventful walk, the reverend convinced himself that God had caused most of the creatures to be absent through his journey. It was good to be in God's favor, he thought.

The turn to the place he sought was just ahead. It would be another mile or so down Skyview Drive before he came to the old school. He quickened his pace, trying to beat the storm and the approaching darkness.

A thick forest surrounded the road now filled with twisted trees and a ground clinging fog. His eyes darted to the woods repeatedly, a feeling on uneasiness building with each unidentified sound. Darkness was descending and a light rain began tapping against his face.

He was within half a mile of his destination. He could not shake the feeling that he was being watched.

Peterson stopped, frozen in place.

A scruffy-faced boy about seventeen years of age jumped in front of him, a rifle trained at his head. Looking to his left, then to his right, the reverend saw two boys with weapons hiding in the woods.

"Stop right there, man, or I'll blow your brains out," the boy on the road said.

The preacher remained still and raised his hands as the other two came from the woods and circled him.

"It's okay, my son. I am a man of God. There is no need for your weapons. I mean you no harm."

The boy reaffirmed his aim and took a step closer. "God is dead. He must be; the devil has control of things now."

"No, young man, that's not true. God has spoken to me and told me of what will pass." The preacher lowered his arms. "Are you from the school?"

"There is no school. Not anymore. It's just a place."

The preacher approached the boy. As he did, the other two closed in on him. He studied his captors. All of them were young, still impressionable, just what he needed if he were to build an empire of God-fearing people. It was easy with children. These youngsters looked quite battered in appearance and mindset. He needed more information in order to gain their trust.

"I am Father Peterson. Where are your teachers? Are they still at the school?"

"No," the first boy said. "They're gone. They're all gone."

"Where did they go?"

"Some left, some are dead."

"I'm sorry," the preacher said. "God has been watching over you for you to survive this long. He sent me here. He told me in a dream where to find you."

The preacher lied. He needed power and could not have found a better place to accumulate it.

The boy lowered the rifle. "You dreamt about us?"

"I was told to come here and make you strong, to lead you into a new world. I can do that, you know. You'll have everything you want and you'll always be happy."

"What's going on out there?" the boy asked.

"It's the end of the world, my son, the end for all of them. The beginning for us."

Rain began to fall in earnest.

CHAPTER 20

Mick drove into the lime quarry where the dead were burned to keep disease to a minimum. The wrapped body of his friend was in the back of the truck. Recent events had caused Mick to think he had become desensitized to the pain and death surrounding him, but now that it had struck close to him he realized that was not the case.

He drove past the spot where Chuck was burning bodies to an area farther in that was surrounded by two hundred-foot limestone cliffs. He stopped the truck and contemplated the task ahead of him. He took a long pull from a silver flask of bourbon. "Shit, I might as well get on with it," he said. "Prolonging it will not make it any easier."

Mick stepped out of the truck and went to the tailgate. Jon's body was wrapped in his sleeping bag; the one Jon had special ordered from Top Of The Drive Sporting Goods before they'd gone out of business. A man Jon's size had to special-order most things. Mick reached in and dragged Jon's enormous body out of the truck and onto the ground.

He stared at the wrapped body of his fallen friend. Amanda had sewn the top of the bag shut with a needle and fishing line, sealed in like a caterpillar in a cocoon.

The day was unusually warm for late fall and Mick worked like a man possessed to dig a shallow grave. Placing Jon's remains in the slight trench, he poured gasoline over it, and then lit a cigarette from a pack Chuck had left on the seat. He sucked on the cigarette until a long shaft of red-hot ash grew on the end and then tossed the cigarette onto the funeral pyre. The gasoline ignited with a loud whoosh and began to consume the sleeping bag.

Mick watched the flames until his emotions gave in to a tightening in his chest. His throat ached with unshed tears as he turned away from the blaze. Rather than break down, he channeled his grief into anger. He cursed God and then denied him. There is no God! What kind of a God would curse his greatest creation with this plague of flesh eaters?

He pounded his fists against the truck to vent his anger. With each strike, his anguish dissipated. He released a bitter laugh and shook his head to clear it of the hot emotion he had allowed himself to feel, then turned his attention back to the task at hand.

From his pocket, he extracted Jon's police badge. Even though the police force had vanished along with the rest of civilization, Jon had kept it with him out of pride more than anything else. Mick examined the badge with Jon's identification number and WCPD insignia inscribed over it. He put it back into his pocket.

Mick removed the small flask from his jacket pocket again and took another long swig. Many things still needed to be done. Another bus still had to be brought in to carry everyone away if and when the situation called for it. Winter would set in soon and they would need to heat the building. If they'd had more time to prepare, maybe they could have been ready for this crisis. Maybe they could have saved more lives, even Jon's.

Mick laughed sardonically. "Yeah, right! Who plans for an army of flesh-eating dead zombies?" He said, as though explaining it to his fallen friend.

He put the flask away and covered Jon's remains with a shovel. After the grave was covered over, he removed the badge from his pocket and placed it on the shallow grave.

CHAPTER 21

Television monitors broadcast satellite-view tactical displays, each showing a different region of the planet. There were close-up observations of Russian missile bases and U.S. cities burning or deserted of everyone but the walking dead.

Gilbert Brownlow stood behind one of the technicians, watching the screens.

Millions of Americans were dying. As the number of living dwindled, enemy numbers grew. Brownlow became increasingly embittered. He believed the situation called for swift, drastic measures. The inability of present leaders to act would, in his opinion, seal their doom.

The technician sitting at the console in front of Brownlow turned and removed his headset. "Sir, I have a transmission from Norad. Emergency, priority one."

"Is it visual?"

"Yes, sir."

"Put it on screen five."

The view of a burning New York City faded, replaced with the communication room at Norad. A young lieutenant Brownlow didn't recognize sat at the communications console, his face pale with fear. "Sir, we have been compromised. The situation is grave."

"I want to talk to the President," Brownlow said. "Where is he?"

"The President is dead, sir. The Vice President is also dead. This facility has been overrun with those—creatures. I've locked myself in this room and for the present I'm safe but there's no food or water here and hundreds of those things are outside the door. I'm trapped."

"Lieutenant, would you please verify that the computer in front of you is on and operational?"

"Yes, sir." The lieutenant acknowledged and executed the order. "Sir, it is operational."

"Good." Brownlow said. "Now below you, to your left, you will see a safe. The combination code is one-five-oh-six-eight-nine. Please open the safe now."

The lieutenant opened the safe and found a red card inside. He removed it.

"The card should say, 'GONE FISHING, can't play.' Am I correct?

"Yes, sir. You are correct."

"Please type that password into your computer as written. Now."

The Lieutenant typed the password into his computer and a page of text appeared with an EXECUTE button at the bottom of the screen.

"Please read the orders out loud, lieutenant."

The lieutenant read the orders. His voice boomed over the room's speakers for all to hear. "In the event of a national emergency and the death of the President of the United States and his cabinet, or the fall of Norad, all command functions will be thereby transferred to the Mount Weather Command Center. The responsibilities of the office of President will be passed to the current Secretary in charge." The card slipped from the lieutenant's fingers and glided to the floor.

"Do you understand that, lieutenant?"

"Yes, sir, I do."

"Please execute the order."

The lieutenant moved the cursor to the EXECUTE button and clicked it. Within seconds the computer screens in the Mount Weather War Room displayed a download bar. When the bar turned completely blue, the computer's soft-spoken female voice said, "Transfer complete. All command functions enabled."

Brownlow was finally content. He allowed himself a small sigh of relief. He would now be able to put an end to this nightmare his own way. It was the moment he had been waiting for. No longer would he be forced to sit idly by while the United States went down in flames.

"Thank you, lieutenant," he told the man on the screen. "And good luck, son."

Brownlow killed the transmission without further thought to the young man and moved in front of the television monitors.

"Gentlemen," he announced with an air of self-importance, "the responsibility and the well being of this great country has been transferred to our post. It is now up to us to find a solution. I want to know the ratio of dead compared to the number of living, first in the major cities, then in rural areas. I want this information by nine tomorrow morning."

Brownlow walked out of the door, leaving the men dismayed. Some were afraid of what the next move would be.

The news of Norad's fall spread quickly throughout the base. Rich Cowen and Sharon were in the lab when they heard the report. It was exactly the turn of events they hadn't dared to imagine. The fact that Brownlow was now in charge of the nation's military arsenal brought an element of even more uncertainty to their dilemma.

Dr. Cowen carefully examined the saliva sample from the restrained creature on the examining table. He had determined that the virus responsible for infection and death was not present in the bloodstream.

"Nothing, Sharon. Still nothing."

Sharon paced the floor, deep in thought. "What would happen if fresh blood were introduced into the saliva sample? Maybe it's something that reacts together."

"Possibly. I'll take some of mine."

Dr. Cowen took a clean needle and held it in his teeth while he swabbed his arm inside his elbow with alcohol. He tapped his arm with two fingers until a vein swelled. The needle stung as it pierced the skin and he winced at the prick. The cylinder turned red with his life liquid. "All right, that should do it."

He took the sample to the microscope. "Now let's see if anything happens."

He focused the image again and studied it for several minutes. He noticed no change. "I'm at a loss," he said, moving away from the screen. "I can't find a single thing that would cause this condition. If we can't come up with something to give Brownlow..." His voice faded.

Sharon knew what he meant. Gilbert Brownlow wanted to push the button and end the problem, destroying half the planet in the process.

CHAPTER 22

Amanda ventured unnoticed down the steps and into the basement of the shelter. Almost a month without a decent bath was too much for her to handle. The guards wouldn't allow any of the survivors outside, much less down to the river for a bath. Water brought into the refuge was only for drinking. It was too dangerous to get enough for bathing, too.

The basement was dark. Amanda could barely make out the crack of light surrounding the door leading outside. The darkness made her anxious. The building was well guarded but there was always the possibility of something lurking-waiting. Her heart pounded. She had always been a little afraid of the dark.

Arms reaching blindly in front of her, she felt her way toward the splinter of light and found the doorknob. The door was locked but she fumbled with it until it opened and flooded the room with sunlight. She breathed a sigh of relief as she turned the button on the doorknob to lock the door behind her.

Amanda hurried down the path, careful of her surroundings as she went. The river was one hundred yards behind the shelter and she eagerly anticipated the cool water running over her body. She began to jog.

The river was calm and clear. Amanda searched for a secluded spot and found one a few yards upstream. The bank sloped gradually into a wide, deep pool. She removed her shoes and unsnapped her jeans and let them drop, kicking them away with her foot. The blouse came off next, leaving only a pair of black panties to hide her nakedness.

Amanda jumped in and submerged herself in the river. She let the water run over her body as she bobbed up and down like a child, pushing off with bare feet against the spongy riverbed. With a bar of Ivory soap she had swiped from Dr. Brine's ration of supplies, she lathered her skin and hair with such relish it was nearly erotic.

She dipped beneath the surface to rinse herself, then leaned against a rock close to shore and closed her eyes. It was well past swimming season but it felt so good to be clean she didn't mind the chilled water or rising Goosebumps.

Twigs snapped and Amanda's eyes flew open. She saw a monster step into ankle deep water, arms outstretched, gaping hole of a mouth open as it approached. Amanda spun around and used her feet to kick off the rock and headed for deeper water. The creature followed until it was waist deep, still reaching, fingers clenching. Amanda looked around in all directions. Her only option was to swim away from it and try to reach the shore before it could do the same.

She began to swim downstream when another creature came out of the tree line, dragging a mangled leg. It started to walk into the water but stopped at the edge, as though it intended to block her way. The other creature continued through waist-deep water toward her. They appeared to be working together, herding her the way ranchers drive cattle.

Amanda turned and swam to deeper water and struggled to keep her head above it. The creature waded until the water was shoulder deep, then stopped and backed away, afraid of the current. It waited there, blocking her path.

She had to do something fast. Her arms had grown weary of treading water to stay afloat. She began to swim upstream but the one on the bank stayed with her. The other creature had waded back to waist-deep water.

Amanda couldn't swim faster than they could move on land. She would have to swim all the way across the river. She was ready to do so when Jim ran from the path and took aim at the one on land. He fired and the monster fell to the ground. The one in the water, confused as to which human to attack, backed away, almost tripping over itself. Jim took careful aim and fired again, hitting the creature in the forehead. Its head whipped back and its body turned in the water before submerging. It surfaced and floated downstream.

Amanda swam back until her feet touched bottom. Jim walked to the river's edge and waited.

"You okay?" he asked, smiling slightly.

"I think so," she said. She suddenly realized her breasts were exposed, nipples erect from the cold water. Embarrassed, she crossed her arms to hide her nakedness. "I'm okay," she said. "Would you...?" She pointed to her blouse, keeping her arms over her glistening breasts.

Jim's eyes were fixed, then reacted. "Oh, of course!" He tossed the shirt to her and Amanda slid the blouse over her head.

"I'm sorry to walk up on you like that but it looked like you could use some help."

Amanda picked up her jeans and shoved one leg into them, then the other. "I feel like a fool," she said, buttoning them. "I'm such an idiot."

"Oh, I don't know. It looked like a pretty good idea to me," Jim said.

A guard ran down the path, out of breath, rifle ready. Jim spun around ready for another fight.

"You all right?" the guard asked, looking at the slain creature.

"Everything's fine," Jim said. He turned to Amanda. "Next time, let me know when you want to come down here. I'll come along." He smiled, "Don't worry, I'll turn my head."

Amanda picked up her shoes and emptied the sand from them before slipping them on. It would be a while before she attempted a bath again. She would deal with the crud before going through another encounter like this. If it hadn't been for Jim, she might have been lunch for two zombies.

The guard pushed the remaining creature into the river and watched it float away. The water around it turned red as the bullet hole released blood and brain matter. A school of minnows gathered around the carcass to feast on its offerings.

CHAPTER 23

Reverend Peterson appraised Skyview School. A large Victorian home with vaulted gables and octagon towers; a large covered porch wrapped around three sides. Several small sheds were in the rear yard; two other teens draped in yellow rain coats, rifles at their side stood on the porch. They lowered the hoods and joined the other three escorting Peterson. Dressed in green military fatigues beneath their raincoats, they were quite surprised to see someone else arrive.

"Who's he?" the taller of the two boys asked, using the barrel of his gun as a pointer.

"Says he's a preacher or something," said the scruffy-faced boy who had blocked Peterson's way on the road.

The taller boy studied Peterson. "He ain't no preacher. He don't look like no preacher. Maybe he's one of them zombies. Maybe he's a spy come here to kill us like you said they would," the first boy said.

Scruffy Face pushed the taller boy in the chest, almost knocking him down. "He ain't no zombie, you idiot. Zombies don't talk and he does. He might be a spy, though."

The tall boy regained his balance and made a dash toward Scruffy Face but he was stopped by the other three. "Don't you push me, Eddie! Don't you ever push me again!" he said, shaking himself free from the other boys' hold. "Or you'll be sorry."

Eddie laughed, knowing full well the kid wouldn't have a chance in a fight. None of them would, one on one. "You'd better behave, Romeo, or else I'll have to put you in the basement. Maybe you *and* Juliet."

The boy he called Romeo backed away, horrified. After a nervous glance at his tormentor, he went inside.

Peterson observed the boy's reaction. That was the kind of power he needed over them to achieve his goal. Eddie, the scruffy-faced boy, seemed to be in charge but that would soon change.

Peterson thought of ways to gain the upper hand. He needed Eddie's trust and faith first, and then the others would follow. Any that counted, anyway. As long as he had the cooperation of those with guns, the others would have no choice.

The preacher went into the school, sandwiched between two of the boys, Eddie leading the way. In the foyer, a curved stairway led to a balcony overlooking the entrance. On the left was a meeting room that contained a television and several chairs and sofas.

Eddie started up the stairs; never once turning to make sure his captive was under control or following. He was fully confident of the boys' loyalty to him. If Peterson tried anything they would shoot him. Peterson sensed this and followed quietly. It was not yet time to make his move. At least they were going upstairs and not to the basement. The boy outside had been terrified at the mere thought of being put there. Yes, that was power indeed, he thought, coveting that power.

Peterson was taken to a room covered with flowered wallpaper and old paintings of people in clothing from a past era. Three single beds were unmade.

One of the boys pushed Peterson into the room and slammed the door. Peterson went to a window on the far side and peered out. It would be easy to use the bed sheets to climb down and escape but that was not his plan. He had far greater things in mind.

At the fire pit in the back yard, Jenny was busy preparing a meal for the twenty-two boys who lived there. The grill was covered with venison steaks and tenderloins, grease popping and cracking as the meat cooked over a wood-fueled flame. The rain had finally stopped, allowing her to do her ordered duty.

She and her boyfriend Jody had been there over a week now after being found by Eddie and two others on the highway as they tried to make their way to one of the rescue stations. Eddie had convinced them that the rescue stations were deathtraps that the authorities were killing everyone they saw. It was better if they came back with him.

Eddie had lied but they had no way of knowing that. In retrospect, going with Eddie had been a big mistake and now they worried over their predicament. They were outsiders to the motley crew assembled there.

Jenny used a spatula to turn the meat over. Tonight it would be deer meat for dinner, tomorrow, too, if it were still good enough to eat by then. There was no food left at the school so they were forced to eat whatever could be shot and carried in.

Jody walked up behind her and put his arms around her waist.

Jenny turned, spatula high, ready to strike. "Damn it, Jody, haven't I told you not to sneak up on me like that?"

"I'm sorry. I didn't mean to scare you."

Jenny relaxed. There was a troubled look on Jody's face. "What's wrong, Jody?"

"Eddie, that's what. I hate him. He's crazy, Jenny. He thinks he's an army general or something. We'd better watch our step around here or we'll be next. We need to get out of here."

"Shhh! Be quiet. Someone might hear," Jenny said, inspecting the area around them. "Where would we go?"

"Riverton," Jody whispered. "The last I heard, there were still people there who can help."

"How will we get there, fly?"

Jody didn't get to answer because Eddie had stepped around the corner with two of his cronies. He picked a small piece of venison off the grill.

"How much longer before the food's done?" he asked, tearing the meat in half. Blood dripped from the hardly-cooked flesh.

"Fifteen minutes," Jenny said, continuing her work.

"Good. The patrols should be back by then. When it's done, get Romeo here to take some upstairs to the new guy. Not too much, though. I've got an army to feed."

Jody glared at Eddie, fists clenched. He didn't like being called Romeo and Eddie knew it but he wouldn't let himself be provoked again.

As the young soldiers continued on their way, Eddie threw his uneaten portion of steak on the ground. Jenny fetched it and tossed it back on the grill to finish cooking.

"Don't let him get to you, Jody," she said. "That's what he wants."

"I think he wants me out of the picture so he can have you, Jenny. Only I don't think he quite knows how to do that without killing me. If he did that, you wouldn't be too fond of him. But if he ever comes up with a way…" Jody paused to let what he said sink in. "We need to think of something soon."

CHAPTER 24

Chuck parked the school bus inches in front of the basement door, ripping the side mirror off in the process. After he made sure the folding doors of the bus were directly in front of the basement door, he killed the engine, retrieved his weapon, and walked down the isle to the emergency exit and stepped out. If trouble arose, they'd be able to escape safely to the bus through the basement and find a more secure location.

The school bus could only carry sixty people. They'd have to bring in another bus to accommodate everyone in the shelter.

As Chuck rounded the corner of the building he saw Mick in the midst of a heated confrontation with Mayor Woodson on the front porch. Woodson's arms flailed wildly as he shouted at Mick and then stormed away. Woodson gave Chuck a withering look as he passed, mumbling to himself as he departed.

"What was that all about?" Chuck asked.

"He's been on my ass to find something with better accommodations. I guess in his own self-righteous, narcissistic way, he's right. I'd chew my tongue off before telling the little prick he's right." Mick grinned, wryly. "Quarters are tight here. If one person gets a cold, everyone gets it. It's just not set up to handle this many people for a long period of time."

Chuck lit a cigarette and leaned against the railing, blowing the smoke away from Mick to avoid another lecture on the evils of smoking. "I know a place. We'd probably have to clear it out first."

"It's not in town, is it? Too many of those damned things around in town."

"Nope. It's about eight miles north of here."

Mick's eyes lit up. "The prison!" Mick said excitedly, slapping Chuck on the back "What a great idea! I don't know why I didn't think of it."

"Maybe because you didn't spend two years there. It seems that carrying five pounds of pot around in your trunk is frowned upon by local law enforcement. Who'd've guessed?"

Mick was surprised at yet another bit of information about Chuck's colorful past. It was something he should have come to expect by now.

"We'll go out there tomorrow and check it out," Mick said, "It should be empty or, rather, without survivors. I'm sure we would've heard something if it was still in operation."

Dr. Brine tossed the needle he'd used to inject acid into the brain of his deceased patient into a wastebasket, relieved at the elimination of decapitating the dead. Decapitation didn't really kill them, since the head still lived. It merely stopped them from chasing you around. Acid was cleaner and more efficient.

The idea of using acid to destroy the brain had come from Mayor Woodson's ten-year-old son. It was a method of murder he had read about on the Internet. No damn wonder the whole world has gone to hell in a hand basket, he thought.

This was the fifth patient he'd lost since coming to the station, three women, and two men, counting Duane. A sixth looked like it may take place soon. An elderly man had pneumonia and his condition was deteriorating.

A lifetime of caring for ailing patients had made Dr. Brine one of the town's most beloved citizens. When other doctors began charging outrageous fees, Dr. Brine kept his low so anyone needing a doctor's advice could have it without sacrificing too much.

He had retired and looked forward to spending the rest of his life working in the flower gardens in the summer and spending time with his daughter and her family in South Carolina in winter. He longed to be with her now instead of maintaining this butcher shop he'd come to detest. Seven years of medical school and over forty years of practice had not prepared him for recent events. He had always thought of himself as an honest country doctor but the procedures he had been performing this past month were more fitting for Dr. Frankenstein.

Dr. Brine grabbed his cane and hobbled over to where his other patient lay sleeping. Mr. Manuel looked every day of his eighty-one years. His breathing rattled with each inhalation and his eyelids fluttered. He had not been attacked by one of the creatures, but his fate after death would be the same nonetheless.

"It won't be long now," Brine said gently, holding the hand of the comatose man. "This ain't no world for you, or me, neither, for that matter. You gotta be young and strong to get through life now."

No sooner had he spoken those words than the old man released one last rush of air and did not draw another. The good doctor had one more brain to destroy.

CHAPTER 25

Amanda returned to the shelter. The smell was worse every day. With over one hundred unbathed people packed into one large room it was almost unbearable to endure.

In shock after Will died, she had wandered about her home like one of the creatures outside. She ate when she was hungry, but mostly she cried. After a while she stopped crying. Crying wouldn't change anything or make her feel better. When she slept, the dreams came where Will died over and over again, pale and sick, falling into spasms and convulsions.

Her life with Will had been brief but nonetheless happy. Married three months after their first meeting, that life was a distant memory now, lived by someone else.

Amanda had been numb for so long she'd been genuinely shocked by the strange flutter she'd felt standing naked under Jim's appreciative gaze. He had made her feel giddy, and had unexpectedly stirred a nearly forgotten warmth deep in her belly.

She was fraught with guilt for having this unexpected need. It wasn't that long ago since Will died, leaving her with the ghastly job of destroying his murderous body and the demon that occupied it. She couldn't allow herself to be attracted to anyone else just yet. It wouldn't be right.

Amanda took some extra clothes out of her bag. First a print blouse with tiny flowers, one she had never been particularly fond of, and another pair of jeans. At least they were clean, she thought, making her way through the crowd to the restrooms.

The two semi-working bathrooms were the only luxuries in the shelter. Water was carried from the river to a fifty-five gallon drum in each restroom to flush away the stools.

Amanda walked into the ladies room and found it empty. Normally at this time of the evening, there was a line waiting.

She laid her change of clothes across the sink and stared into the mirror above it. She had to wipe off a thin film of grime in order to see her reflection.

The person on the other side of the glass was a stranger. Something about her didn't look the same. It was the reflection of someone who looked like her but didn't have her thoughts, a twin or an impostor. If she spoke to the reflection, would it answer? Would it give her solutions to the problems that filled her mind?

Amanda shook off the strange thoughts and ran her fingers through her still-damp hair, slicking it back, away from her forehead. Her adventure at the river had both frightened and exhilarated her. Jim had come to her rescue like the hero in a cheap romance novel, saving her, half-naked and vulnerable from the bad guys. He escorted her back to the building and then walked away, returning to whatever it was he had been doing, as if rescuing damsels in distress were part of his day-to-day activities.

Jim was a mystery in many ways. He kept his emotions and thoughts to himself, which only served to make him even more intriguing.

She donned her fresh clothes and left the bathroom for the large room buzzing with conversation. Mick had positioned himself several feet above everyone else by standing on a barstool. Jim flanked him on his left. Amanda went back to her spot by the wall where Felicia and Izzy waited.

"What's going on?" Amanda asked.

"I don't know yet," Felicia said, craning her neck for a better view. "Some kind of an announcement, I think."

Mick waved his arms for quiet and the chatter softened. Everyone's eyes rested on Mick, waiting for news, whatever it may be. Mick lowered his arms.

"I know it's been a very unpleasant experience for everyone this past month. The world has fallen apart around us. We've all witnessed the deaths of friends and loved ones and all of us live in fear of what is to come. This rescue operation was put together hastily to help people get to safety fast. We thought the situation would be dealt with promptly and everyone would go back to their homes. Obviously, that has not been the case. The emergency has gotten out of hand in populated areas, including our town. The major cities of the United States have been evacuated and martial law is in effect across the nation. Local governments have total authority."

"How did this happen?" a man asked. "Are we at war? Did an enemy country do it?"

The crowd buzzed at the man's questions but Mick quickly silenced them. "No, I don't think so, though no one seems to really know. It's worldwide."

The crowd buzzed again and Mick had to raise his arms to regain their attention "Now quiet down so I can give you what information we do have. We don't have much to tell you about why or how it happened. Television and radio stations are no longer broadcasting so we can't find out anything new. What we can tell you is this; we're trying to find a better place to move everyone. This building is insufficient to handle the amount of people crammed into it. We should have something ready within the next few days. We'd like you all to please be prepared to leave here on short notice. That means gather your belongings and be ready to go. In the meantime, please be patient. Things will get better."

Mick stepped down and he and Jim went to the office. The babble rose again as everyone anticipated a safer site.

The snowy television was on in the office but the sound was off. Mick collapsed into the swivel chair behind his desk and leaned back so his head rested against the wall. Visibly exhausted, he closed his eyes and released a deep sigh.

Jim sat across from the desk. He pulled the .44 Magnum from its holster and absently cleaned it.

"I want you to go with me to inspect the prison tomorrow," Mick said, his eyes still closed.

Jim stopped cleaning the gun and studied the bags under Mick's eyes. The lack of rest and the strain of his job were taking their toll on him. He shouldn't be going anywhere. He needed to sleep.

"I can take Chuck with me to do that. Maybe you should stay here and get some down time," Jim said.

"No!" Mick snapped. "I'll be fine. I need to do this myself. I don't want anyone else lost. I can handle it."

Jim went back to cleaning his gun. Mick seemed to be an intelligent man; he should know his limits. Jim would trust his decision.

"Okay, fine," Jim said, "but you've got to be alert, so get some sleep tonight. We could be walking into a mess out there."

"Shit, Jim, we'll be walking into a mess anywhere."

CHAPTER 26

The door swung open and Jody walked in with a piece of deer meat Jenny had prepared on a small plate. He walked to the nightstand, put it down, and backed away.

"So, you're a preacher?"

Peterson took the plate from the stand and took a bite of the meat. After he swallowed he said, "I am a man of God. I'm here to do the Lord's work."

"And what might that be, preacher man?"

Peterson put the plate back on the table and walked to the window. He looked down into the yard. "To cleanse the earth of evil. To start over."

"You plan on killing all those things by yourself?" Jody asked, hoping.

Peterson turned swiftly to face Jody, a stone cold expression on his face. "Not them," he thumbed to the window, "the others. The real evil."

Jody's hope faded. The preacher's remark had taken him by surprise. What other evil? There was something sinister about this man. He caused Jody to lose all thought. The preacher gave him the creeps.

"When you're finished eating, Eddie said you could walk around. Just don't try to leave."

Jody turned and ran into the closed door; face first, before finally getting out of the room.

The preacher smiled at the boy's blunder. Fear. The ability to create fear is power.

The preacher left his room after his meager meal and started down the steps, thinking about his conversation with Jody. The boy had been scared but not in the way Peterson wanted him to be. He should have been in fear of him because he was an instrument of God. What he'd seen in Jody's eyes was the fear of a madman. There would be people like that, people who would fail to recognize him for what he was, but they would be dealt with accordingly.

Peterson exited the building through the front door and searched around the grounds until he found Eddie sitting on a tree stump looking down the road that led away from the school. He walked up behind him, startling Eddie when he got close enough to be heard. Eddie whipped around, his rifle pointed at the preacher's head.

"What the hell are you doing here?" Eddie demanded. "You're not supposed to be this far away from the house. Sneaking up on me is a good way to get your head blown off."

"I'm here to help."

"What do you mean?"

"I'm here to keep all of you from being killed."

"We're doing just fine," Eddie snapped. "We can take care of ourselves. Those things won't come up here."

"Those things aren't your problem. Your problem will be when the live ones come and shoot you all."

"Why would they do that?" Eddie asked, remembering the tall tales he had told Jody. But that's all they were, tall tales.

"I saw it for myself," Peterson said. "They think that anyone who didn't come in at the beginning is either sick by now or out to loot the town. I saw them kill two innocent people, a boy and a girl." The Preacher continued his lie. "Shot them dead while they pleaded for their lives. They hadn't done a thing wrong except not come in right away.

I'm telling you, boy, no matter what I said earlier, the devil *is* in charge now and he's getting stronger."

Eddie blinked hard at the preacher's words. Were they really shooting innocent people? The preacher was telling him things he wasn't aware of. If those things were really happening, they could be in for serious trouble.

"How many weapons do you have here?" Peterson asked.

"Not many." Eddie confessed. He was beginning to question his own decisions. "We got a few from some houses down the road."

"Well, we'll have to change that. We need more guns or we won't be able to fight back. Come," he commanded. "We need to make plans."

Eddie obediently followed the preacher back to the school. He was confused and, for the first time, afraid. Hiding from the dumb creatures had been easy but live people were smart enough to find them.

The preacher sensed Eddie's uncertainty as he led him toward the house, confident of his plan and how it would end. Start with Eddie and the rest would follow.

Peterson stopped and turned to Eddie. "What's in the basement? I heard you tell the boy who brought me my food that if he wasn't careful you'd put him there."

"Three of our old teachers."

"You locked your teachers in the basement?"

"They're dead. They're the walking fucking dead," Eddie grumped. "I keep them there to threaten. You know, to keep people in line."

"That's good," Peterson told him. "We'll keep them there for now."

"What can we do to keep the people in town from coming up here and killing us?" Eddie asked, and stopped walking, to face Peterson.

"We get strong," Peterson replied. "We get strong and we kill them first."

Eddie's eyes widened and Peterson sensed his reluctance. He put his hand softly on the boy's shoulder. "Don't worry son, it's God's will."

CHAPTER 27

Jim nudged Chuck in the side with the toe of his boot. Chuck rolled over and groaned, pulling his covers up higher. Jim waited a moment before trying again. This time he let him have it hard in the shin.

Chuck threw the covers away with a jerk, growling and ready to pounce until he saw Jim standing over him with a crooked grin and two cups of coffee.

"What time is it?" Chuck asked, rubbing his eyes.

"It's five o'clock. You're gonna sleep half the morning away. We've got a lot of work to do." Jim handed him a cup of coffee.

Chuck moaned and took a sip, wrinkling his nose. "I like mine with cream," he grumped. "And a little sugar."

Jim took a sip of his own coffee and looked around the room cluttered with sleeping bodies. Most of them only had a blanket or two between them and the concrete floor. A lucky few had mattresses or sleeping bags. A few people were already awake. This arrangement made for strange hours and sleep patterns for a lot of the survivors.

"Coffee's better without them. Now come on, we need to get going," Jim said, walking away.

Chuck took another sip of coffee and took a pack of cigarettes from his shirt pocket. He stuck the cigarette in his mouth and crushed the empty pack. When panicking people had cleared the stores of food, cigarettes went too. Nobody wanted to be without smokes. Chuck had only one full pack left. He hoped that when they went to the prison today, he would find a generous occupant willing to share.

Not a chance, he thought. What a terrible time to have to quit.

Jim opened the door to his truck and the dome light came on. It was still another hour until daybreak and the light shined brightly. He wanted to drive his truck to the prison because he trusted it to not break down and because it was the only real thing he had left of the way things were. That gave him comfort. The iron bars welded over the windows made him feel caged but it was still his truck.

He turned the key to the ON position and the fuel gauge began to climb, stopping when it reached the full mark. Jim was unaware the tank had been filled but relieved that it had already been done. Getting gas was an easy task as long as there weren't too many creatures around. A small hand pump straight into the tanks at a service station or any car filled a truck in minutes.

Jim removed the key from the switch and went to the office. Mick was drinking a cup of coffee. Jim watched him move around the room in preparation. He seemed in better spirits, more rested. Jim drank the last of his coffee.

"Anymore coffee in the kitchen?" he asked.

"There's plenty," Mick said. "The coffee machine holds fifty cups. Chuck took it from a restaurant in town."

"Yeah, but the night watch has been drinking from it all night." Jim turned to get a refill but Mick stopped him.

"I've been thinking about something, Jim."

"What's that?" he asked, setting his empty cup next to the television.

"This town had over twelve thousand people living here. The county, another ten thousand or so, and that's a low estimate. Still, it totals twenty-two thousand people. We have a little over one hundred here."

Jim nodded. "Okay, so what's your point?"

"Let's say there's a thousand or so hidden in the mountains or left the area completely."

"I follow you."

"That still leaves us out numbered two hundred to one by the damned things. And only fifteen of us are properly trained to use guns. If those bastards ever find us and come after us, there's no way we can defend ourselves against those odds."

"I was concerned with that when I came here, remember?"

Mick strapped on the last of his weapons, then took another swallow of coffee. "We've got to have that prison, even if there's still prisoners in the cells. They'll have to make room for us."

Jim grabbed his empty cup and started for the coffee machine. "If there's prisoners still in the cells," he said over his shoulder, "we'd better let them out to help. At least they won't be afraid to use guns."

"As long as they don't use them on us," Mick said.

The morning sun began to rise. The sky was a pale blue in the east but still a deep purple in the west. Crickets chirped noisily in the thicket around the shelter as Chuck loaded the items Mick had specified onto the back of the truck.

He counted three tool belts, one for each of them. Each belt contained flashlights, screwdrivers, hammers, and wire cutters. If the prison was deserted, they would have to break in.

That's a new idea, Chuck thought, breaking into a prison.

Mick and Jim joined Chuck after he had finished loading the truck. All three were armed to the teeth. Neither of them had less than three firearms each. Each had a rifle strapped to their backs, two pistols around their waist, and a machete for good measure. It was becoming the standard post-plague fashion.

They got into the truck without saying a word and drove off to find a better, safer refuge.

One hundred yards away, a lone zombie raised its head at the sound of the truck leaving. It moaned a song of confusion and desire.

PART TWO

WOUNDED MAN

CHAPTER 28

Jenny packed a small amount of clothing and food into a paper bag and rolled it shut. She and Jody would sneak away that night while everyone else slept and make a run for a rescue station. Since their arrival, Eddie's hold over the others had become alarming, his actions frightening. The preacher, who had shown up a week ago, was never far from Eddie's side. He had developed an eerie power over everyone, including Eddie.

With the exception of she and Jody, everyone was now armed with guns taken from homes long since deserted by their owners. Jody's rifle was taken away soon after his clash with Eddie so the two of them were now defenseless. This, Jenny noticed, caused Jody to be edgy and frightened, although he denied it.

Jenny stuffed the bag under her bed and left to find Jody. She went to his room first and found him there. Several days before they were told they could no longer sleep in the same room. Jenny guessed it had been the preacher's idea to keep them separated. He had some crazy notion that all of this was the Armageddon foretold in the Bible. Maybe it was but he was definitely not one of God's messengers. Who was he to judge them? She thought angrily.

Jenny quietly closed the door and sat on Jody's bed. He tiptoed to the door, opened it a crack, and peered out to be sure the hallway was clear. When he shut the door, he turned the lock so they wouldn't be caught off guard. It was impossible to be too careful.

Jenny bounced her crossed leg up and down and bit at her fingernails with a vengeance. She studied her hands between vicious attacks, wincing at how much she had chewed away. What had once been lovely nails were now ragged edges.

"Stop that!" Jody whispered. "Don't let them see how tense you are. They'll suspect something."

"I can't help it. I'm afraid. What if they catch us?"

"We're not going to stay here. It's getting too crazy. We leave tonight."

Jenny got up and paced the room, biting viciously at her nails. The decision to leave is the right one, she thought. It wasn't necessarily the safest.

"Eddie wants everyone to be in the TV room this afternoon." Jody said, "He's got something to say."

"What's it about?"

"I'm not sure. Something he and the preacher came up with."

Jody lifted a corner of his mattress and pulled out a large hunting knife. He took the knife from its sheath and held it up. Sunlight glistened off the eight-inch blade.

"What's that for?" She said, a bit too loudly.

"Shhh! Quiet down!" Jody gave her a disapproving look. "It's to take with us. We need to have some kind of protection." He returned the knife to its sheath.

"That thing won't kill those monsters."

Jody tied the knife to his ankle with an old shoestring then dropped his pant leg down, covering the weapon. "Maybe not but it will sure kill anyone else. I won't be left completely defenseless."

Jenny bit her nails with newfound enthusiasm. She was worried, not only for herself but also for Jody. It would be just like him to go off half cocked if things got rough.

CHAPTER 29

Sharon Darney peeled off the rubber gloves and threw them into an overflowing waste can. It was one o'clock in the morning. She and Dr. Cowen had been working all day trying to isolate the virus. So far there was no sign of anything in the creature's bloodstream that would cause the condition. Dr. Cowen had finally given up and gone to bed. Sharon would not be far behind.

She went to her desk and opened the third drawer with a hard jerk. The drawer always stuck so she only used it for things she didn't need too often. This was one of those times.

Sharon pulled out a bottle of Jim Beam and rested it in the palm of her hand, label up. She considered putting it back in the drawer but she twisted off the cap and poured a shot into a Styrofoam cup on the edge of the desk. She hastily downed the first shot and poured another before sitting in her chair.

"It's got to be there." She glanced at the creature still strapped to the table. "There's got to be a reason. Something's got to be killing you. But if it's there, it must be invisible because I haven't seen the damned thing. So where the hell is it?"

Sharon downed the second shot and went to the creature's side, as though waiting for a response to the question she had just asked. "What makes you tick, you son of a bitch? What's your secret? Is that little bug hiding or…" Sharon stared at the zombie, her eyes brightening. "That's it, you tricky little bastards! It has to be!"

Bolting for the intercom, she glowed with newfound hope as she pushed the TALK button. "Doctor Cowen, please come to Lab One! Doctor Cowen, please come to Lab One!"

She tied a surgical mask to her face and slipped on another pair of gloves. After a few minutes, Dr. Cowen ran in, buttoning his lab coat.

"Get that tray of instruments and bring them over here," she told him as she checked the restraints on the creature.

"What's up? Did you find something?"

"Maybe, maybe not. But I have a hunch."

Sharon used the scalpel to cut the shirt off of the creature, and then began to make an incision into its chest before Dr. Cowen grabbed her hand, stopping her.

"Hold on! Let me kill him first before you do that!" he said.

"To hell with *him*," she bristled. "I need it alive, or functioning, or whatever it is they do."

Dr. Cowen stepped back and held his hands up in submission. "Okay, have it your way."

Sharon cut from breastbone to waist, laying open the entire torso. The zombie squirmed as she cut, groaning and pulling at the straps, its body twisting this way and that. A ghastly putrid smell wafted from the open cavity, penetrating the masks they wore. Sharon choked back the bile that rose in her throat. Dr. Cowen watched with a combination of fascination and revulsion, still trying to figure out what she thought she'd found.

"It's hiding from us," she explained. "It's posing as something else, blood cells or something. I don't know. But I do think we can find it in its true form."

"How? Where?"

"In the organs. That's where it does the real damage. That's where the virus kills. It doesn't matter if they're made useless. Most of the organs aren't even used when the bodies revive."

Sharon cut away the tissue surrounding the living cadaver's liver and removed it, carefully carrying the foul-smelling prize to a nearby worktable.

"You see? I think the reason we can't find anything is because it assumes the appearance of something else, something non-threatening. It may even change its appearance from one thing in the saliva to something else in the blood. It stays one step ahead of us. We may have looked right at it and not even known."

"You may be right but why do you expect to find it now, in that liver?"

"Because," she said, slicing through the organ, "it may have to revert back to its original form to do its damage, to kill."

She took a small sample from the center of the organ and smeared it on a slide. "You know, an infected person doesn't even develop antibodies to fight this thing, whatever it is. I think it's because the body's defenses don't even know it's there."

"Until it's too late," Dr. Cowen said.

"Exactly! Somehow it inhibits the body's ability to defend itself, like the AIDS virus."

Dr. Cowen puzzled over the hypothesis in his sleep-fogged mind.

Sharon carefully put the slide under the electron scope and focused. A computer screen displayed and enhanced the image to its utmost clarity for viewing. The electron scope magnified viruses that were far too small to be seen by anything else.

The image came into focus and to her delight found something new in the middle of the slide. The normal tissue cells from the creature's liver was motionless, dead as it should be, but there was something very small, hardly seen even through the electron scope. Dark and shadowy in appearance, it darted across the slide with great speed, and then disappeared into thin air. Sharon typed commands into the computer in an attempt to find the elusive microbe.

Dr. Cowen moved closer to the screen. "What the hell was *that*?"

"I don't know but I'm going to try to get it back. I've never seen anything like it."

"It didn't look like a virus, and it scurried away like a bat out of hell. Like it knew we were watching."

"A bat out of hell isn't far from being an accurate description of this thing, Rich. If we want to find answers, hell might be a good place to start looking for them."

Dr. Cowen dashed to the computer on Sharon's desk and brought up a library of images for every microscopic organism known and cataloged. As Sharon continued in vain to locate the suspect organism, Dr. Cowen searched through the data for something similar.

"I'm telling you, that's not any kind of microbe or virus I've ever seen. This is something new. Nobody has ever seen that before. Nobody."

"Someone has. We have."

CHAPTER 30

The drive to the prison took about ten minutes. There was no sign of living humans on the way but the walking dead wandered the fields along the road, mostly in small groups, except for a health club where about thirty of them aimlessly shuffled about.

Jim drove the truck into the entrance of the prison and came to a stop at the gate of the main security fence. The prison was a two-story brick structure surrounded by a twelve-foot chain link fence topped with razor wire. Thirty-foot unmanned guard towers were located at the north and south ends of the yard. The outer fence was also twelve feet high but it had no razor wire. The electronically controlled gate was open. After scanning the area for imminent danger, Jim drove the truck through the outer gate and came to a stop at the second gate. It was locked with heavy chains and padlocks. A sign over the gate said WHITEPOST CORRECTIONAL CENTER. Another sign warned visitors about leaving keys in their car when visiting.

Jim, Mick, and Chuck got out of the truck and walked to the main gate. Chuck yanked on one of the heavy chains. It clanked and fell free, the lock plunging to the ground.

He turned to the others and smiled. "This may be easier than I thought." He grabbed the other chain and pulled but the chain held firm. Chuck grimaced. "Guess I jinxed it."

Chuck went to the truck and then quickly returned with a pair of bolt cutters. It took him several minutes to cut through the lock before it broke free. He pulled on the chain, swung open the gate, and began walking through. Jim seized him by his arm and pulled him backwards.

"Just hold on, Chuck!" Jim snapped, "We're breaking into a prison. You don't want to be shot by one of the guards."

"Look around, Jim. There's no one here."

"Maybe not, but you're still reckless. Calm down."

Chuck's shoulders slumped. He tossed the bolt cutters to the ground and stuck his hands in his pockets like a petulant child. "Okay. Sorry."

Mick shook his head at the display. Correcting Chuck had become a part-time job for Jim but he didn't seem to mind. As a matter of fact, he had taken quite a liking to Chuck.

Jim rubbed the stubble on his chin, and then got the binoculars from the glove compartment and carefully studied all of the doors and windows on their side of the building. Each window had iron bars spaced about four inches apart.

"Looks abandoned," Jim said, lowering the binoculars, "although I thought I saw something in a window on the second floor. Just a glimpse, possibly nothing."

Mick took the binoculars and looked for himself. He scanned the front of the building from left to right paying special attention to the windows. After a minute, he lowered the glasses and returned them to Jim, then un-holstered one of his pistols. "Well, there's only one way to find out." Mick said, as he checked his weapon "Let's go see."

The three walked cautiously through the gate and up to the massive metal door in front of the prison. Chuck rummaged around in his tool belt for something that could pick the lock. "I don't know if I have anything to open this one up," he said, still searching.

"How about using the knob?" Jim inquired in a droll tone.

Chuck looked up flustered. Jim was holding the door open for him. "What?"

"It wasn't locked," Jim grinned. "Why do you always have to do things the hard way?"

"It's more exciting." He answered, hiding his embarrassment. "Now why would they lock the gate over there and leave this door open?"

Jim shrugged, "Who cares," he said, and moved ahead. Mick and Chuck followed without giving it another thought.

They entered a drab and shadowy room. An area to the left was used for checking visitors in and out of the prison, a small window to take or return their belongings. Ahead, a barred door led into what they assumed were the cellblocks and the rest of the prison.

Jim checked his rifle and straightened his baseball cap. "All right, everyone," he said, "stay together. Chuck, you keep an eye out behind us. Mick and I will take out anything that lies ahead."

Matthew Ford knelt next to the cot in his prison cell, his head face down on the mattress. He was weak and very hungry. He had run out of food three days ago and the water in the toilet was almost gone.

When the dead first walked, prison procedure continued as usual, but as things got worse the guards deserted to be with their families. The desertions left a skeleton crew to care for the prisoners. Because of this, the prisoners were confined to their cells. All yard and exercise privileges, revoked. Food was brought to them in their cells less and less frequently. Matthew feared starvation and began to hoard his food.

The inmates pleaded to be set free but the guards ignored them. Then, with only three guards left to care for the entire population his fears became reality. Shots were fired from another part of the building. It was the last time they would see a guard alive, or get fed. Later they got their first glimpse of the walking dead as they found their way into the cellblocks. Most of them twisted and disfigured, the bloody apparitions strained against the bars to reach their prey.

A big man, known throughout the prison as Kong, occupied the cell across from Matthew's. Large and hairy, the nickname was given to him because it rhymed with his real last name, which was Long, and because it fit.

When the creatures first came, most of the prisoners lost control. They screamed and prayed, but not Kong. Hate filled Kong's heart. He focused his hatred on the creatures and cursed and spat at them.

The prisoners in A Block became frantic. Growing ever weaker they cried out for help, which only excited the creatures more. Not wanting to waste energy, Matthew stayed quiet and rationed the food he had hidden in his cell. At night the only light came from the moon shining through windows up the corridor. Movements and moans of the creatures sliced the darkness as they roamed the corridor, hoping to get at the prisoners locked behind bars.

Three days after the disappearance of the guards, Kong had had enough. "Come here, you sons of bitches! Come and get it!" he roared, raking a metal cup across the bars to get their attention. "I might die in here," he screamed, "but I'll take a few of you with me!"

It worked. Several of the walking dead closed in on his cell. Arms outstretched, their fingers clenched at empty air. The first one to reach his cell was greeted by Kong's hand gripping the monster's hair. With great force, Kong slammed its head into the bars. It fell silently to the floor, dead at last.

"Dead fuckin' meat!" Kong's voice echoed. "Now stay dead!" he said, pointing down at the corpse.

Matthew half expected Kong to start pounding on his chest after such an impressive feat, like the real King Kong. Perhaps he'd let loose with a Tarzan yell at the same time but he merely grunted in his offish way.

A second and third closed in. Once again Kong's arm thrust through the bars grabbing the one closest by the hair. He pulled hard to repeat the first kill. The creature's head hit the bars but not with the ferocity of the first. Another creature seized his arm and held steadfast and Kong released his grip and fought to break free, but with both creatures holding him, his efforts were in vain. He pulled and thrashed against their hold and in turn the creatures jerked at him as if trying to pull him through the tiny openings between the bars.

Matthew watched in horror as Kong wrestled with the hunger-crazed monsters. Upon realizing that they couldn't pull him through the bars and out of the cell, one of them simply lowered its rotten head and bit down on two of Kong's fingers, tearing them away from the rest of his hand. Blood jetted from the stumps and the creature released its hold. It staggered backwards to relish the morsels dangling from its mouth.

With only one creature still holding him, Kong was able to pull his injured limb through the bars and retreat to the back of his cell where he quickly wrapped a towel around the painfully gushing wound.

"Mother fucker!" he ranted. "You mother fucker! I'll kill you!" His voice was higher pitched and more wild than before.

Kong wrapped the towel tight and again charged the bars, screaming at the ghouls. He thrust his good arm through the bars with uncontrolled anger, recklessly grabbing the shirt of the nearest one. The monster's mouth came down on Kong's wrist and tore away a large chunk, much the same way a hungry person bites into a meatball sub. The bite severed arteries and caused tremendous blood loss. Kong fell to the back of his cell and collapsed to the floor, writhing in agony. His life-giving blood gushed freely from his body into large puddles on the floor. Kong cursed softly until he became too weak and died.

That had been days ago. Now the big man stood bewildered in his cell, one of the flesh eaters himself. His milky eyes watched Matthew.

It won't be long now, Matthew thought. His food was gone and he would soon die himself. He would die and be like Kong, pacing his cell like the rest of the inmates who were now walking dead, looking just as stupid. Maybe he and Kong would stare at each other with vacuous eyes and drool for eternity. What a lovely thought.

Matthew grew too weak to care now. He might be the last one alive; none of the other inmates had answered his calls since early yesterday morning. All of the creatures that had made their way into the prison block were now in front of his cell, waiting.

Matthew closed his eyes and let his mind wander back to his freedom, back to the days when he'd had a life, when he had no idea how trivial his problems really were. He thought about his family and how he had let them down. Why had he always hurt the ones who loved him? He hoped they were safe.

Surviving on the run or in a prison cell appeared to be his lot in life. He hadn't meant any harm. Neither had he intentionally hurt anyone. In the end, the only person he'd hurt most was himself. To end his life like this was futile yet just, he supposed. Sadly, his life would end the way he had lived it, without meaning and in vain.

His thoughts dwindled away and his body trembled in a warm sort of way as he was giving in to death's grip. Suddenly, a shot sounded from somewhere inside the prison. He pulled himself to his feet with a renewed energy and hope he thought was long gone. Leaning against the cell wall for support he yelled as loud as he could.

*   *   *

A spray of blood and brains splattered the wall behind the zombie's head as it crumpled to the floor. "We've got company!" Chuck shouted.

Jim spun around and saw one of the prison guards Chuck had killed. It was still in the uniform. From the looks of things he was long dead before Chuck shot him. His clothes were torn, his body mangled.

"Goddamn it, we're walking into a trap in this hallway!" Jim said. "If the guards are zombies, this whole place is probably crawling with them."

At that moment a plea for help came from somewhere nearby. The man's voice was weak and desperate. It faded into the wails and moans of the dead, which grew louder and closer.

"Move out!" Jim shouted and the three men hustled down the hall the way they had come. They turned the corner and ran into the entranceway in time to see another walking corpse at the door. Its head was tilted to one side but its eyes stared straight ahead. One arm was outstretched; the other hung limply like a broken wing.

Mick raised his weapon and promptly dispatched it in mid-stride. It spun around and fell to the floor seconds before the men raced past it and outside.

"Chuck, go start the truck and pull it away from the gate another hundred feet or so!" Jim shouted. "It's too close. We'll need more room to retreat while we blow these bastards back to hell. Leave it running though. We've gotta get that guy outta there before we can leave."

"Gotcha," Chuck said, taking off.

"You got plenty of ammo?" Jim asked Mick.

"What do you think?" Mick answered, a little peeved that Jim had even asked. It was a question more suited for Chuck. Mick carefully watched Chuck from over his shoulder as he drove the truck to the other side of the gates and then returned to stand beside them. He nodded his approval at where Chuck had decided to park it.

The cries from the building grew louder and louder until the first zombie blundered out. It was a woman who appeared to be in her twenties, with blond hair and an exposed, pregnant stomach. She staggered, and nearly fell down when she stepped from the doorway. Mick and Chuck stared in shock. Jim took aim and ended her existence.

More creatures appeared in the door and they opened fire. The present state of the world had made crack marksmen out of them and the well-armed threesome dealt with the slow-moving rabble quickly. When all was said and done, thirty-two bodies lay rotting in the prison yard. Jim, Mick and Chuck stepped over them and returned to the front door.

"Oh my God!" Chuck whispered, a horror sounding in his voice.

Mick and Jim turned, their eyes following his to the pregnant woman on the ground. Her stomach moved and bulged. The baby inside her was one of them, one of the undead. Chuck began to choke and gag before turning away to vomit. Mick turned away and did his best to hide the sickening feeling in his gut. Jim performed the painful duty without hesitation.

He fired two shots, and then covered the woman's remains with his jacket. The others waited while Jim lowered his head and closed his eyes to block the horrible vision from his mind.

Once again the threesome entered the building. The pleading voice no longer echoed through the prison and they feared they might be too late.

Cautiously, they made their way down the wide hall and through two open but heavily barred doors. They were the same kind of doors as the jail cells but these kept the entire cellblock separate from the rest of the prison. A sign on the wall leading to a corridor of cells said CELL BLOCK A.

In the cell on the right, a large, hulking man crashed into the bars and growled at them, eyes glazed, his face a deep blue. Chuck jumped away, startled by the swift movement as it reached for him through the bars. In the cell to the left, a black man in his thirties, all but dead himself raised his head from the cot and laughed softly, a tinge of madness in his voice.

At first, Matthew thought he was having a cruel dream, delivered by a vengeful, heartless God, one last stab at past sins. Then, as his vision and head cleared a bit, he realized that living; breathing people were actually there. His mind swam with hope and relief.

"I'll be damned," he said, shaking his head. "I'll just be damned."

CHAPTER 31

Jody walked uneasily into the TV room, the knife strapped to his leg was rubbing him raw. He would have to position it better later. He saw Jenny standing alone in the corner and squeezed his way through the crowded room to stand by her side.

Almost everyone at the school was present to hear what Eddie had to say. And why wouldn't they be? Eddie had let it be known that attendance was mandatory, and everyone did what Eddie said, everyone except Jenny and himself. They were not part of this rowdy, ill-mannered band of delinquents, nor did they want to be. They complied with his demands out of self-preservation and nothing more.

Eddie and Reverend Peterson stood in the front of the room whispering to each other before Eddie finally pounded the butt of his rifle against a lamp table, quieting the room.

"Everyone, pay attention!" he shouted. "Father Peterson has something to tell you. Listen to him. He speaks the truth."

Peterson stepped forward and surveyed the room, smiling like the proverbial cat who got the canary.

"You don't have to have the gift of a prophet to understand the significance of the recent catastrophe, or to foresee its conclusion. I have explained it to Eddie and now I will explain it to you." He paced the floor for a moment, then stopped and pointed a finger toward the ceiling as though the thought he had been searching for finally came to mind.

"God has chosen you to survive." He lowered his finger. "But to survive, we must become as one. We must forget about what we want as individuals and strive for the good of the group. There must be no exceptions or we will all perish."

Peterson stood well over six feet and his stature and appearance intimidated some of the youngsters as he moved among them, talking to each one to maximize his effect.

"There is a great evil swelling the earth. Not the dead but the living. They shall be consumed and sent to the final death, their desires eaten up! Their sins, eaten up! Some of you may fear the same fate. That's good because if you falter you, too, shall die a horrible death." His tone was urgent, full of dark power.

The young assembly displayed signs of awe. This was what he'd been waiting for. He moved to force his will upon them. "Your little world here is nothing. Your life here is nothing. Soon the wicked living will come and kill you, as they have so many others. Why? Because they are jealous! Jealous that you have been chosen to survive and that they will die. They will kill you with no more remorse than the demon corpses who rot on their feet. Driven by Satan, they are all one and the same."

Jenny listened to what the preacher said but she didn't buy it. This was some built-up tale for the sole purpose of creating fear, to bend the will of everyone here to do his bidding. For what purpose she didn't know but she was sure that the entire world hadn't gone mad. Surely they would realize that killing would only create more of the monsters to rise and kill again, a scenario that could only end in the extinction of humanity.

"We can't stay here forever!" the preacher said. "We will run out of food. We are already running very low. We will have to destroy the wicked and take their food before they destroy us. We have to do this together, as one. You will find that I have an unconcealed impatience and will treat any opposition with scant courtesy to say the least."

"We have to go find the other survivors and warn them," Jenny whispered to Jody. "This guy's a lunatic! We can't let them do this."

"We won't," he said. "Tonight."

CHAPTER 32

The man in the cell was weak. Jim couldn't tell how long he'd been without food and water. From the look of him, it had been at least a few days. Most of the new prisons had electronically controlled cell doors but this block wasn't that new. These doors had to be opened with keys. Not that electronic doors would have helped, the power was off.

Jim jerked the door, knowing it was futile before he tried. How else would the man have survived the uninvited guests? All of the other eight-by-ten cells were now occupied by zombies, prisoners dead of starvation and dehydration. Their clothes hung loosely from their bodies, each face sunken and discolored. Many of them thrust their arms through the bars in an attempt to reach the objects of their passion. Others trudged their cells, oblivious to their surroundings. The lone survivor, the black man, was lucky to be alive.

Jim remembered the guard-turned-zombie they had killed in the hallway. He turned to Mick. "Keep an eye on things here. I'll go see if the dead guard has any keys that will open this cell." He walked down the hall and around the corner, leaving Mick and Chuck with the prisoner.

"Anybody got a bologna sandwich?" the prisoner asked, stumbling to his feet.

Chuck reached into a pouch attached to his belt and pulled out a Baggie. "How about peanut butter?" he asked, holding it at arm's length.

Matthew reached through the bars and took the offering. "Right now I'd eat a shit sandwich if you used enough bread." Half of the sandwich disappeared with the first bite.

"Be careful. Don't eat that too fast. You'll end up puking it back up," Chuck warned.

Matthew consumed the sandwich in two bites. He used the small cup on the sink to scoop water from the commode tank and gulped it down. There was no need to ration the water any longer. Help had arrived.

Minutes later Jim returned, jingling a key ring. He thumbed through them, trying each one until he found the key that made the lock click. The door swung open.

Matthew, exhausted but anxious, wasted no time stepping outside. His legs trembled and buckled from the exertion. He collapsed at Jim's feet.

Jim pulled him up, holding his arm to prevent it from happening again. "You all right?"

Matthew took a deep breath. "I am now."

"What's your name?" Jim asked.

"Matthew Ford. Ca-ca-call me Matt." He stammered weakly.

"Okay, Matt, let's get you back to the shelter and put some food in your belly. We need you to get on your feet again. We'll need your help."

Matt looked back at the other cells and their pale, animated occupants. "What's happening?"

"I'm afraid we probably don't know much more than you do, Matt," Jim said. "These things are killing people and the people they kill come back and kill. They're not alive but they're not really dead, either. I can tell you this; they're not the people they used to be. I don't think they're even human anymore."

"Holy Christ, how did it happen?"

"I don't know. Nobody does. But I doubt Christ had anything to do with this one."

CHAPTER 33

Mount Weather
6:50 P.M.

Computer screens flashed an endless stream of information to their operators who frantically banged away at their keyboards. The huge satellite monitors that hung from the ceiling zeroed in on cities and military posts around the world.

Gilbert Brownlow flipped through the pages of a report he had asked for a week ago but hadn't received until now.

His face grimaced when he found the statistics worse than he had expected. After only six weeks, the report showed the following:

Worldwide Emergency Report
EYES ONLY
Week Six

COUNTRY	UNINFECTED POP.	MILITARY STATUS
Afghanistan	0%	Nonexistent
African Cont	3%	Nonexistent
Britain	5%	Failing
Canada	2%	Nonexistent
China	1%	Nonexistent
France	1%	Failing
Iran	0%	Nonexistent
Mexico	3%	Nonexistent
Russia	4%	Unknown
Spain	4%	Nonexistent
USA	5%	Failing

Brownlow threw the report on the console in front of him and went to Donald Huff, a technician on the control panel of the main tactical displays. "What are the surviving population figures from city to city in the United States?"

Huff fed several commands into his computer and the information popped up. "This shows that there are less than twenty thousand people around New York City. However, most of them have fled the city, taking refuge in surrounding suburbs and rural areas. The city is all but deserted. The Los Angeles area has fifty thousand. Reports have five or six thousand still in the city itself. Chicago has forty thousand or so in its immediate area and—"

"That's enough. Are there any U.S. cities showing more than that?"

"No, sir, but Fairbanks, Alaska, is still showing an uninfected population of fifteen thousand."

"What's so special about that?"

"Well, sir, Fairbanks only had a population of just over thirty thousand before the plague. That's only a fifty-percent rate of infection in a heavily populated area. It's unique to the information we have on U.S. cities. Even cities with only thirty thousand people are showing a much higher infection percentage than that."

"Hmmm. Find out why but before you do I want to meet with all upper-command personnel in one hour. Make sure they're all notified."

"Yes, sir, but we believe we know why."

"And why's that soldier?"

Donald Huff swallowed hard and continued. "We think it's because of the climate. The cold weather causes the reanimates to move more slowly. This makes it more difficult for them to get to their victims. The reanimates are also weaker than they normally are in the cold. The process may be slower, but they will eventually win out nonetheless. We've compared the Fairbanks data with information from areas in northern Russia and other cold climate regions. The percentages are similar."

Brownlow's face hardened. "What do I have to do to make it clear that any new information that comes to our attention here at this facility," His eyes scanned the room and its occupants, "and I mean to anyone—is to be immediately forwarded to me."

Donald Huff coughed slightly and turned back to the tactical display. "Yes sir. It won't happen again."

Brownlow turned his attention to the hanging screens. The first screen on the left displayed a bird's-eye view of New York City from a satellite. Some fires still burned, the result of rioting, looting, and a population out of control. Even though the riots had been quelled weeks ago, some fires still burned and continued to eat away at the once-great metropolis.

The next screen displayed Los Angeles. Brownlow watched in wonderment at just how close and clear a satellite camera could render an image from hundreds of miles in space. Los Angeles was fairly intact. A few buildings burned here and there but largely the city was unravaged. It struck Brownlow as bizarre, given their recent history with fires and riots.

Animated bodies of the dead roamed through the city in large numbers. Their shuffling, aimless steps and lack of body temperature on the infrared views identified them for what they were, and what the city was—a giant graveyard occupied mostly with the unearthly demons.

8:01 P.M.

Gilbert Brownlow donned a pair of bifocals and opened the folder in front of him. His assistant, George Johnston, sat to his right; sixty-eight years old, George had been a war hero in Vietnam and an important strategist and advisor during the Gulf War. George was also second in command, outranked only by Brownlow.

Six other men of various positions and responsibilities also sat at the table. In cases where major decisions were made, all eight were needed to vote a plan into action. Brownlow addressed the committee.

"Nuclear missiles will be launched at the following U.S. cities," he said.

George Johnston leaped from his seat and pounded the table. "My God, Gil! Have you lost your mind?"

"We have to stop this now!" Brownlow said. "Those bastards are thriving in the cities!"

"There are also thousands of people in dire need of help in or close to those cities," Johnston countered. "If we drop bombs, we'll kill them, too, not to mention the damage to the ecology."

"It can't be helped. We must act now," Brownlow said in a more subdued tone.

"Well, I won't let you do it, Gil! I won't let you kill people who still have a chance to—"

"To what—become the enemy? They have no chance! The order is given. At nine tonight nuclear missiles will be sent to their targets. If anyone tries to interfere, they will be charged with treason and shot. This meeting is over!"

Brownlow stormed out of the room, slamming the door behind him.

Johnston looked at the rest of the men, wondering how each of them felt about Brownlow's decision to bomb American cities. "We cannot allow this to happen," he said, straight to the point as always.

General Albert Jessup, a trigger-happy, gung-ho who had been in favor of instituting Marshall Law even before the plague hit, walked out without a word. Donald Walker, a former Secretary of Defense who had been forced to resign in order to avoid prosecution over covert foreign affairs, cleared his throat and then rose and followed Jessup the way he always did. This left four others beside Johnston.

"I agree with you, George," one of the remaining men said. "But how do we stop him? He has the support of some of the men."

"Not all of them and certainly, as we've just witnessed, not the best of them," Johnston said. "Goddamn it, I'll fight him to the death on this!"

"It's eight o'clock now. What the hell do you plan on doing in an hour?"

George bit his lower lip. He felt a headache coming on. There wasn't much time to act. "Whatever I have to in order to save those innocent people."

*   *   *

"You know, when this plague first started," Sharon told Dr. Cowen, "it only took about five minutes before the bodies re-animated in some cases less. Now it takes three times as long. Decomposition has quickened a bit, too."

The cafeteria was empty, except for a couple of soldiers in the far corner. Dr. Cowen took a bite of his sandwich and wiped the corner of his mouth with a napkin.

"There's definitely a change taking place," Sharon said. "Maybe it's weakening. It could be burning itself out."

"I don't know—maybe so. It's true that the dead take longer to revive now but the acceleration of decay is minuscule at best. I'm not sure if it will really make a difference how long they can remain mobile."

Sharon pushed her tray aside and eyed him as he stuffed in another mouthful of bland army food. He obviously enjoyed it more than she did.

"Do you think it's possible for everyone to have the virus, Rich? I mean *all* of us."

Dr. Cowen stopped eating. "What do you mean?"

"I mean, what if we all have it, even now? What if it's hiding in our bodies, kept in check by something? I don't know—body temperature or something—and only thrives in the cold, inactive state of death?"

Dr. Cowen squinted, an odd expression forming on his face. "Where did *that* come from?"

Sharon pushed her chair closer to the table and leaned toward him, her eyes fixed on his. "Don't you see? It's the only way to keep this scientific. Even those who die a natural death come back. You don't have to have one of those things come up and bite you. If that's not it, it would take an act of God."

"Maybe it is," Dr. Cowen said, opening his mouth for another bite. The emergency warning buzzer blared loudly, startling him.

A radio one of the soldiers carried sprang to life but Dr. Cowen and Sharon couldn't hear what was being said over the sound of the alarm. Whatever it was caused a look of disbelief on the soldiers' faces as they ran from the room, weapons drawn.

Dr. Cowen and Sharon looked to each other.

"Jesus," Sharon said, "now what? A break in?"

"Good God, I hope not," Dr. Cowen said. "Let's go find out."

He got to the cafeteria door first and peered out; only a few soldiers were on the subterranean street but gunfire erupted from somewhere within the complex.

"Shit, it must be a break in!" Dr. Cowen shouted.

At that moment a soldier burst through a tunnel opening connected to another part of the underground complex. Sharon and Dr. Cowen ran back to the cafeteria, fully expecting to see a drove of creatures on his heels. Instead, they were shocked to see two soldiers pursuing the first soldier. One of the pursuers shot him in the back almost in front Sharon and Dr. Cowen. The two pursuing soldiers then ran to the fallen man to make sure he was dead.

"What's happening?" Sharon demanded.

"It's Brownlow," the corporal said. "He's gonna drop bombs on our own cities! He's lost his fucking mind; shit's really hitting the fan!"

No sooner had the words left his mouth than a shot tore through the back of the corporal's head. It exited his forehead and grazed Sharon's cheek. Her head whipped back and a trickle of blood flowed from the cut on her face. Instantly the street was filled with warring men and a hail of bullets.

Dr. Cowen shoved Sharon in the direction of the lab. "Go, Sharon! Go to the lab! Run!"

They both raced for the lab, staying low to avoid bullets as they ran.

Sharon reached the hallway and turned to see Dr. Cowen lying face down in the middle of the street. Her first reaction was to go back and help him but even from where she stood it was easy to see where a bullet had exited his skull.

Overwhelmed with shock and panic, Sharon raced toward the laboratory door. Once inside, she slammed it closed and slid the heavy bolt across.

CHAPTER 34

The nearly full moon hung just above the treetops, casting shadows on the ground below Jenny's window. Too much light, she thought, anxiously. The moon made their mission even more dangerous.

One of Eddie's minions walked from left to right around the building, patrolling the grounds. Jenny closed the curtains and sat on her bed. Jody was supposed to meet her at midnight and he was a half hour late. Jenny was worried. It wasn't like Jody to be late. He was always so punctual.

Jenny's mind swam with thoughts of doom. Maybe Eddie had caught him. Maybe I should go check for myself. She stood up, having finally strengthened her resolve to find Jody, when the door cracked open and he appeared. Jenny tiptoed to him and wrapped her arms around him in a desperate embrace.

"Oh God, Jody, I was so worried! Where have you been?"

"Shhh! I'm okay. I thought I heard noises outside my door. I had to be sure the coast was clear."

Jenny tightened her arms around him, not wanting to let go. She felt safe with him.

Jody placed a gentle kiss on her upturned nose, and then he kissed her long and passionately. He loved her and would do whatever he had to do to keep her safe.

He put a finger to his lips and opened the bag he had brought with him. Removing a length of rope, he crept to the window.

"One of the guys is out there, walking around," Jenny whispered.

"I know. Don't worry."

Jody took the rope and tied one end around the radiator, then returned to the window and waited.

"We'll wait until he makes his next pass," Jody whispered, "then we'll do it. We'll have about five minutes to climb down and run away before he returns, okay?"

Jenny didn't answer so he turned to face her and repeated his instructions. "Okay?"

Jenny nodded her acceptance, her mind snapping back to what he had just said.

It was only another minute or so until the sentry returned. His steps were slow and deliberate as he made his way around the school, weapon raised, ready to defend against any intruder. As soon as he was out of sight, Jody slid open the window and dropped the rope to the ground.

"You go first. I'll follow," he said.

She pulled the small bag of her belongings from under the bed and returned to the window.

"What are you gonna do with that?" Jody asked.

"It's some extra clothes and a little food. I'm taking it with us."

"I'll take it," he said. "You won't be able to carry it down the rope with you. The food's a good idea."

Jody took the bag from her, unbuttoned his shirt, and stuffed it next to his chest.

Jenny climbed onto the windowsill and began her twenty foot-decent to the ground. Her hands burned from the rope and she momentarily lost her grip. She squeezed tighter until she came to a stop, her hands burned raw from the rope.

"Wrap your legs around the rope!" Jody whispered.

Jenny pressed the outside of her feet against the rope like a brake and slid safely to the ground.

Jody slid down behind her. He scanned the yard for trouble and saw none. "Run for the road," he whispered, "as fast as you can! Now!"

Jenny dashed across the yard, Jody close behind. She raced down the drive, away from the school, her legs propelling her over the moonlit terrain. She stumbled and fell to the gravel road, peeling a layer of skin off of her forearms as she slid.

Jody knelt beside her. "Are you okay?

"Ooooh! Yeah, I'm okay." she grumped, but her scratched arms hurt as badly as her bloody hands.

"I wouldn't bet on it," a familiar voice in the shadows said.

Jenny raised her eyes to see Eddie, the preacher, and two of their teen goons emerge from the darkness.

"I dare say that you are far from okay," Eddie said.

The preacher circled the two fugitives, a wolf ready to pounce on an injured lamb. "What do you think you're doing?" he asked.

"We're getting out of—" Jenny began, but Jody stepped between her and the others.

"We want to go," he said. "We don't want to be here anymore."

"If you're not one of the Chosen Ones," the preacher said, "then you're part of the wicked and the wicked will be judged!"

A slight nod from the preacher and the two goons shackled Jody and pushed him toward the school. Eddie roughly grabbed Jenny by the arm and dragged her, swatting and kicking, to the meeting room. To their surprise, everyone was there when they entered.

Jenny and Jody were taken to the front of the room and forced to face the assemblage of young soldiers who stood at military attention, eyes forward, faces tight expressions of antipathy. They were no longer the kids Jody had known upon his arrival. Their minds and wills had been changed, molded to fit the agenda of the preacher and Eddie. He and Jenny would not find any support among them.

"Who among you can cast the first stone at these sinners?" the preacher thundered.

"I can, Father!" the soldiers said in unison.

"Evil has many faces! Sometimes it can even find its way into your own house, and into the house of the Lord, disguising itself as one of our own. And what is the penalty for sinners and evildoers?"

"Death, Father! The final death!"

"Then death it SHALL be!" the preacher proclaimed.

The boys roared their approval

"To the final death!" the preacher commanded.

"This is lunacy!" Jody cried, "What is wrong with you people? This is a sham!"

Several youths seized them both and started to take them away. "Not her!" the preacher said. "We need the women. The New World will need women. Take her to the attic room in the octagon tower and lock her in. Do not violate her lest you suffer the same fate as this heathen," he warned, pointing to Jody.

The two lovers were dragged into the hallway, each struggling against their captors. Jody was taken to the basement door while two others carried Jenny up the staircase, but not before Jenny was able to witness Jody's final defiance.

When one boy went to open the basement door, Jody broke free from Eddie and the two others holding him. He snatched the knife from beneath his pant leg and with a swift upward thrust, sank it deeply into Eddie's side. Despite his shackles, Jody stabbed Eddie again and again before being restrained. Eddie staggered and fell against the wall. He slumped to the floor in a pool of blood and died without uttering a word.

While one boy brandished a length of 2x4, another opened the basement door. Without delay, one of the old teachers, eyes glazed and skin a greenish-gray, tried to force his way through the door. Two more creatures lumbered up the cellar steps behind him.

The boy with the board slammed the lead ghoul in the stomach, sending him backwards into the other two. All three tumbled to the bottom of the stairs in a twisted pile of mangled limbs.

Without a hint of remorse or hesitation, Jody was tossed down the cellar stairs.

Jenny screamed and pleaded for his life but the door was slammed shut and locked. Unable to endure the horror any longer, she screamed his name and passed out, Jody's screams echoing in her mind.

When Jenny came to, she was in the attic tower room, an octagonal chamber with a wood plank flooring and unfinished walls. The room was empty except for a gallon jug of water and a note that said:

IN ORDER TO HELP CLEANSE YOUR BODY OF PAST SINS,
you will not be permitted sustenance
for forty hours and forty minutes.
At the end of that time, if you yet live, you
may be deemed worthy of God's judgment.

—Father Peterson

Jenny smashed the note in her hand and threw it in a corner. Everything was lost. There was nothing left to live for. Her whole existence was foggy and unclear, a dream world without emotion or desire.

She went to the only window and stared at the concrete patio more than forty feet below. Her fingers mindlessly found the latch on the window. Without further thought, she climbed into the opening and jumped.

Chapter 35

It had been more than five hours since war had broken out in the Mount Weather complex. Sharon Darney sat in her chair, staring at the ceiling, wondering what to do next. What was happening on the other side of the lab door? Was anyone left alive? Did Brownlow launch his missiles?

The test ghoul strapped to the examination table made a low moaning sound. Sharon focused her attention on him. It was no longer excited by human presence and appeared to have lost the urge to attack her when she entered the room. It had become docile.

Just as they were beginning to uncover the cause of the extraordinary super virus, all hell had broken loose. Why is it, Sharon wondered, that humans failed when so close to greatness? Was it man's destiny to rise from stone knives and bearskins to almost touch the stars and then disappear forever like the dinosaurs? The answer seemed suddenly clear to her. In spite of all his knowledge and tools, man had not the wisdom to direct his steps.

Sharon pressed her ear against the door. She heard no gunfire. The battle had raged for an hour but it had been silent for the last four. She had to find out what the situation was on the other side of the door.

She slid the bolt back, opened the door a crack, and saw no one. She stepped into the long hallway leading to the main street of the complex and surreptitiously made her way toward Dr. Cowen. His brain destroyed, he would not come back as one of the undead.

Sharon turned the corner and almost walked into an approaching creature. From the look on its face, it was just as surprised as she was at the sudden confrontation. Turning, she saw that the street was full of the undead. Now that they knew she was there, they turned, enmasse, and moved in her direction.

Sharon backed away, keeping several yards ahead of the nearest monster bent on tearing her apart. She could not escape through this mob. Her only option was to return to the lab. At least they couldn't break through the three-inch steel door.

From the lab door, Sharon took one last look down the hall. The creatures shuffled toward her with stiff ungraceful steps, plodding along with only one objective, one goal; to devour her flesh.

Sharon opened the door and was about to retreat inside when another zombie turned the corner from the other direction. It's ungainly remains staggered this way and that as it trudged down the hall toward her. She couldn't resist a fleeting smile at the perfect irony; Brownlow had become the very object of his destructive obsession.

Satisfied that Brownlow was at least defeated and may not have been able to carry out his insane plan, she entered the lab and locked the door.

Now she faced the problem of finding a way out. Maybe they'll just go away when they realize they can't get to me, she thought. Maybe they'd waltz right through the front door. But if almost two months of constant study had taught her anything, it was that they were inclined to mimic the repetitive patterns of their former lives. The creatures on the other side of the door were dead soldiers whose main duty in life had been to guard this installation. They were not going anywhere.

Sharon's eyes scanned the room. If there was a weapon, a club—anything—that she could use to fight her way through them, maybe she could make it.

She went to her desk and pulled out each drawer, dumping the contents on the floor. Nothing. She found nothing of use at Dr. Cowen's work station either. Frustrated, she turned a table on its side, sending instruments crashing to the floor. She slumped to a sitting position amid the jumble, her head in her hands, giving in to tears of frustration and despair.

She cursed herself for being too cautious. If she had left the room and made her escape as soon as the gunfire had stopped, she might have had a better chance. But she had waited five hours. That gave the dead plenty of time to re-animate and fill the corridors.

After several minutes of sitting on the floor, berating her perfect hindsight, she went to the refrigerator and pulled out a soft drink. They were too sweet for her taste but she may be stuck here a while. The sugar would keep her energy level up.

She wondered how long she would last. There was enough junk food for several days in the refrigerator, courtesy of her dead associate. The sinks still worked and the air would be fresh until the circulation system shut down from lack of maintenance.

On that thought, her gaze lifted to the grated cover above the fridge. The air return ducts! The installation was laced with a network that ran to every room, including this one. The return was about eight feet from the floor, large enough for her to crawl through.

Sharon grabbed a chair and placed it under the grated opening. Four screws held the cover in place. She would need a screwdriver. She remembered seeing one when she dumped the desk drawers. She rummaged through the mess on the floor until she found it.

The screws came out easily and the cover popped right off, but the opening was too high to climb into. The old refrigerator would give her the height she needed, if she could push it close enough.

Sharon climbed down and tossed the chair aside. The refrigerator needed to be moved three or four feet. It was an old model without the convenience of rollers on the bottom. It took all of her physical strength and many rests in-between but she managed to push the refrigerator into position beneath the air duct. Pushing the hair from her sweaty face, she gathered her thoughts. "Be calm," she said out loud. "Now is not the time to be rash. What do I need to take with me?"

She studied the room. There was nothing to use as a weapon. Once she left, she would be unable to return. The situation outside wouldn't be much better than in here. One thing had to go with her—her research. She had to continue looking for an answer. She may have been the only one to get as far as she had in discovering a cause.

Sharon downloaded everything she had on the virus onto several optical disks and slipped them into a protective case. The satchel beside her desk contained her laptop and backup power packs. She put her research into the satchel as well as several packets of peanut butter crackers and two pieces of cold fried chicken Dr. Cowen had left in the refrigerator.

From one of the empty examination tables she pulled a nylon restraint out of its metal guide and ran the strap through the satchel's handle. She fashioned a harness of sorts and strapped the satchel over her shoulders and secured the buckle. She was ready.

Sharon grabbed the chair and climbed up onto the refrigerator. She took one last look around to be sure she had everything the room had to offer. The creature she had been using for her research was still strapped to the table. It was still alive, despite the missing liver. The only organ vital to its survival was its brain. As long as that was undamaged, the ghoul would not cease to function.

Sharon crawled into the passageway and began her journey through the maze of airshafts.

Soon she came to a register overlooking the street and cafeteria front. The re-animated soldiers were still there. Some roamed aimlessly, others sat in doorways or against walls, devouring the remains of some unfortunate soul, oblivious to her observation.

Sharon followed many paths in the passageway, turning this way and that for what seemed like hours. They all led to uninviting places or dead ends, until she came upon a passage that went straight up for a hundred feet or so. This one was twice the diameter as the rest and had a metal ladder attached to the wall.

She climbed the ladder to the top. A horizontal shaft went another fifty feet. At the end of this shaft was a covered opening. She crawled to it and peered between the grates. She was at ground level, not far from the bench by the flowerbed she had sat on many times.

It was still dark outside. There was no way she was going outside while it was still dark. She would wait in the dimly lit shaft.

When Sharon opened her eyes, the sun was shining and a chilling wind blew into the shaft. There was no sign of danger as far as she could see. It was now or never.

She examined the cover. It was attached from the outside, hopefully not welded shut. There was only one way to find out.

Leaning back with her feet against the grill, she kicked as hard as she could. Her efforts produced a loud racket that echoed throughout the chamber. She kicked it again and again. On the forth kick the grate broke free and swung down, held by one rusting screw. Making sure her satchel was secure; she climbed up and out of the ventilation system onto solid ground.

There were no creatures in sight so she started toward the main gate, hoping to find a vehicle to make her getaway.

The guard shack at the main gate was abandoned but the gate was open. Two vehicles were still parked in front of the shack. One, a wide, sturdy-looking four-wheel drive with the word "Hummer" airbrushed on its tailgate was closest to her but there were no keys inside. The other vehicle, a ragtop Jeep, had a set of keys in the console between the seats.

Sharon quickly climbed inside. She inserted the key and the motor roared to life. Sharon hadn't had much experience with manual transmissions but it would have to do.

Grinding the shift into first gear, she stared at the road on the other side of the gate, unsure which way to go. One thing was certain; she wanted to go in the opposite direction of Washington, D.C. Away from the hungry hordes.

She popped the clutch and the Jeep lurched through the gate.

CHAPTER 36

Amanda checked her meager possessions and returned them to the pack. Nothing was missing this time. She carried the backpack with her wherever she went now. A couple of days before she discovered someone had helped themselves to a pair of her jeans and a can of corn. People would never change no matter what the circumstances. A bad situation usually brought out the worst in people.

Felicia sat nearby, running a brush through the mute child's golden locks. The girl scribbled in a notepad she had picked up somewhere, enjoying the attention Felicia showered on her.

"God, I'll be glad to get out of here and to a place where you can at least take a shower," Felicia sighed.

Amanda looked up and smiled. "Yeah, me, too." She snapped her backpack shut and slung it onto her shoulder. She wasn't sure the move to the prison was going to be any better than where they were now. The murdering corpses increased in numbers every day. Each new death took one away from the living and added one to the measure of the dead. She was beginning to feel that it was a hopeless situation. The dead would find you and get you no matter where you hid.

Amanda got to her feet and met Felicia's gaze. Felicia's nervous posture and childish grin gave Amanda the impression that Felicia was younger than her years. Her sudden change in attitude lately puzzled

Amanda. She wasn't as fearful as she had been. She was more at ease, almost cheerful.

Amanda smiled again, this time more sincerely. "Yes, it will be nice to bathe and have a little privacy. I hear each of us will have our own place to sleep. Even if it is a jail cell, it'll still be better than what we have now."

"Mick asked me if I wanted to ride out with him." Felicia said. "Should I?"

So that was it, Amanda thought. That's the reason for her lift in spirits. Mick.

"Yes. I would. What would it hurt?"

"It won't hurt a thing," Felicia said.

*　　　　*　　　　*

"Is that the last of them?" Jim asked.

"That's it," Chuck said, lighting a cigarette. "That's the last of the bodies. The whole place has been searched. They're all gone. All of the cells are empty, too.

"Good. Where did you get cigarettes? I thought you were all out."

"Off the bodies of the prisoners. Hell, I found over fifty packs, either on them or in their cells. That'll last me another month or so."

"You're a sick son of a bitch, you know that?"

"That's what they tell me. I don't see it though. But then again, us sickos never do."

"Come on. Let's go see if we can get the power back on before they start bringing people out here."

Chuck crushed the cigarette butt beneath his boot, making sure it was out. "I've already checked it out, Jim. All you have to do is flip a few switches and fire up the generators. There are two ten-thousand-gallon fuel tanks underground over there," he said, pointing to a gas pump and utility shed. "They're full—plenty to last us for months if we use it sparingly. And guess what else I found?"

"What's that, Chuck?"

"The inner fence is e-lec-tri-fied! All we have to do is turn it on and crank up the juice. No one will want to touch it, dead *or* alive!"

"Really? Show me."

Chuck took Jim to the main guard shack by the front gate. Inside was a room with four video monitors that hung above a console of controls and communication equipment. A locked wall cabinet contained several hand-held radios and key rings. The controller's chair lay on its side and a box of rifle shells were scattered across the floor, indicative of a post left in haste.

"Look here," Chuck said. "These buttons open and close the gate in the outer fence. This one here electrifies the inner one."

"Why isn't the outer fence electrified?"

"Because it's older. It wasn't designed to be powered. But when they put the new one in five years ago, they went the extra mile. You see those screens?"

Jim looked at the monitors hanging above the console. "There are video cameras on all of the guard towers," Chuck told him. "The whole prison grounds can be monitored from here just by moving the cameras with these four rotating knobs."

Jim absorbed everything Chuck told him, pleased with the information. His former life as a builder was all but forgotten. The only ambition he had now was to protect the survivors. The prison seemed the perfect place to do it.

CHAPTER 37

The Riverton Rescue Station buzzed with excitement. Some told of their narrow escapes from the roving dead while others spoke with renewed hope that their new prison home was safer than the overcrowded, unsanitary pig sty they had endured for the past two months.

The Riverton building had been adequate in the beginning, when the assumption was that the emergency would be dealt with quickly.

The building wasn't safe now, or adequately equipped for a prolonged stay. In recent weeks morale had sunk into depression. But with the coming move, Everyone's spirits had improved. All were doing their part with the packing and loading of supplies in order to hasten their departure.

Mick closed his suitcase containing everything he had left in the world. He checked his watch. It was time to call Jim and get a report on their progress. Jim had done a competent job in everything Mick had asked him to do. There was no doubt that today would be any different. Mick had come to depend on Jim quite heavily since Jon's death. It was a great relief to him to have another take-charge, levelheaded leader to help share the load.

The radio on his desk was to be one of the last things to go to the prison. Mick picked up the microphone and pushed the CALL button.

"Jim, you read?"

When no response came, he waited a moment and tried again.

"Jim, this is Mick. Do you read me?"

After a long silence, Mick tried to keep dread from creeping over him.

He was about to try again when Jim said, "Yeah, go ahead, Mick."

Relieved, Mick continued, "How's it going out there?"

"We're ready. Power's on and the place is secure. You can start the evacuation whenever you're ready."

"Ten-four. That's what I wanted to hear, Jim. I'll be taking down the radio at this end so we won't talk again until I see you. Is there anything you need?"

"Everything's fine here. I'll see you when you arrive."

"Ten-four and out."

Mick clicked off the radio and unplugged it from the extension cord that ran to the generator. Carefully, he placed it in a box and carried it outside, putting it on the back of his truck with various other things that had been crammed in.

Returning for his suitcase, he saw Felicia using a brick to nail a ply-board sign on the wall by the front door. The sign said, GONE TO WHITEPOST PRISON FOR SAFTY in red paint. The paint dripped from the bottom, making it look as though it had been done in blood, like the title on a late-night horror movie.

Upon completing her task, she turned with a satisfied grin to see Mick watching her. "Hey, Mick."

Mick inspected her work. "Good idea. Maybe someone'll still show up."

Felicia tossed the brick over the porch rail and inspected her work again. "You don't think they can read, do you?"

"What?"

"You don't think those—things—can read, do you?"

Mick thought their reasoning power was almost non-existent but what if somewhere, in the back of their minds, that ability still remained in a subconscious, splintered way? The sign might become a dinner bell. "Well, if they can I doubt they'll notice that you spelled safety wrong."

"Ahhh!" she moaned, then giggled to hide her embarrassment. "I did, didn't I?"

"Don't worry about it. I think the meaning is clear."

Sharon stopped at an intersection in Warren. Her indecision of which way to go created a lump in her throat, making it difficult to swallow.

An inner voice advised her to find safety among friends and family. Alone, she was vulnerable. But home was in Chicago, a world away. An unaided trip there would surely prove fatal.

She eased through the intersection and coasted the Jeep through Warren. The street she was crossing seemed to be in the village Center, where all the creatures seemed to congregate. A bizarre caricature of humanity, they existed in a twisted semi state of consciousness, unaware of who they once were or what they had become. Only a driving urge, the uncontrollable instinct, remained.

Sharon drove on, leaving the nightmarish scene behind only to witness more of the same whenever she passed through a populated area. She had not been in open territory since the beginning of this great plague and she was shocked at how far reaching and absolute the progression had been.

Until now she had not been confronted with the possibility that there may be no one left to aid her.

In her sleep-deprived state, she wondered what new horror had befallen mankind up ahead. Then she realized that the dinosaurs were merely life-size fiberglass copies of the terrible lizards that once ruled the earth, a tourist attraction. She laughed softly at her blunder and stopped the Jeep.

She was at a crossroads. If she turned right, the road would take her to the city of Winchester, ten miles north. She knew of it, a small city of about forty thousand. Too populated, therefore too dangerous. The sign also said that if she went left, it would lead to Shenandoah National Park, a mountain park. If there were any survivors, they may have retreated there.

A slight movement caught her attention near one of the dinosaurs. Three ghouls emerged from behind it and moved toward her. Sharon popped the clutch and turned left toward the park. The clumsy creatures chased after her but they faded into the distance as she drove away.

With the walking dead behind her, she relaxed. She was determined to survive. It didn't matter if there was no one left on the planet, she would not allow herself to become prey to those evil-smelling harbingers of death, nor would she allow herself to lose rationality. She would turn her fear of them into hatred, intense antipathy. They were, after all, the enemy. You had to hate the enemy, not fear them; otherwise you lacked the capacity to overcome such insurmountable odds.

Sharon was so caught up in re-training her thoughts she almost missed what she had been searching for. Massive movement from the left made her bring the Jeep to a tire-squealing halt. Files of people exited school busses and entered a large brick building. High chain link fences surrounded the structure. A sign told her it was the White Post Correctional Facility.

Quick, vibrant motion indicated living, breathing humans. Her heart banged fervently against her chest and her skin flashed hot from the adrenaline rush.

She had found survivors!

PART THREE

JUDGMENT DAY

CHAPTER 38

December

"I wouldn't have thought for a second that I would get out of this place, only to return again, much less be *happy* about it!" Matt said, scanning the countryside through binoculars from the north guard tower.

Chuck scanned in the opposite direction, grunting in response to Matt's conversation. Heavy dark clouds and a ground-hugging fog moved in from the east. It had been a nasty day, with periods of misting rain. The day was almost over as the last glow of light faded and gave way to darkness but their shift wouldn't end until six in the morning.

Chuck let the binoculars drop against his chest and rubbed his tired, bloodshot eyes. He stretched and then leaned against the rail, propping a foot on a metal folding chair. He lit a cigarette, enjoying the first drag.

"You got an extra?" Matt asked.

Chuck looked at the ground thirty feet below. "Go buy your own." He waited for the stunned look to fill Matt's face before cracking a sly grin and flicking his wrist, shaking several cigarettes from the pack opening. "Go ahead."

Matt took the smoke and Chuck produced the fire. "Just don't make it a habit," Chuck said.

"Ahhh," Matt said, enjoying the smoke's flavor. Though stale, it was still an almost erotic feeling to his lungs. "Don't worry, I don't smoke that much—not anymore. I'm not addicted—anymore."

"No. I mean, don't make a habit of borrowing them from me. They don't make this particular brand anymore. Know what I mean?"

"I think I do," Matt said. "This brand or any other brand."

Matt watched the fog grow thicker on the ground. It began to rise higher and higher until it filled the deck on which they stood.

"Eerie," he said. "I can't see a thing. Not even the ground right under us."

Chuck took the binoculars from around his neck and laid them on the flat handrail that wrapped around the watch area. "I guess I won't be needing these anymore. It's as thick as pea soup out there, too dark anyway. Speaking of soup, I'm hungry. Are you?"

Matt didn't feel like eating. He was trying to see through the fog that got thicker by the second. It was so thick the lights that normally shined so brightly around the prison yard now barely glowed through the haze.

"How'd we get stuck with the night shift anyway?" Matt asked.

"We volunteered."

"Volunteered! I didn't volunteer. You might've but I didn't! What's this volunteered shit?"

A moan echoed through the mist, silencing them. The moan turned to a whimper. It was almost like a baby's cry but it was the unmistakable wail of the dead. Unseen through the fog, some had found them, drawn by the light or some kind of primal sixth sense. Regardless, their cries now filtered through the night.

Chuck and Matt listened to their whines. The December chill penetrated Matt's clothing but that was not what made him shiver. The eerie wails that echoed through the fog and the fact that visibility was so poor that the ground beneath them had disappeared worried him. Mounting anxiety creased his face.

"Don't worry," Chuck reassured him. "They can't get through the gates. It doesn't sound like there are enough of them. Not yet, anyway."

"How can you tell they're on the outside of the gates?" Matt whispered.

"Where else would they be?"

Matt flipped up his jacket collar and sat on the edge of the folding chair by the rail.

The forlorn sound of walking death haunted him.

Chapter 39

The fog and clouds were gone the following morning. The sun blazed and it was unseasonably warm for early December. The ghouls who had found their way to the prison were quickly dealt with once the fog lifted and revealed their location. A bevy of crows picked at the decaying corpses, scattering when a crew arrived to load them onto the dump truck for disposal.

Sharon Darney quickly settled in as a member of the ragtag band of survivors at the prison. Her first priority was to continue her work on ending the plague, or at least to slow it down. The infirmary had been made into a makeshift laboratory but it was hopelessly short of the equipment essential to her work. At the last meeting it had been decided that a small group of volunteers would risk going into a populated area to get what she needed. A hospital should have almost everything necessary.

The prison was ideal for their needs. Easily defended, well stocked and powered, several wells supplied enough water to drink and for occasional showers. They were totally self-sufficient. It wasn't the Ritz but under present circumstances, it was most welcome.

The large food pantry was fully stocked. With what they had brought with them, there was plenty of food to get them through the winter and most of spring if rationed properly.

*   *   *

Amanda scribbled numbers in the ledger Jim had provided and resumed counting the various items that filled the shelves. She would make this count each day to make sure no one stole any of the food stored there. The fact that she had been stuck with the job was supposed to have been a testament to her dependability but she thought it was a deliberate plan to prevent her involvement in the more dangerous tasks she had volunteered for.

Only moments ago Jim had set her up with the task at hand, then he had disappeared. A plea for help had come over the citizen-band frequency. Jim was off to find the sender before it was too late, a job she was perfectly capable of doing. She supposed giving her this tedious post was Jim's way of keeping her out of harm's way.

"Everyone here must do his or her part," he had said, "and you have a better head for this kind of thing than anyone else." He had smiled so sincerely that she begrudgingly accepted the dull task.

All things considered, there were some pretty good items in the pantry. There was no fresh meat but there were plenty of canned hams, chicken, and pork, an abundance of vegetables, flour, and sugar. She wondered why prison food had a reputation for being so bad. Certainly some pretty good meals could come from what was stored there.

The fault had to lie with the cooks. Slop it in, spoon it out. Don't worry about how it tastes. If anyone thought she was cooking, they had better think again. She'd take no part in that.

CHAPTER 40

A cloud of black smoke loomed on the horizon as Jim maneuvered his truck through the streets on the outskirts of town. Chuck sat quietly in the passenger's seat staring out the window at the scenery devoid of human life.

The revived dead roamed the countryside in their search for warm flesh. They passed empty houses and businesses, a mangled child's bicycle. Even the absence of wildlife testified to the immense desolation that now ruled a once-thriving world. In a million years it would be covered beneath layers of earth for some future digger to find and ponder.

The closer they got to town, the greater the creatures grew in number until they resembled a freakish festival crowding the streets, yards, and parking lots, a sea of rotting flesh. Excited by the sudden appearance of the truck, their wails began to rise. They grabbed empty air in vain attempts to reach their prey. They were leery of stepping in front of the speeding truck. Instinct or experience had taught them to hesitate.

"Damn," Jim said. "The smoke! I think it's coming from the hospital."

Chuck looked at the smoke rising over the hill ahead and alarm made him sit straight in his seat. "Shit, that's where the call for help came from! What now?"

Jim slammed the gas pedal to the floor and raced toward the burning structure. Creatures who were fast enough or fortunate enough to get out of the way, scattered. The ones who weren't bounced off the fenders as Jim weaved around them.

They topped the hill and the hospital came into view. Smoke and flames billowed from the second-story windows and rolled into a column of black smoke that rose high into the air. Waves of zombies circled the burning structure, keeping a safe distance between themselves and the raging fire.

Jim crashed through the mob, sending one of the ghouls flying and crushing another beneath the tires.

They skidded to a halt in front of the Emergency entrance. The glass doors looked as though they had been shattered, refortified, and broken again.

Jim and Chuck leapt from the truck, weapons at the ready. The creatures, though agitated, made no attempt to get near the burning structure.

"You ready?" Jim asked.

Chuck grinned. "Let's rock-n-roll!"

They entered the smoky building, taking up positions at every corner before moving ahead. Each and every room was checked as they moved through the hospital with lightning speed, not throwing caution to the wind even as the building began to come apart.

The ceiling gave way in some areas and large pieces of burning debris fell around them in furious fire blasts. The smoke thickened. Time was running out. In a few minutes, the whole place would fall on their heads.

"There's no one here," Chuck choked. "They either left or they're dead."

"No! There's gotta be someone here. That distress call came minutes before we left."

"Then where are they?" Chuck shouted above falling bits of fire and rubble.

Jim thought fast. Where would he go if he couldn't get out of a burning building? "Downstairs! They must be in the morgue. There will be less smoke there. I saw a staircase back down the hall."

Jim pulled his shirt up over his mouth and nose and motioned for Chuck to do the same. "Now move!"

They ran down the hall to the stairway and opened the door. There was less smoke in the stairwell and they took the stairs two and three at a time, racing to beat the fire. In a dead run they slammed through the door at the bottom and found themselves in another hall.

Chuck, who came through second, was immediately whipped off his feet and slammed to the floor, face first. Groping hands pulled at his collar and face. A throaty, gurgling groan echoed in his ear as he rolled onto his back, bringing him inches away from the mangled, puss-dripping maw of a ghoul intent on taking a sizable chunk out of his throat.

Jim tried to get a clean shot on the creature without hitting Chuck but the way they thrashed about made it impossible. Chuck fought fiercely to break the monster's grip. It began to get the upper hand, drawing closer for the fatal bite. With a swift upward thrust of both knees, Chuck sent the zombie careening backward into the wall where Jim put a bullet in its brain.

"Chew on that, you son of a bitch!" Chuck screamed, getting to his feet.

"You all right?" Jim asked.

Chuck checked himself for injury and, to his relief, found none. The knot that had suddenly formed in his throat prevented him from speaking so he nodded.

"All right," Jim said, noticeably relieved, "let's get a move on."

Again they hurried down the lower hall, checking rooms as they went. They heard the crashing of falling debris as the building continued to come apart. The thick black smoke was now beginning to filter into the basement where they searched.

The last door at the end of the hall was locked but Jim remedied that with a skillful shot into the lock. He swung the door open. Huddled in a corner were a man, a woman, and two children.

"No time to waste!" Jim shouted. "Back upstairs now! This whole place is gonna be down on our heads in a few minutes! Run!"

When they opened the ground-level door it was like opening the door to a blast furnace. The intense heat and smoke almost knocked them over. It burned their lungs as they ran for the exit.

An explosion erupted at the far end of the ground floor and fire mushroomed in their direction, consuming everything in its path. The force of the heat and the explosion pushed them forward just ahead of the burning inferno.

They ran to the truck. The man and woman each carried a child over their shoulders like a sack of grain.

Jim grabbed a child in each of his large, work-hardened hands and tossed them unceremoniously into the cab, shouting over the roaring fire, "You two climb in the back and lie low!"

The zombies kept their distance, more afraid of the fire than the desire to seize the fleeing humans.

The truck sped through the mob again, mowing down the walking dead as it bounced wildly over fallen bodies.

"We thought there'd be help there," the little girl said to Jim once they were out of immediate danger. "Daddy said there were good people at the hospital but they were all gone. Lots of bad people came instead."

Jim looked at the two children nestled between him and Chuck. He was struck by how defeated they looked. He wondered where they had been. This nightmarish ordeal had been going on for months now yet here were four survivors. They were beaten but they were alive.

"I know, honey. Everything's gonna be better now. You're going to a safe place."

"The monsters got inside but daddy made them go away with fire. But then the hospital started to burn up, too," she said, trailing off to sleep as the words left her mouth.

The boy, a year or so younger, put his head on his sister's shoulder and promptly fell asleep.

Chapter 41

"I don't know much about what you're doing but I'll help you as much as I can, Doctor Darney."

"Thank you, Doctor Brine. I can certainly use all the help I can get."

"You say that you found a bug that might be doing this?" he asked, hobbling closer on his cane.

Sharon looked up from her laptop. Dr. Brine was old, in his late seventies maybe. She didn't know if he possessed enough knowledge to give her any real help but he did have countless years of experience, coupled with an ability to make you feel that he was an old family friend, one who would never abandon you.

She could imagine him taking chickens or goats for payment, or walking through heavy snow in the middle of the night to help the sick. A forgotten virtue in the present time, she thought.

"I think the organism I found is in some way responsible for what's happening."

"Hmmm," Dr. Brine said, rubbing his chin, pondering the possibility. "That may be, pretty lady, but I ain't never seen no bug that can make a dead man walk."

"Neither have I," Sharon said. "But I won't find out anything else without the proper equipment."

The infirmary door opened and Jim led the four bedraggled survivors in. The children clung to their mother's legs, their eyes darting about the room, their safety still in question.

Jim led them to an examination table and gently lifted each of the children onto the table. "I'd like you to give them all a check up, Sharon. Just to be sure they're okay."

Sharon patted the boy's head then glanced at Dr. Brine. "I think this is a job more suited for you, Doctor Brine. Would you see to these nice people?"

"I sure will." He responded in a cheerful tone and hobbled to their side as quickly as his decrepit legs would allow.

Sharon pulled Jim aside. "How about the equipment?" she asked. "Did you get the things I need to continue my research? This stuff is—"

Jim raised his hand to stop her barrage of questions. "I've got some bad news for you. These people were holed up in the hospital in town. At this moment it's a three-alarm blaze."

Sharon's mouth dropped in disbelief. It was one thing after another. She was blocked at every turn, as if an invisible hand relentlessly pushed her backward. "What now? Where's the closest one?"

"Winchester, I think. But it may be too dangerous to try it."

"It may be too dangerous not to try it," she said. "We've got to stop this!"

Jim frowned and picked up his rifle. "I'll check it out. But I won't promise you anything."

CHAPTER 42

Felicia walked into her grandmother's kitchen. Her grandmother had been dead for many years but there she was, sitting at the table, drinking a cup of tea the way she'd always done, humming a song Felicia vaguely remembered from childhood.

Though Felicia knew she must be dreaming, it felt real, as though she'd stepped over a time threshold and into her past. She was oddly comforted and joyous at the thought of spending this fleeting dream-time with the woman she loved dearly; the woman she had shared an unbreakable bond with in life.

Felicia eased herself into the chair across from her grandmother, hoping nothing would waken her and break the spell.

Isabelle Smith folded her hands on the table in front of her and smiled at Felicia with the same loving smile she'd always bestowed on her favorite grandchild.

"Hello, my children," she said in a soothing voice. "How are you?"

Her words made Felicia aware that she was not alone. Izzy, her ethereal shadow in life, had followed her into her dream world.

"Grandma, this is Iz—"

"I know who she is, sweetheart. She's like us in her gift, only more so. See how she glows with it?"

Felicia looked down at Izzy clinging to her hand. The aura around her body was truly brilliant, like the aura surrounding Christ in the picture on grandma's bedroom wall. Felicia was stunned. How had she missed it before? She had known from their first meeting that Izzy had the sight but somehow she hadn't realized the magnitude of the gift.

"I'm afraid, Grandma. Afraid of what's happening here. I'm afraid of dying."

"I know you are, honey, but you will be fine. You have to be strong now. Listen to your heart and the things it tells you. It will lead you, just as mine led me. And listen to this child."

"But, Gran—"

"Shhh. Listen now, Felicia. There are more ways to listen than with your ears. Have you forgotten?"

"No…yes. I just…I haven't—"

"Shhh, child. Listen."

And then Felicia heard it. Whether it was in her head or in her heart or in her ears, she couldn't be sure. It came upon her suddenly and unexpectedly. A musical, childlike voice said, "I lift up mine eyes unto the mountain from which cometh my help."

Felicia looked around the room. In spite of the morning sunshine streaming through the lace curtains and the presence of her grand-mother, thoughts from the real world began to filter into her mind.

"It's all right, my child. You're safe here," her grandmother said with the familiar smile. "There's nothing to fear here."

"Where am I, Grandma?"

"You're here with me for now."

"I've missed you so much," Felicia sobbed. For the first time she began to truly remember reality that her grandmother was long since dead and buried. "You're dead. This is only a dream."

"You of all people should know that dreams and reality are inter-laced, Felicia. A day's thoughts return to cleanse the mind and allow you to focus on the next day. Sometimes lives are built on dreams. Sometimes dreams come true. A dream can be many things."

Felicia walked to the window, wiping tears as she went. Her grandmother's flowerbeds bloomed as they always had. Birds sang beautiful spring songs and were answered by others from afar. She was in a world she knew from long ago.

"Is this the end?" Felicia asked.

"Do you mean Judgment Day?

"Yes."

"In a manner of speaking, yes. We are all being judged, the dead and the living. Beware! An apostle of evil is coming to you Felicia, one who has been judged and sentenced. He will come as a sheep but he is a wolf. Do not let him enter your flock. He is one of many. There are more like him. Don't let him trick you. He will if he can."

"Why is it happening?"

"Hate has consumed the earth. Hate is what's really being destroyed, washed away by its own rage."

The room began to spin and darken and Felicia held tight to the back of a chair to keep from falling. Her grandmother's voice began to get fainter and fainter as the dream world slipped away.

"I've got to go now, Felicia, but I will always be near...always be near...always be..."

Felicia tried desperately to hold on to the world she had found herself in, a world of beauty and security, a world where pain and death had no meaning. But her hold was fragile. The harder she held on, the faster it faded to darkness until it disappeared.

She awoke with tears flowing down her face. She choked back sobs as she opened to her eyes to the real world. She saw her reflection in the blue, teary eyes that stared back at her.

Isabelle reached out and silently wiped the tears from Felicia's face.

*   *   *

Mick entered the guardhouse at the gate near the inner fence. All of the radio equipment had been set up there so the guard on duty could always monitor it.

Pete Wells, an older man of about sixty, sat at the console, his ear close to one of the speakers, listening to an even stream of pink noise.

"How's it going?" Mick asked. "Anything new?"

"Not yet Mick, still the same ol' shit. A weak signal hidden behind tons of static."

"Damn. There's got to be others out there somewhere."

"If there are, they don't have a radio or are too far away. I finally got that satellite dish working, too, nothing on it either. I'm starting to believe that maybe we're the only ones left."

Mick glanced toward the road. The trees had lost their leaves. Winter was setting in. The bleakness of the landscape and the grayness of the sky did nothing to better his mood. The holidays were approaching but none of that mattered now. There would be nothing to celebrate this year. He was surprised he had even given it a thought. It was about the least important thing he could think of.

"Let me know if anything changes," Mick said and walked out.

The prison yard was quiet. No creatures had appeared for a couple of days. Maybe they would be safe, Mick thought. As long as they were careful and rationed the food, it might work. There was no reason to think otherwise. It would take a virtual army of those monsters to compromise the perimeter.

With that thought in mind, he relaxed a little and turned toward the main structure. Jim, who had walked up from behind, startled him. The sudden surprise was enough to rob Mick of his momentary comfort.

"Sorry, I didn't mean to startle you, Mick."

Mick drew a deep breath and rolled his head around his shoulders to relieve some of the tension. He allowed Jim a small smile. "It's okay. I was just looking around."

"We're gonna be okay here, don't you think, Mick?"

"We'll be fine." Mick said, continuing toward the building. "As long as we stay put."

"I'm afraid I can't do that, Mick."

Mick stopped and faced Jim. "What do you mean by that? What's up?"

"I have to go to Winchester to get a few things."

Mick studied Jim for a moment. Apparently Jim feared nothing. At least it didn't show on his face. If anything, Mick thought he looked forward to the excitement.

"You don't know what you'll be walking into, Jim. What's so important that you have to risk that?"

"That lady doctor needs some equipment in order to continue her research for a solution to this mess."

"What can she possibly do to stop what's happened?"

"I don't know. Maybe nothing. But I think we have to try, even if nothing does come of it."

"I won't try to stop you. You're gonna do what you want anyway. You know the drill. Just be careful."

CHAPTER 43

It was no use. Sharon could not continue her work without the proper equipment. There was no way to combat something she couldn't see. The microscope on the table would never magnify the organism enough to be visible. If she couldn't see it, she couldn't kill it. Disgusted, she slammed her laptop shut and paced the floor.

"Don't let it whip you," Dr. Brine said, slurping the last bit of coffee from his cup. "This ain't no new bug, or radiation, or anything else made by man," he said matter-of-factly. "This is God's doing."

Dr. Brine put his cup to his lips for another sip and frowned at the empty cup. "Or it might be Old Scratch's. Either way, it's beyond us fixing. All's we can do is hope to see our way through it."

"I won't accept that," Sharon said. "There's got to be a *logical* reason."

"That's the problem with all you young scholars today; everything has to be logical. Well, I say to hell with logic! Since when has logic got anything to do with it?"

"Logic has everything to do with it," Sharon argued. "Any problem has to have a logical solution. When they bite you, you die. That's because the virus infects your body and quickly turns your organs to mush. Logical answer! What I can't figure out yet is why the dead corpse revives after death, or why they hunger for human flesh. But that, too, has to have an answer, a *logical* one. And I'll find it."

Dr. Brine lightly tapped his cane against the floor. He couldn't quite fathom why the notion of the phenomenon being supernatural was so hard for her to believe. He had found through the years that things didn't always have tidy explanations attached to them. And this one…this one just isn't meant to be figured out.

"You want answers?" he said, "I'll give you answers. They attack, they bite, but they rarely devour you. They're trying to reproduce in the only way they can, by increasing their numbers. Everyone they bite dies and becomes one of them. It's their only way. As far as why they're coming back, well, you better pray to God for that answer. I think He's the only one that can tell you."

Sharon stopped blocking out the old doctor's ramblings and thought about what he said. Procreation? Was that their way of continuing the species? Could that be the answer?

"But they also attack other living animals," Sharon said.

"Yeah, they do," Dr. Brine agreed. "A dog prefers a dog but he'll take just about anything when the urge hits."

CHAPTER 44

The preacher sat on a far away hill and watched. They were quite safe and secure behind the high prison fence and barred windows it would seem. Safe and probably well fed. Most times the hunting parties he sent into the woods for fresh game came back empty-handed. His followers were becoming less and less content. Something had to be done soon.

The sign at the place in Riverton was nice. It saved him the trouble of looking for them. Now that he had found them, they were well defended. No matter, he thought. God is on my side.

A man in his early twenties came to the preacher's side and sat down. He was thin and unshaven and his clothes hung loosely from his malnourished body. Sunken cheeks and dark circles beneath his eyes gave him an appearance that could easily be mistaken for one of the walking dead if it weren't for his fluid movements. The grumbling in the young man's stomach grew louder by the minute and he was becoming weaker each day. He stared at the encampment, eagerly anticipating a meal. They wouldn't just give food to them; they would have to fight for it; the preacher had told them that. He had told them how greedy and selfish these people were, that their destruction was inevitable.

At first he fought the idea of killing living, breathing humans, but hunger helped sway him to the preacher's way of thinking. These people must truly be evil as he had been told, and evil must be destroyed. They would destroy them and take what was rightfully theirs as God and Father Peterson intended.

Peterson studied the encampment through his binoculars, taking in every detail. Guard towers; each manned. Ten or twelve-foot chain link fences, two of them, surrounded the encampment. They would have to cut their way through. Yes, it would be difficult but God would surely guide his hands and lend strength to His Chosen.

"When?" the young man asked. "When do we do it?"

The preacher lowered his binoculars. "At night. The darker, the better."

CHAPTER 45

Matt threw supplies on the back of the truck, then wiped the sweat from his glistening forehead and he leaned against the fender. His strength was finally back, most of it anyway, but the crates of ammunition and toolboxes were still heavy. He bent to pick up another box.

Chuck lit another cigarette, his third in less than a half an hour. He leaned his head back as he exhaled, savoring the flavor. His obvious intention was to avoid anything that vaguely resembled work.

"You people sweat a lot, don't you?" Chuck said.

"What?" Matt asked, picking up on the racial stereotype.

"What is it? Your skin's black so it soaks up more heat?" Chuck took another deep drag. "But what makes you smell so much worse?"

Matt pushed away from the fender and walked to where Chuck stood, towering a good six inches over him. "You son of a bitch!" he sneered. "You try doing a little work and you'll sweat, too, goddamn it! And speaking of smells, I think I smell the blood of an inbred, chain-smoking redneck!"

Chuck looked at Matt. He had intended to spark a reaction from him but not a violent one. All he had really wanted was for Matt to tell him to "go the hell on" so he could avoid the dismal manual labor.

"Cool your jets, big guy. I was only kidding. I didn't really mean any disrespect to your people."

"My people? My people are decent, God fearing, hard working Americans! Or they were until this shit happened." Matt paused to check temper "What do you think about that, you ignorant little bastard?"

Chuck looked at Matt, momentarily stunned by the big man's tirade.

"Before you answer that," Matt advised, "now would be a good time to keep your stupid, bigoted mouth shut."

"You mean a closed mouth gathers no feet?" Chuck smiled, hoping to ease the tension.

"Exactly!"

"I'll keep that in mind," Chuck said, taking another drag. "I'm sorry, man, I really didn't mean anything by it."

Matt relaxed. "So what are we gonna do today?" he asked. If this whole "dead" thing had taught him anything it was that life was too short to waste on bullshit.

"We're going to Winchester to get some things for the new doctor."

"Winchester-in this truck? What things? I ain't going to no Winchester. That place will really be fucked up. We don't wanna go there."

"We'll be fine," Chuck said. "Those things can't get inside that truck."

"Yeah, and we won't be able to get out. Those things will be a swarm in the city. I ain't going," Matt said, turning back toward the prison.

"Okay, suit yourself. Me and Jim will do it ourselves."

Matt stopped but didn't turn around right away. He stared past the towers to the foothills in the distance. They looked so calm, so normal. He could just as easily hike up the trails to the mountain's highest peak and camp there until this mess was finished. But Chuck's words had made him feel guilty. What if they went and got killed just because they needed one extra hand to get out of a bad situation? It would be his fault. There was no way he was going to live with that on his conscience. Chuck would be a small loss but he couldn't live with it if anything happened to Jim. He'd have to go. Besides, Jim was going, too, and that made him feel much better.

"I'll go," Matt said, spinning around on one heel to face Chuck. "But you better hope I don't get bit because then I'm gonna bite you. You got it?"

Chuck shrugged and lit another cigarette.

✳   ✳   ✳

"Do you really think you'll find the answers you're looking for?" Jim asked Sharon.

"I don't believe in witchcraft, Jim."

"Maybe you should."

"There's a logical reason and if I live long enough, I'll find it."

"So, you don't know anything yet?"

"I know a little."

"And what's that?"

Sharon flipped open her laptop and the screen came to life. After she entered a few commands, the information she was looking came up and she turned the screen to face Jim.

"I found a foreign organism that I believe is the cause. It was a tough one to find but I found it."

"It looks like a shadowy black tadpole," Jim said, squinting at the digitized image of the culprit.

"Sort of," Sharon said, seeing the slight similarity. "But this tadpole doesn't turn its victims into frogs. That would take witchcraft and I don't believe in that, remember?"

"Yes. What does it do?"

"It turns many of the major organs, including part of the brain, into mush. It spreads throughout the body at lightning speed, killing its victim in less than seventy-two hours, that's what it does."

"Killing you and making a person get back up to kill after the body is cold are two different things. Are you forgetting that this whole thing started with the dead rising, not a living person being a carrier? How do you explain that?"

"I'm not sure." Thinking Jim was about to make a crack about witch-craft again, she said, "There could be several reasons. It could be that it was there before the dead actually started resurrecting. Maybe we're all carriers, even now, before we die. Maybe only after death does it mutate into the image you see on the computer."

"That certainly is logical, if nothing else, but it still doesn't explain why they want to *eat* us."

"I'm stumped there, too. Doctor Brine's explanation sounds as good as any, though, reproduction of the species. It's their only way. Nature finds a way—in this case in an unnatural way."

Jim took the rifle that never left his side from the table and slung it over his shoulder and walked to the door. "I guess we'd better get going so we can be back here before it gets dark."

"Jim?" Sharon said.

Jim turned.

"Be careful."

"We will."

CHAPTER 46

"Okay, two out of three. Winner drives," Matt said.

"No way!" Chuck said. "I won the toss, so I'll drive."

"Yeah? Well, I've seen you drive. You drive like a fucking nut!"

"I'm a good driver and I won the toss so—"

"I'll drive!" Jim said, coming up from behind. "I don't trust either one of you behind the wheel."

"Sounds good to me," Chuck said, giving in.

Matt nodded. "Works for me."

"You two just try to keep your heads on straight. It might get hairy."

Five miles outside of Winchester, the scenery changed. No longer was the roadside lined with fields and farmhouses. Large housing subdivisions and strip malls now cluttered the landscape. They passed a large graveyard on the left and Jim stared at the multitude of gravestones, wondering if the dead there had awakened. Were they fighting to be released from their dark boxes, waiting to climb up through the earth and thrust a decayed hand into our world? One thing was certain; they couldn't escape a covered six-foot hole.

Strangely, they hadn't seen that many of the walking dead yet. A few here and there lumbered about in their mindless manner but there weren't nearly as many as they had expected. In a city the size of Winchester they had thought the dead would surely rule.

They continued on toward the city proper, zigzagging in and out of the abandoned cars littering the road. At one point the road was barely passable and Jim was hardly able to squeeze through because of an accident that had happened many weeks before.

One creature, a longhaired hippie type wearing a shirt bearing the slogan "Shit Happens" was attempting to open one of the abandoned car doors.

Chuck couldn't control his mirth at the irony of the shirt's message. "You can put that on my headstone when you put me in the ground," Chuck laughed. "Shit Happens! Don't it, though?"

Jim brought the truck to a sudden halt in the middle of an intersection, throwing the two distracted passengers into the dash and then back into their seats.

"What the hell are you doing?" Chuck yelled.

Jim smiled and pointed to a building on the corner of the intersection. "Gentlemen, I believe we may have just hit the proverbial jackpot."

A large nameplate above the front doors said, U.S. ARMORY. Jeeps, tanks, and covered vehicles filled the parking lot around the army reserve depot.

Jim eased the truck forward and climbed the curb in front of the building, then came to a stop once again, this time less abruptly.

"How do you even know it hasn't been cleaned out?" Chuck asked.

"I don't," Jim said. "We won't know until we check." He opened his door and stepped out.

Matt began to fidget. He cleared his throat loudly. "What are we doing, Chuck? We ain't stopping here, are we?"

"We sure are my friend. The boss man says we're gonna check it out."

"That's what I was fucking afraid of," Matt grumped, sliding out behind Chuck. "Jesus Christ! Man, this is fucked up."

Jim reached into the truck and took his weapon from the gun rack in the rear window. He checked the rounds and then checked his revolvers.

Several zombies were in the area but not too close. They could be in and out before they closed in, if all went well.

"You stay out here and keep an eye out," Jim told Matt, handing him a walkie-talkie. "Let us know if they get too close. If you have to, take a few out."

Matt stuck the radio in his jacket pocket and clutched his rifle. "Right. Take them out. I can do that," he nodded, doing his best to remain calm.

Jim and Chuck trotted toward the building as Matt reminded himself, "In the head. Shoot them in the head. I can do that."

The doors were unlocked and swung open when Jim pushed against them. The two men leaped inside, crouched in military fashion, and surveyed the corridor. It was empty except for countless pieces of paper covering the floor, along a few rotting bodies. The sickening, sweet-smelling rot overwhelmed their senses. Chuck gagged as they stepped over corpses.

Room after room was void of anything useful. Frantic people had cleaned out the Armory when things fell apart. Then Jim saw a metal crate in an office behind the door. Dried blood covered part of the lid.

Jim bent down and opened it. The crate was filled with twenty hand grenades, maybe more. Jim and Chuck exchanged a victorious smile and Chuck grabbed the crate, grunting as he got it shouldered. They quickly exited the room.

They ran down the hall, Chuck's breathe heavy, his heart pounding from his heavy burden. Jim was in the lead as they turned the last corner before the main doors. Three creatures waited there. The first one grabbed Jim as he made the turn. Caught by surprise, he dropped his weapon and it clattered across the tile floor. Quickly pinned against the wall, the three ghouls pawed at him, wide-eyed and eager.

Jim butted his head against the ugly monster directly in front of him, pushing it a few steps backwards, giving him some room to work. The monster on his left lost his grip but instantly reached out for another hold.

Shots rang out from Matt's gun and Chuck's radio sprang to life. "They're coming! They're coming! Oh my God!" Matt screamed.

Chuck put his heavy load down but before the box of grenades hit the floor, Jim grabbed the ghoul on his left and held it at arm's length. The other creature moved behind him, ready to strike. In one fluid motion, Jim rammed an elbow into the forehead of the ghoul behind him and shot his fist into the face of the one in front of him. Both ghouls dropped to the floor, dead. Jim withdrew his revolver and shot the third between the eyes before it could close in again.

Chuck grabbed the box and Jim retrieved his rifle. Without so much as a glance at the dead creatures on the floor, they headed for the front door.

Outside, Matt swung his rifle back and forth, unsure of what to do. Jim swallowed hard and stopped in his tracks. The area was surrounded with thousands of monsters, all closing in.

Jim ran for the truck. "Throw the grenades in the back, Chuck! Carefully!"

All three piled into the truck and Jim started the engine. Wheels spinning, he burned rubber back to the street as the massive horde continued to close in.

Jim dodged as many as he could but sent others flying over the truck as he plowed into them. The thought of going deeper into the city was ridiculous now. There were just too many ghouls.

Sharon wouldn't get her equipment today.

CHAPTER 47

Mick walked down the darkened corridor toward the cell he now called home. He paused at an unusual sound. The plague, as he thought of it, had heightened all of their senses to unidentified noise, had heightened their awareness to any danger. What he heard was the soft, incessant crying of a woman. He moved in the direction of the sound, unsure of whether or not his presence would be welcomed.

"Felicia, is that you?" he asked the form huddled in the corner of a small cot.

She sniffed and tried unsuccessfully to stop crying.

"What is it, baby? The dreams again?"

He entered her cell and moved toward her. Perhaps he was overstepping his bounds but he couldn't control the overwhelming desire to protect and comfort her.

Felicia shook her head as Mick sat beside her. He reached out to touch her hair, then her face.

"It's okay, darling," he soothed. "I promise you I will die before I let anything happen to you, or to Izzy."

Mick knew that Felicia had been having prophetic dreams more frequently. Felicia had told him about her "family curse" as she called it. She told him about her grandmother's warnings of coming doom, of a wolf in sheep's clothing bent on revenge, that he was a sick man with evil intentions, one of many. The clairvoyant dreams were more intense with the passing of each day.

Mick pulled Felicia into the comfort of his embrace. Felicia held tightly to him, a sob escaping her quivering lips. He stroked her hair and listened to her latest vision. Most of what she said didn't make sense to him but he listened anyway, rocking her gently to comfort her.

Holding her close, his heart pounding from the nearness of this beautiful but troubled child-woman, he realized his desire for her ran deeper than passion. It was almost too much to bear. He lowered his head and she raised hers until their lips met. The kiss sent waves of desire through Mick's body.

He caressed her shoulder down to the curve of her slender waist. Her thin gown barely veiled her skin beneath. Felicia snuggled closer into him, pressing her body against his.

Felicia's cell was at the end of that particular block. Amanda slept soundly on the other side of the wall. Izzy, who normally stayed very close to Felicia, was "sleeping over" with her new friends, the children who had been rescued from the burning hospital.

Mick eased Felicia back onto the cot and their bodies moved in heated unison. A candle on a small table illuminated their blinding need for comfort, passion, and love.

Mick awoke with a start. A small alarm clock on the nightstand beside the spent candle said it was six a.m. It was actually five o'clock but no one had bothered to turn the clocks back to Standard Time in October. It had been rather pointless, considering.

Mick looked at Felicia, who still slept soundly, temporarily rid of the strange dreams that haunted her. She was beautiful and he couldn't take his eyes from her, nor did he want to. Usually he was making his rounds to make sure all was safe and secured by this time of the morning.

An unfamiliar feeling wrenched his gut. It was like a hand twisting and pushing up against his heart. Unfamiliar though it was, he easily identified it; he loved her.

Perhaps he had loved her for some time now but last night had sealed his fate. He had fallen deeply, almost painfully, in love with her. Looking down at her, he knew he would never let anything hurt her. He *would* die first.

Felicia began to stir, and then opened her eyes. She smiled at Mick, who still leaned over her.

"Good morning sleepy head," he said, "did you sleep well?"

Her smile broadened. "Very," she said, still half asleep. "What time is it?"

"It's late. After six."

"That's not late, silly." She laughed, and then wrapped her arms around his neck, drawing him close. "Don't leave me yet," she whispered seductively.

Mick pulled away and gazed deeply into her sky blue eyes that sparkled in the dim light of the cell. "I will never leave you," he said. "As long as I live, as long as you'll have me, I will be by your side."

Felicia's eyes teared. "I love you, Mick. I have since I first saw you."

"And I love you, too, Felicia. More than you can imagine."

CHAPTER 48

"We are an endangered species," Jim snapped. "I'll be damned if I'm going to risk lives in search of a cure that probably won't make a difference if it's found."

"I'm not asking you to risk lives, Jim," Sharon pleaded. "All I'm asking you to do is try."

"We tried. Winchester is overrun with countless thousands of those things. There's no way we can get to the hospital in the city's center and get out alive. We barely got out as it is."

"Then I'm stuck," Sharon said, defeated. "There's nothing else I can do."

"Go on what you've already got."

"I've got nothing!" she cried, swiping her hand angrily across the table, scattering her notes to the floor. "I've got nothing!"

Jim stared out at the prison yard. The way he saw it, their failure to get her equipment was the least of his worries. With so many creatures all around them now, it was only a matter of time before they were in a desperate situation.

Jim watched Sharon slump into the chair in front of her computer. "Maybe you're right Jim. Maybe—but maybe it's time to circle the wagons."

"Yes." He said and moved closer. "Listen to me when I say that Winchester was a walking graveyard. Thousands of them were at the

Armory alone. Only one thing drives them—the urge to eat. Since we're
at the bottom of the food chain, they'll come this way. They'll find us
and when they do, those fences won't hold them. That's my first priority."

Sharon looked up at him. "How long do we have?"

"I don't know. Days, weeks maybe. It all depends."

Sharon straightened her disheveled white lab coat. "Okay, what do we
have to do?"

CHAPTER 49

Reverend Robert Thomas Peterson stood in the doorway, watching his followers tear greedily at two half-cooked rabbits. It was the first food they had eaten in two days. He watched happily, his own belly full from his secret private stock.

It was good that they were so hungry, he thought. Half starved as they were, they would do anything he asked in order to obtain food. Even kill.

Cleanse the earth of evil. Yes, that's what is happening, he thought. The resurrection of the dead was foretold in the Bible. No one understood it as completely as he did. The earth was being cleansed of its defilers, of those who would defile God. It had fallen to him to lead the multitudes of righteous survivors into the New World; a more controlled one. As Moses had led the Israelites, he would also command this new life. A virtual god, he would be worshipped by all. Second only to the God of Heaven, he thought, vanity swelling his chest.

The time was almost upon them. Preparation was needed if the plan was to be a success. The prison was needed for its fences and food. Kill the goats and the sheep would be easily led. Any male above the age of sixteen or carrying a weapon must be dealt with swiftly. Once that was done, the rest would follow his law or die.

The preacher smiled at the thought of his congregation swelling with the ones he allowed to live after the prison attack. They would thank him for their salvation. The tribulation sent upon man would be finished.

The dead would once again be dead and he would rule the earth, bringing peace for a thousand years. He would be seated at the right hand of God, by God.

The hall door leading outside swung open and one of the preacher's young followers stood in the doorway, hunched over and out of breath. He pointed behind him, toward the driveway. One hundred yards away were two of the resurrected tools of God who had strayed from their given tasks. It happened sometimes, the preacher thought, watching them. Falling from God's grace, they were in error.

The preacher turned to the followers who were finishing off the rabbits. He chose four of the biggest and strongest. "You know what to do." He told them.

The four bigger boys grabbed clubs and baseball bats and ran outside in a rush. The preacher followed and watched from the porch.

The two ghouls, one an old man, the other a younger one, lumbered on, unaware of their doom as the boys approached. The first of the boys to arrive, a tall fellow with a flare for the job, swung low at the younger ghoul's legs as it reached for him and beat it to the ground, where he proceeded to smash away until the skull split like a melon.

The older ghoul was grabbed by one of the rushing lads and whipped to the ground by the tail of its un-tucked shirt where it too was slain. When they had finished, they stood over their kill, disgusted by their thoughts but desperate enough to consider them. The two rabbits had not been nearly enough to satisfy their hunger.

The preacher saw them falter and walked toward them. "Father?" the bigger of the boys asked, his eyes showing his torture. "Why can't we—"

The preacher raised a hand, quieting him. "You must not eat of this," he said, "for in that day, you will surely die. They are unclean. Take them to the woods a good distance from here and dispose of them. And be quick about it so their filth doesn't invade your soul."

The four boys carried the bodies away as the preacher watched.

It was time to prepare.

CHAPTER 50

Amanda waited for Jim to arrive in the large pantry next to the kitchen. She had checked her inventory book over and over, it couldn't be wrong but there it was; food was missing. Several canned hams, vegetables, flour, and various other items were gone. She couldn't understand how this had happened. She locked the door herself each time food was removed. It was her job, but numbers don't lie.

Amanda heard the clicking of Jim's boots as he walked across the hard floor of the kitchen. With a creak the pantry door opened and Jim walked in. His eyes scanned the room at first in an attempt to discover an alternative way inside. Amanda waited patiently as he did what she had already done herself.

"I've already checked," Amanda said. "There's no other way to get in here."

"Then they're using the door," Jim said. "They must be."

"It stays locked."

"Who else has a key?"

"No one. Just me."

"Then I'll have another lock added to it. A deadbolt, maybe."

"We would've run out of food about mid-May anyway. What then?"

Jim didn't know what they would do then. Once the food ran out there would be no choice but to go in search of more, and that meant going out into the hostile environment again.

"Don't worry, Amanda. I'll figure it out before it gets to that. Who knows? Maybe this will be over by then."

"Sharon Darney doesn't agree. She said those things could go on for years before they finally rot away and die."

Jim had heard that too. Years could pass before everything got back to normal again. A bleak thought but not necessarily true. For some unforeseen reason the creatures could simply drop over and cease to exist in the same inexplicable manner they had risen.

He checked the room again to be sure he hadn't missed something. He inspected the lock on the door to see if it had been picked but there weren't any telltale scratches on the lock.

"It's best to have someone watch the pantry at night for a while." He shut the door behind them. "We don't need anymore food disappearing. I'll get someone on it."

Amanda gathered her things and followed Jim into the hall. He seemed preoccupied with something else this evening. Something bothered him and it wasn't just the disappearing food.

"Jim, is there something wrong? Has something happened?"

"No, Nothing's wrong. I'm just a little tired, that's all."

Amanda looked into his eyes. He was lying. He wasn't very good at it but she wouldn't push it. Jim was a hardheaded man. If it was that important, she would know when the time came.

Jim left Amanda and stepped outside. It was early January but a slightly warm wind blew from the south. The sun was still above the Blue Ridge Mountains several miles to the southwest. It was beautiful scenery beyond the fences and guard towers, even in mid-winter's grasp he couldn't imagine a more beautiful place on Earth than the Shenandoah Valley.

Mick and Pete Wells were busy repairing a portion of the inner fence when Jim walked to them, he watched silently until Mick noticed him.

"What's up, Jim?" He asked, not lost to him was the troubled expression creasing Jim's face.

"Maybe I should ask you the same thing. How'd that happen?" Jim asked, pointing at a torn section in the fence.

"I don't know. I never noticed it before. I guess it could have been there all along."

Jim glanced to the two school buses parked by the main building. Mick followed his gaze.

"What's wrong?"

"We're going to need another school bus."

"What on earth for? What's worrying you?"

"Two buses won't hold everyone. We need another to get these people out of here, if it comes to that."

"Look around, Jim. This place is as safe as it can be. We're fine."

"You know, Mick, I remember a conversation we had similar to this a while back. I was right then. I'm not sure if I'm right now but I'll be damned if I wanna take that chance."

Mick grabbed Jim's arm and pulled him away from Pete, who was still mending the broken fence. "Maybe you had better tell me what this is all about."

"The other day, when we went into Winchester...remember I told you that the place was swarming with thousands of them?"

"Yes."

"There are thousands of those bastards not too far to the south, in Warren. Not as many as in Winchester but, nonetheless, we're pretty much surrounded on all sides."

"Yeah, I know, but we've always known that. So what's the emergency?"

"None yet, Mick, but if they all happen to find their way here, there could be an emergency. A big one that we're not prepared for."

"Do they have a reason to come this way? I mean, how would they know we're here?"

"I don't know. Maybe they don't but they've managed to practically wipe humanity off the face of the planet. I just don't want the job finished."

"Can I make a suggestion?" Pete Wells asked.

Mick turned to see Pete, tools in hand. "Sure, Pete. What do you have?"

"Get the goddamned school bus. If Jim thinks it's necessary then we should probably do it. He's right. We won't fit everyone into those two over there. I know that I don't want to be the one standing outside the bus waving bye-bye to you guys because there isn't enough room for me to be saved too. Get the damned bus."

Mick sighed, "It just worries the hell out of me anytime we have to send someone out there to do something. It's inviting trouble."

CHAPTER 51

A small group of survivors in Winchester huddled together in the corner of a church basement, awaiting the end. For five months they had survived the rampaging hordes that had decimated the city. Kept awake each night by the endless pounding and moaning of the demons that needed no sleep, they prayed continually to no avail. Their torment remained until the bitter end.

Their prayers unanswered, their faith shattered, the barricaded doors and windows collapsed and countless ghouls filled the room. There were so many more outside that escape was impossible.

The room filled with the smell of rot and evil that accompanied the soulless, uncaring creatures. The group remained huddled together, their eyes closed to their approaching doom. The final horror of so many cold hands pulling and tearing at warm flesh forced their eyes open as they experienced the final seconds of their lives.

They had hoped that finding refuge in a House of God would protect them from the fate of so many others. They had hoped to be spared this awful fate by the all-powerful hand of God, and that their worship of him would be full of that same power and truth; the gift for their troubles, a divine sword to slash their enemies.

In the end it would seem that it was merely a form of worship, its power false, the truths of their religion apparently misleading, a Babylon of lies.

Maybe it wasn't Armageddon or anything sent by God. Perhaps it was sent from hell. Only the devil could orchestrate such a horror.

That was Denise Givens' last thought before her blood cooled. Winchester was now completely "dead."

CHAPTER 52

Once again Jim's pickup was loaded and ready for another dangerous mission into a populated area. Jim, Chuck, and Matt were off to get a another bus so everyone could be safely evacuated if the prison fences were not strong enough to hold the thousands of creatures roaming so close by.

Matt worked out quite well as the third man on these outings, allowing Mick to stay behind if something went drastically wrong at the prison. It also guaranteed that Mick would survive to lead the rest.

Jim drove toward the north end of town, past the old Riverton Rescue Station that had housed them in the beginning. A large number of undead wandered around the property, loiterers not quite aware of their own existence until the truck alerted them to the presence of live prey. Only then did they seem eager of anything. Oddly unified, they moved slowly but steadily after the moving vehicle.

The truck easily left the slow-moving gaggle behind as it made its way across the last bridge and entered town. Jim, Chuck, and Matt had become desensitized to the large numbers of walking dead that now filled the streets. Their bodies had grown more deteriorated and the rotted, decayed flesh caused them to move in a most grotesque manner. The smell of death and decay permeated the air.

They saw more of the same all the way through town. There were hundreds more creatures milling about now than the last time they had been in town. Exactly why rural ghouls gravitated toward town was a mystery. There wasn't a living soul left in town to attract them.

Jim watched them as he drove on. One by one they turned toward the truck and attempted to follow. Jim wondered if what he was beginning to suspect was true, that it wouldn't be long before they discovered the prison. If so, then this would be the last trip he would permit to a populated area so close to the prison.

He had seen the same behavior from the ghouls in Winchester; they had been attracted to the truck and followed.

Jim turned on to the road that led to the school board offices. The creatures were as thick there as any other place in town. One of them, a woman, pushed a shopping cart with another creature inside. Chuck laughed as they drove by, amused by the sight.

The bus parking lot was fairly free of zombies. Jim counted only six so he nosed the truck as close to the front of the bus as possible in case it needed a jump-start.

The three men sprang from the truck, ready to do their jobs. Jim grabbed the toolbox from the back. "I'll hot-wire the bus. You two take your positions and keep those bastards at a good distance."

Chuck strapped on his machete, un-shouldered his rifle, and went to work. One creature, a black man who looked as if he was a fresh kill, came too close. Chuck raised his gun but Matt fired a bull's eye to the ghoul's head before Chuck could pull the trigger.

"Good shot, Matt."

"Thanks," Matt said with a grin that quickly faded as he saw more creatures approach from behind the buses and behind the office. The parking lot was now becoming quite populated and Matt became a bit unnerved.

"Look out behind you, Chuck!" Matt shouted.

Chuck turned to see three of them almost within arm's reach of him. They were too close to use his rifle so he quickly abandoned it in favor of his pistol. As he raised the weapon to shoot the closest aggressor, the creature grabbed his arm, causing the shot to ricochet off the pavement.

Matt tried to shoot but Chuck and the creature were intertwined in a wrestling match he couldn't risk it. Two others were also getting closer. Matt knew Chuck couldn't fight off all three so he sprayed the two approaching creatures' brains into the air.

More creatures came from behind the bus as it roared to life and Jim hurdled through the door into the fray, both revolvers drawn, bullets flying. Zombies dropped all around him but Jim couldn't get a shot on the one attacking Chuck without hitting him; he ran to help hand to hand.

Chuck had the creature by the shirt collar trying to push it away. It bulled forward and he lost his balance and fell backward. Chuck's head hit the asphalt with a dull thud, dazing him momentarily. That was the opportunity the creature needed. The brown, flesh-caked teeth clamped onto the top of Chuck's left hand.

At that moment Jim reached down and grabbed the creature by the hair and yanked. To Jim's horror, the skin from Chuck's hand tore away, exposing tendons and red meat. Jim pulled the monster from Chuck and slammed it to the pavement. He withdrew his pistol and shot it dead.

Chuck screamed back to consciousness. Jim ripped his shirt and wrapped the wound as Matt shot at more of the undead in a futile attempt to keep the area clear.

"Jesus, Jim, we gotta go, man!" Matt cried. "There's just too many!"

Jim helped Chuck to his feet and saw that the undead were closing in on all sides. "Matt, can you drive that bus?"

Matt glanced quickly at the bus idling in front of the truck. "Yeah, I think so."

"Don't think so, man! Can you DRIVE it?"

"Yes!"

"Then do it! I'll take Chuck in the truck."

Matt bounded for the bus and closed the doors behind him. Several wide-eyed creatures banged on the glass panels, attempting to break through.

Jim rushed Chuck to the truck and pushed him inside. He pulled his revolvers one last time to avenge his friend's horrible fate. Shot after shot pierced the skulls of countless creatures. There were no cries of pain from the mortally wounded as they fell. The same emotionless expressions they carried with them in their mindless lumbering followed them into the stillness of true death.

When his pistols were empty, Jim flung himself inside the truck and drove away.

"It's my fault!" Jim said.

"It's not your fault, Jim."

"It is! I should've—"

"It's nobody's goddamned fault!" Chuck's said, his voice cracking with emotion, "Goddamned shit just happened!"

Jim angrily pounded the steering wheel. It *was* his fault. The situation should have been checked out better before they actually made the attempt. Chuck was now a walking dead man because of his failure to ensure the safety of his men and it ate at his gut.

CHAPTER 53

An eerie silence befell the infirmary as Dr. Brine wrapped Chuck's hand with gauze. Chuck hunched over on top of the table, his injured hand outstretched bit at the fingernails of his good hand and stared at the floor. Jim and Mick were close by. Neither said a word. There was nothing to say.

Chuck knew what awaited him and that knowledge made him want to scream but he wouldn't show his weakness. Not to anyone, especially Jim. He would not be remembered that way.

Dr. Brine pulled the wrapping tight and Chuck cringed from the pain. The bite was beginning to burn like a raging fire. He could almost feel the infection as it spread up his arm and into his system.

"That too tight for you?" Dr. Brine asked, noticing Chuck's recoil.

"No," Chuck said, not looking up. His eyes watered as his will faltered. He glanced upwards just enough to see Jim pull the doctor away. They spoke quietly but Chuck knew what they were discussing. Why did they even try to keep it a secret? He knew what was to come.

Jim whispered to the doctor "Is there anything you can do for him?"

"I've seen a lot of people get bitten by those things Jim. Nothing could be done for any of them."

"Are you sure?"

"He'll become one. That's for certain. He'll have to be watched when the time comes. About the only thing I can do is ease the pain."

Dr. Brine held up a syringe and squeezed the plunger until a stream of fluid squirted out. Chuck watched the doctor swab his arm with alcohol. Dr. Brine smiled as he brought the needle close but Chuck grabbed his hand before he could administer the shot. too much. I'll be damned if I'm gonna ride this out doped up and blowing spit bubbles."

The doctor pulled the needle away for a moment. "Don't worry, son. It's just enough to ease the pain. I wouldn't do that to you."

Chuck let go of his arm and Dr. Brine sunk the needle into the protruding purple vein. Almost immediately the rush hit Chuck's brain. He leaned his head back and his eyes closed as the pain faded.

Dr. Brine gently laid Chuck back on the table to rest. "Just stay there a minute. Your head will clear up in a little bit."

Chuck heard the doctor's voice as it echoed in his head. For a moment he was completely content to lie there and enjoy the warm fuzzy feeling that engulfed him.

CHAPTER 54

Mick and Jim walked through the main doors and out into the prison courtyard. The cold air stung their faces and a light snow began to fall. Winter had finally descended its icy hand over the state.

Jim pulled his jacket closed but didn't button it as they walked to the north fence. This was one of Mick's daily rounds. Each day he walked the perimeter of the fence, checking every square inch for signs of weakness.

Mick stopped and stared across the large field that spanned that side of the prison. In the distance, they counted ten creatures sluggishly moving closer. They were pretty spread out and far away, but there was no doubt they were the walking dead.

Mick turned to the guard tower covering that direction. There was no one on the upper deck to give an advanced warning. It was Chuck's turn to keep watch.

"They're coming this way," Jim said quietly.

Mick focused his attention again on the lumbering group. "Yup. Fifteen, maybe twenty minutes."

Jim drew his revolver and checked his load. "I'll go take care of them."

"Take this." Mick held out his weapon, a silencer attached. "You need some help?"

"No, I'll be all right." He answered somberly and took the weapon. "There's not that many."

Mick watched as Jim walked through the gate and trudged across the field, moving steadily toward the small mob, his gun at his side.

Jim stopped just ahead of them and waited. He could see their twisted, grotesque features clearly. In the lead was a woman in a business suit. Torn and tattered, it hung in strands from her disemboweled torso. Her eyes were blank and emotionless.

He raised the gun and fired and she fell to the ground, face down. His hate for these monsters grew as he continued to end their miserable existence with fatal shots to their heads, sending blood and gray matter spewing out in red mists.

Nine were down and only one remained. Unlike the rest, it turned in the other direction. Jim followed, running to get in front of it. Once more it attempted to flee. This one had learned, and was trying to escape its fate. In some way, it valued its own existence.

Jim realized this and circled it until he was again facing it. The creature stopped and stared at Jim but made no attempt to attack. There were unmistakable signs of fear on its pale gray face.

Pity momentarily welled up in Jim, if not for the creature itself then for whatever remained of the man it once was. Nevertheless, he knew what he had to do.

"This is for your own good," Jim said. "For who you used to be."

The creature's face relaxed and his expression of fear eased. Jim fired and it fell, dead at last.

Jim scanned the area; it was finally clear and he started the walk back. As he passed the others lying on the ground his attention was drawn to one in a policeman's uniform. He used his foot to turn the creature over. Patches on the front of the blue jacket indicated he'd been with the Winchester City Police.

This group was from Winchester, fourteen miles away. They must have been drawn in this direction by the truck during their last visit. His worst fears were now more than a frightful hypothesis. There was no telling how many others would follow, or how far behind they were. It was true that they wouldn't know their exact location, but their fragmented thoughts would most likely keep them to the road. With nothing in Winchester to hold them there they would have followed the truck. There would be nothing along the way to deviate them from their course. They were coming!

Jim jogged back to the prison yard where Mick waited. His mind raced with possibilities, none of which were pleasant.

Mick walked to meet him as he came through the gate.

Jim stopped in front of him. "Our future is growing more uncertain by the minute."

CHAPTER 55

There was no question in Reverend Peterson's mind about what had to be done. If he was to be a leader, a god, as his Father in the heavens intended, there must be no opposition. And that is what the people at the prison were; they would stand in his way. He would only allow the weak minded and the females to live. They would certainly follow him but the men, the ones in charge, would have to die.

If he died in the process, so be it. It would not be the first time his Father had used him thus. Better to be dead. But that would not happen, not with the Father on his side. This was his purpose.

It was almost time, the day of final Judgment was almost at hand. Soon he would take his rightful place as the Supreme Authority, as well he should. He knew all about sinful man, how to shepherd him. He would be glad when it was over so he could relax a bit. The dead would once again be dead and he would choose for himself the biggest house in the county, perhaps even go to Washington to live in the White House and build an empire. A thousand-year reign!

Soon, he thought. Soon he would accomplish what he knew his Holy Father wanted. The reign of the dead would end and his would begin.

CHAPTER 56

Dr. Brine carefully wrapped clean bandages around Chuck's hand. He wore surgical gloves for protection against the possibility of the virus infecting him through skin contact.

Chuck fidgeted and flinched at the slightest touch from the old country doctor. The bite had caused the entire arm to swell and turn a deep blue. The pain was unbearable. Even morphine did little to ease his suffering.

He had slept through the whole evening and night, something he had asked them not to let him do. He was aware that there wasn't much time left but he didn't want to sleep his last hours away. That he assured himself and everyone else would not happen again.

Dr. Brine put Chuck's injured arm in a sling, then went to the cabinet and returned with several pills in a bottle. "Here," he said, handing him the bottle. "When it starts to hurt, take one."

Chuck took the bottle with his good hand. "What are they?"

"Percodan."

"They won't make me sleep, will they?"

"If you wanna sleep, take three."

"I don't."

"Then take one or two."

Chuck slipped the bottle into his shirt pocket, got down from the table, and gathered his things. He really wanted to get back to work and keep himself busy, anything to take his mind off his aching arm and his fate.

"Son?" the doctor said. "When it's time to sleep, you gotta come back here. You understand?"

Chuck nodded. He understood. If he died in his sleep, there needed to be someone around to blow his stupid brains out.

Jim was in the cafeteria drinking his morning coffee when Chuck walked in. He was surprised to see his friend. He was even more surprised to see the toll the zombie's bite had taken on him. His face was ashen and there were dark circles under his eyes.

Without a word, Chuck walked to the coffee machine, poured himself a steaming cup, then sat down across from Jim. For a moment neither said a word as they drank their coffee. With a forced grin Chuck leaned across the table toward Jim. "Who's gonna win the Superbowl this year?"

Jim stared at him blankly before it occurred to him that it was close to Superbowl Sunday, or it would have been.

"Football fan, huh?" Jim asked.

"Hail to the Redskins! Hail victory!" Chuck began to sing the team's fight song. He swung his cup rhythmically back in forth, splashing coffee over the rim.

Jim laughed, not because Chuck thought the Skins would've stood the slightest chance of winning the big game this year but because his singing was so bad.

"What are you laughing at?"

"Your singing is almost as bad as your choice of teams. The Redskins wouldn't have won shit this year. They have no talent."

"What are you, a communist? They're America's team."

"I'm a Dallas fan! The *real* 'America's team.'"

"Good God! Well, at least this shit wouldn't have affected them much. They already played ball like the walking dead."

That brief moment was a time warp into the past; Jim sitting with a good friend, trading jabs about football. He shuddered inwardly to clear the surrealistic feeling that had crept over him.

Jim sipped his coffee. "Well, we'll never know who would've won it now."

"Ummm," Chuck agreed and popped one of the pills Dr. Brine had given to him.

"You feel okay?"

"I feel like shit."

"Why don't you take it easy, Chuck? Go find a place to rest a while."

"I can't rest. I'll have plenty of time to rest when I'm dead." He slid his cup back and forth between his hands, trying to put his thoughts together. His body was being invaded he could feel it. He felt worse with the tick of each minute.

He had seen what others had gone through after being bitten. First they grew ill. By the end of the second day, they were hallucinating, unable to control bodily functions. The third day was usually their last. This was Day Two.

"As long as I can walk, I want to help out around here," Chuck said. "And when I get bad—" His voice cracked. "You'll see to me? I mean, you—you'll—you know what I mean, right?"

Jim nodded. "Sure man. I'll see to it myself."

Chuck nodded, relieved. At least that was one thing he didn't have to worry about.

CHAPTER 57

The weather changed. It had been cold all week but then a warm front moved in from the south and rain began to fall. It rained hard and continuously through most of the night.

Jim sat in a chair and watched it through the barred window in the prison infirmary. Chuck had taken a drastic turn for the worse. He was sleeping, finally, in the bed next to where Jim sat vigil.

It was unlikely Chuck would make it through the night. At one point his temperature had shot up to one hundred and seven degrees and then just as quickly it began to plummet. His skin turned gray and was cold to the touch. His breathing was thick and labored. His once full cheeks were now sunken and drawn, pulling the corners of his mouth into a scowling frown. This horrible curse had taken no more than thirty-six hours to rob him of his health.

Jim held the revolver on his lap, the same weapon he had used to eliminate the ten ghouls.

How long ago his trip into the new and horrible world seemed now. It had been about five months but it seemed like a lifetime ago. So much had happened so much had changed. He'd forgotten the cabin in the mountains, his life in Manassas.

His thought went back to his brother in Montana. It was the first time he had thought of him in months. He wondered if his brother was safe. Montana was pretty sparsely populated and David was a survivor, like himself. They were both forced to be survivors after their parents died in a fatal car crash when he was thirteen and David was twelve. They lived with one relative and then another until they were old enough to get jobs and places of their own.

Jim rubbed his tired eyes and forced himself to focus on the present. The rain splashed against the windowpane with a hypnotic effect. Pitter-patter, pitter-patter it gently thrummed. His eyes fluttered shut, then opened wide at a stirring from Chuck's bed.

Chuck shrieked and his eyes opened. "They're coming to get me, Daddy! They're in my closet!" Chuck pointed to a corner in the room, his eyes wide, but distant.

"It's okay, Chuck. I won't let them get you."

Chuck reached out and took Jim's hand. For a moment his eyes cleared. "The monsters! You'll keep them away?"

"Yes, I will."

"Because I don't wanna be taken away with them. You'll keep them away?"

"I'll keep them all away. You can rest now, Chuck."

Chuck took a deep breath, sighed, and became still.

Jim pushed the lids down to cover the blankly staring eyes.

He left Chuck's face uncovered. Jim sat by the lifeless corpse for almost thirty minutes. He was beginning to think that maybe Chuck had beaten it. Maybe he wouldn't rise as one of the undead. Maybe he had willed away the curse. Jim had often thought he could do the same. Simply stop the evil transformation by sheer determination and refuse to let his body be used in such an obscene manner.

Jim's meditation was interrupted by the faint sound of rustling linen. There was movement beneath the cover that lay over the lower half of Chuck's body but the eyes remained shut. There, again. A twitch! He was coming back.

His hand tightened on the weapon as Chuck's body continued to move. The eyes opened. Glazed, blank, and soulless, they focused on him. A gargling sound bubbled from Chuck's throat as he strained to sit up.

Jim raised his weapon and targeted the center of Chuck's forehead; the corpse that less than an hour ago had been Jim's friend fumbled awkwardly to gain its feet. Jim squeezed the trigger. The bullet whined past the silencer and penetrated the skull, sending body and army cot crashing to the floor.

Jim continued to aim at the creature. He took a slow, deep breath and felt a hot tear escape the corner of his closed eyelids. In a moment the nausea would pass.

CHAPTER 58

The rain continued to fall the next day. Dreary clouds, layer upon layer, dark and menacing, filled the sky. Banks of ghostly gray fog blew across the land, obliterating any color that lent substance or form to the surroundings.

Jim stood over Chuck's grave as the rain slid down his face and plopped to the ground. There was only one thing left to do.

He picked up the handmade wooden cross with the words "Shit happens" etched into the crosspiece and drove it into the soft wet dirt with the back of the spade shovel he had used to dig the grave. Chuck's life was complete in a sense. He had lived recklessly but he had died helping others survive. He contributed more then most and received less. Jim would miss him.

*   *   *

That night, Jim sat in the southern tower. He'd had a very uneasy feeling. Nothing he could put his finger on, just a gut feeling. Maybe it was the way things had gone this past week. Both the fear of the creatures following the truck and Chuck's death weighed on his mind. It could be nothing, just worry and fatigue. In any event, there was little he could do other than what had already been done.

He strained to see across the prison yard. The fog had grown thick he could no longer see the fence that enclosed them. At least the rain had lessened.

"Midnight," he said softly, glancing at his watch. He'd been awake for nineteen hours. In an hour he would be relieved of his guard. Not too soon for him. He had gotten only three hours sleep the night before yet he felt he shouldn't sleep, not tonight.

He felt suddenly alone, even homesick. He shuddered as a cold chill ran up his spine and his loneliness gave way to unaccountably cold dread.

Mick was asleep when one of the guards found him and gave him the news. They had caught the thief responsible for stealing the missing food. Mick quickly jumped up from his bed and dressed, then followed the man to the pantry, his head still foggy.

Upon entering the cafeteria, Mick saw the man sitting at a table, the gun-toting guard who had staked out the pantry standing over him. Mick wasn't surprised, he should have known. A feeling of loathing and contempt flashed over him like a heat wave.

The man in the chair was Stan Woods, the former mayor.

CHAPTER 59

The kitchen looked the same. Felicia had been there many times during her childhood until her grandmother died. She had never gone back to the house after that.

Felicia looked through the window that, in her past dreams, allowed a flood of sunshine to stream through. This time, it was pitch dark outside, except for strange lights in the distance, like a ballpark or something. Her fascination with the lights was broken by a voice that sounded from outside; it was the voice of her grandmother. Felicia followed the voice to the back porch, where her grandmother, Isabelle Smith, was looking toward the lights.

"They're in danger, Felicia. The devil himself has a hand over their domain."

Felicia stared at the lights in confusion. "I don't understand, grandma. Whose domain?"

"Yours, darling. He's there now."

Felicia stared again at the distant lights and it became suddenly clear. The lights in the distance were the lights that surrounded the prison. They were all on, like a beacon showing them the way through the night.

"You need to go now. Wake from your sleep and warn them before it's too late."

"Who is it, Grammy? Who's coming?"

"An incarnation of the evil one himself! You mustn't let him in. Warn them, Felicia. Warn them now. Go! Run!"

The voice faded away and with it the strange dream.

Felicia sat bolt upright in her bed, suddenly wide-awake. Izzy was also awake, standing by her bed. The little girl trembled with fear, pure panic in her eyes. Felicia's motherly instinct took over and she pulled the waif close to her.

"I know, Izzy. I already know. We have to warn them."

Jim's duty relief, a burly man known only as Griz, climbed the ladder to the deck of the tower. Griz was six-three with a large beer belly and long whiskers. As quietly as possible, he walked to where Jim was leaning over the railing, listening.

Except for the wind, Jim heard nothing. Then there was a small rustling noise that sounded like it had come from outside the fence.

Jim recoiled suddenly and leaned toward the big man. "Go down and turn on the power to the fence," he whispered.

Griz's face paled. Big as he was, he wasn't a brave man. He had turned down a request to help the others with their tasks in the undead jungle.

"What's wrong?" he asked, trying to see through the fog. "Are more of those things out there?"

"I don't know—just hurry!"

Without asking another question, Griz swiftly but silently dashed to the ladder and disappeared.

Jim again focused his attention in the direction the noise had come from; they were faint, barely audible, like the constant threnody of an airplane engine in the distance.

*   *   *

Mick circled Stan Woods, unsure whether to pounce on him and pound him mercilessly in the face with his fists or wait for an excuse.

"This is an outrage!" the mayor cried.

Mick yanked him out of the chair and tossed him against the wall like a rag doll.

"You selfish son of a bitch!" Mick spat. "I'll kill you!"

Drawing back a clenched fist, he heard Amanda say, "That won't help anything, Mick. It won't change a thing."

"It will sure as hell make me feel better!"

"He has a wife and a son."

"They're better off without him."

"Let him go, Mick," Amanda ordered. "There are plenty of cells. Let's lock him up. He won't get into any trouble in a prison cell."

Mick paused momentarily, unable to release his pent-up rage. He relaxed his fist and begrudgingly settled for a stinging face slap across the mayor's face before releasing his grip on the whimpering bastard. The only thing he hated worse than a thief was a thief who stole at the expense of innocent, needy people. Stan Woods was that and more.

As he motioned for the guard to take the thieving scoundrel to a cell, the warning alarm sounded outside.

"Something's wrong," Mick said. "Jim would never use that alarm without good reason. It will wake the dead for miles around."

CHAPTER 60

Mick bounded through the doors and into the courtyard, Amanda on his heels. A spotlight was aimed at the south side of the fence. Jim hurried down the ladder from the tower and took position in the middle of the yard. Griz dashed from the guardhouse, slipping in the muddy grass several times before reaching him.

"Power's on!" he gasped. "They try to get through there and they'll be cooked zombies."

"Then kill the alert siren. It's getting on my nerves and making way too much noise," Jim said, continuing to watch the fence. "There's a switch beside the power to the fence. It must've been set to ring when you powered it."

The spotlight shined through the fog enough to illuminate a thirty-foot area. There was still no sign of movement. Guards who had been sleeping were awakened by the alarm and scurried, half asleep, from the main building, along with many others.

Mick spotted Jim and hurriedly ran to his side. He struggled to see through the fog but if Jim thought there was reason for concern, he would not question him.

"Who and how many, Jim?"

"I don't know. I still can't see but there's something, or someone, out there."

"Zombies?"

"Maybe. Get some of the guys up in the other towers. I want all of the lights on. Instruct everyone to stay away from the fence. It's powered."

Jim crept closer to the fence to get a better look as one by one the lights were turned on, flooding the same area. There was still no sign of anyone or anything. Jim was beginning to believe that he had been mistaken, fooled by his own weariness. Then a lone figure emerged from the mist in front of the fence. He wore a long black robe and stood silently before raising his hand before speaking.

Reverend Peterson assessed the situation. He had failed to surprise them completely but all was not lost. He was ready for this contingency. Even now the alternate plan was in motion. It would take longer to reach his goal but the result would be the same; the death of these wicked fools who allowed Satan to blind them to the Truth. Victory would be his, gained from within their ranks. Standing amongst them, he would see their throats slashed.

Peterson studied the man standing before him. A tall, bold-looking fellow with a strong face obviously set in his ways and full of himself. This one would have to die. It was plain to see that he would not follow.

"We request entry," the preacher said in his most earnest voice.

"We?" Jim asked. "How many is 'we'?"

"There are ten of us," the preacher lied. "Please, may we enter?"

Jim studied him. Why did he feel distrust toward a man he was seeing for the first time? Was there a real danger? Or was it simply the night playing tricks on his troubled mind? In any case, here were survivors that needed help. He couldn't turn them away.

Jim took a few steps back to where Mick was listening. For some unknown reason, Jim was still not convinced of this man's intentions. He needed Mick's help.

Mick had the same troubled expression on his face when Jim asked for his opinion. He, too, felt the uneasiness.

Jim scanned the crowd huddled around the main doorway. They were cold, wet, and nervous. No one seemed to be at ease with this. Everyone appeared disquieted by this unexpected turn of events, everyone except the man at the fence.

He showed no signs of worry or concern but his pleas for help seemed less than genuine. There was something dark and unsettling about him. Where were the others who were supposedly with him?

Jim had waited as long as he could. A decision had to be made now.

Felicia burst through the crowded doorway. "No, Mick! Don't let them in." Felicia ran full tilt toward Jim and Mick. She held a piece of paper high as she screamed, "They're the ones! They're the ones!"

Out of breath, she shoved the paper into Mick's hand. "You can't let them in here! He's the one, the wolf in sheep's clothing!"

Mick glanced at the paper. It was a picture of the stranger. Hand drawn, it perfect in every detail. No one but Izzy possessed the talent for such work.

"Izzy did it last night, Mick—last night, before he came. I felt the foreboding but she KNEW!"

Mick remembered Felicia's warnings, the dreams she had experienced. This strange sixth sense was no longer limited to Felicia. Even he and Jim sensed it. There was danger here.

Mick turned to face the man again. "I can't let you in here, mister. Maybe tomorrow I can—"

His words were cut off by a sudden burst of rage from the preacher. "You have now earned the wrath of God! ALL OF YOU! And you, witch, shall be first to receive Judgment for your sins!"

Shots sliced through the fog and bullets whizzed through the chain link fence. Felicia felt a sharp, intense pain as one slammed into her, tumbling her backward. More shots were fired blindly into the darkness from the few guards who had thought to bring their weapons with them when the alarm sounded. Others scurried about to find safety or to find weapons of their own.

Mick reached for Felicia, who had been standing at his side. To his horror, he found her on the ground holding her chest. He quickly dropped his body over hers, protecting her from the flying bullets.

"Felicia! My God! You're hurt!"

"I'm fine," she said through the pain. "I can make it."

Mick scooped Felicia in his arms and dashed toward the front door. Sharon Darney grabbed Felicia. "I've got her, Mick. Go help the others. I'll see to her."

Mick was torn. Should he leave her or not?

"Go!" Felicia urged. "It's just a scratch. I'll be fine."

Still he hesitated. He grabbed Felicia's hand and pressed his lips to the long, slender fingers he had come to know so well. "All right, I'm going." He leaned over and gently brushed her lips with his. "It's taken me thirty years to give my heart to someone. Don't you leave me now. You hold on for me. I'll be back."

He turned and dove through the front door into the fray in the courtyard before his emotions completely overwhelmed him. He would see to it that that man, and every single one of the bastards with him, was killed for what they'd done.

Jim dashed through the fog like an apparition and stopped in front of Mick. "We're going to war. Are you ready?"

"Get the sons of bitches, Jim! Kill them all! Goddamn it! KILL THEM ALL!"

Jim took the AK-47 from his shoulder and disappeared through the panicking crowd.

The guards fired blindly through the fog at the perimeter. Jim and Griz stood behind a waist-high concrete wall. Every few seconds, a flash could be seen from an enemy gun and they would target it and fire. Sometimes they heard cries when their bullets hit home but most of the time they missed. Jim continued to fire at any movement outside the fence. He took down several of the intruders when they strayed into the light.

The low hum of an engine grew in strength. Jim could hear it now even above the popping gunfire. He skittered from behind the wall and found cover behind a barrel. He turned an ear toward the swelling sound. It grew in strength until it closely resembled the roar of a freight train. Its direction was unclear but it seemed to be all around them.

Then a great crash split the night. The twisting and tearing of chain link mingled with the roar. The outer fence was being torn to ribbons. The invaders could break through it but it would be a lot harder for them to get through the inner, electrified one. He needed to see what was happening.

There was a burst of blue sparks. Someone who had gotten through the outer fence had unknowingly latched onto the inner one and was fried for his trouble.

Jim smirked in momentary satisfaction as he watched the sparks dance into the air. One less to worry about, he thought.

Then the appalling reality hit home.

Blue sparks exploded on all sides. They were bright enough to brighten the entire area. Jim slumped in hopelessness. The gunfire stopped as everyone froze at the spectacle before them.

The faces of the dead were pressed up against the fence in all directions. Every inch of the fence had a face pressed against it. The monotonous groaning that had been mistaken for a distant engine was in fact the chorus of the undead. There was literally a sea of thousands of walking corpses, the end of which could not be seen.

The first line of creatures was electrocuted against the fence. As they burned and fell, more took their place and were burned to a crisp.

Jim assessed the situation, his mental wheels spinning almost audibly. Soon the fence would short out and fail from the load. They would be totally defenseless. Then he remembered the three buses parked by the main building. There was still a chance.

CHAPTER 61

Reverend Peterson was surrounded. This was not the way the Father had intended it to end. Not at the hands of these demons. They were judges, God's judges, and he was not to be judged. He had done everything expected of him yet here he was, with no way to escape as the creatures closed in. Could it be that he would be saved at the last moment, a test of faith? Raised to the heavens before the monsters clutched him? Yes, that must be it. Don't curse God now, he thought. You will be saved.

But his feet did not leave the ground, nor did he see the brilliance of God arrive to save him. Instead, he felt the cold hands and hard, tearing teeth of the dead as they moved in to devour him.

They pulled and ripped at his flesh, their rotted faces looking up to him as they removed large chunks with each bite. The preacher screamed in agony and watched, horrified, as his left arm was chewed through and pulled from the rest of his body. Several creatures greedily fought over which would claim the arm as their bounty.

A familiar voice rang loudly in his head. *Come on to hell, you little brat. You've got a lot of whippings due. Come on to hell* said the voice of his earthly father. He wasn't digging at the lid of his coffin, tormented by his thirst for flesh. He was waiting patiently in hell for his son!

A suppressed memory flooded the preacher's mind as he fell beneath a swarm of frenzied demons. He remembered a day long ago when his father, clutching his chest as he fell to his own fate reached out to him begging for his life-saving heart medicine. He could have brought the medicine to his father but he didn't. He watched him die instead.

"Oh! The beatings will be severe," the preacher cried pitifully. "NO! This was not the way it was to be at all!"

Another putrid creature piled on top the rest to help tear him limb from limb. They went their separate ways to consume their hideous meal.

Jim found Mick still firing vainly at the overwhelming number of walking dead pressing against the fence. Mick possessed the look of a wild animal, cornered and determined to fight to the death if necessary.

"It's no use, Mick. There's way too many. We've got to leave."

Mick stared blankly at Jim. It took a moment for him to come back from the place his mind had skipped off to. Only then did he realize the futility of his actions. "Where, Jim? Where will we go?" he said angrily.

"Any place but here," Jim said. "The fence won't hold them much longer.

"Where in the hell did they all come from Jim? Look at them. There must be thousands of them out there. How'd they all find us at one time? What did they do, have a meeting? God help us! What are they thinking now?"

"We've gotta use the buses. We've gotta get these people under control and loaded up, now!"

Dr. Brine and Sharon Darney worked quickly to get Felicia ready for travel. The bullet had lodged in her right lung, collapsing it. Dr. Brine was old and his hands were unsteady but he had managed to retrieve the bullet.

Felicia was unconscious and they were dressing the wound when Mick burst into the infirmary. His first reaction was to rush to her side and hold her close but there was no time. He couldn't allow anything to slow them down for a second. "We've got to move her! Can she be moved?"

Dr. Brine glanced through the window at the turmoil outside. "Don't look like we've got a choice, Mick."

"No, we don't."

Brine grabbed his bag. "What about everyone else?"

Jim's taking care of them. We're evacuating."

Sharon pulled a stretcher from the closet and carried it to where Felicia lay. They shifted her limp body onto it and carried her from the room. In the hall outside the infirmary, people ran this way and that; shouting for loved ones in an uncontrollable frenzy, afraid and desperate.

The three maneuvered the stretcher through the unruly crowd as best they could without getting knocked down. After several close calls, they came to the front door and stopped. They put Felicia down away from the turmoil.

Mayor Woods burst out of the door behind them and raced to one of the buses. Mick watched as he ran to the first one in line and entered. At first Mick thought the Mayor was acting in his usual self-serving manner to ensure himself a seat but when the bus engine came to life, he realized it was more than that.

The bus began to move toward the front gate, Woods in the driver's seat. Alone in the bus, he had not even waited for his family. He was going to flee the prison on his own.

Mick un-shouldered his rifle and yelled to Jim, who was still rounding up survivors, and pointed to the moving bus. Jim took aim as the mayor approached the gate. The blue sparks of electricity that scorched the creatures against the fence stopped abruptly just before the bus crashed through the gate. Jim fired and Woods was thrown from his seat. The impact of the AK-47 tore away most of his right shoulder.

The bus crashed through the main gate, exposing a gaping hole for the dead to enter as the bus skidded out of control and down an embankment before flipping onto its side.

Creatures surrounded the bus like ants at a picnic. Others awkwardly stumbled through the opening and made their way for the panicking group of survivors. It was now or never. They had to get as many as they could in the remaining two buses and make a run for it.

Amanda searched through the crowd for Izzy but the little girl was nowhere to be seen and Amanda wouldn't leave without her. She had seen her just before the shooting began but Izzy must have gotten scared and went back inside to hide.

Amanda scrambled through the halls to the cellblocks. She would look in Felicia's cell first.

The hall and the cell was dimly lit, but to her relief Amanda saw Izzy curled up in a corner, her hands wrapped around her legs, her head resting on shaking knees.

Amanda tugged on the cell door but Izzy had locked herself in. Suppressing panic that now tried to rob her of her rationality, Amanda collected her thoughts. Izzy must have the key. Maybe she could talk her out.

"Isabelle," she said softly, "we have to go now honey."

Izzy didn't respond. She remained in her position, rocking back and forth.

"Izzy, please open the door. Let me help you."

When there was still no response, panic began to get the best of Amanda. How could she get her point across to this frightened child?

"Izzy, Felicia's hurt. She needs you. We have to go to her so we can help her. Don't you want to help her?"

Izzy raised her head. Tears were streaming down her face.

"Come on Izzy. Bring me the key so we can go to her."

Izzy stood and walked to the door. She gave Amanda the key, then returned to the table beside Felicia's bed and picked up her drawing book and pencil.

Amanda fumbled with the key until the door opened. She scooped up Izzy and ran.

CHAPTER 62

The scene outside was ghastly. Hordes of rotting corpses entered the compound, descending like vultures on the frightened survivors. They attacked in organized groups as the survivors crammed into the buses.

Jim was directing them to safety when he saw Amanda run from the building, Izzy bouncing under her arm like so much dirty laundry. He passed his task on to Griz and ran to help her taking Izzy so Amanda could run at a faster pace.

He pushed Amanda into the bus and handed Isabelle up to her. He took another quick look around and saw Matt fighting his way through the mob of zombies. He pushed and shoved, dodging reaching arms as he ran toward the bus.

Jim shot a few zombies to clear Matthew's path. The last fifty feet were a straight shot to the bus and Matt leaped breathless through the door.

Except for the unlucky survivors who had been dragged to the ground by the demons, there was no one left to get to safety. The ghouls were closing in on the buses. If others were left inside the building, their fate was sealed. The prison yard was swarming with walking dead.

Jim climbed in and got in the driver's seat. He started the engine and revved the motor for maximum speed. He popped the clutch and lurched forward. Mick followed suite in the other bus.

Both vehicles sped through the gate, past the overturned bus, and away from the carnage.

Mayor Woods stood beside the wrecked bus, partially eaten. He was now one of them.

PART FOUR

UNCERTAIN FUTURE

CHAPTER 63

The morning sun peeked above the Blue Ridge Mountains as the buses pushed on, leaving their once-secure safe haven overrun with marauding dead. Never did they think the creatures would break through the two-layered, electrically fortified fences, except for Jim, who realized the probability too late.

There was nowhere to go, no new refuge to conceal them. If they did find something, security was a luxury they would never take for granted again.

Jim led the way and Mick followed close behind. At first count, which had to be estimated on the run, it appeared they had saved approximately sixty-five of the more than one hundred people who had been at the prison.

A half an hour had passed since their departure. There hadn't been a creature in sight since leaving the prison. They surmised that all of the creatures within a twenty-mile radius must be at the prison. They were safe for now but danger was never too far away. They had no food and only a few had firearms. There was very little ammunition.

Jim was out of ideas. Their situation had deteriorated so quickly there had been no time to think things through let alone formulate a plan. His mind clouded from lack of sleep, he hadn't a clue what to do next.

Jim found a secure place to stop. He pulled off the deserted highway and into an area that had once been a Park and Ride for commuters. Several cars were still there, abandoned months before. From the large fields surrounding them, they would be alerted to any danger. They'd have plenty of time to react.

Jim stepped out of the bus. His legs were rubbery and weak and he had to grab the doorframe to keep his balance. His nerves were shot. Everything was catching up to him now that the immediate crisis had passed.

Mick was already out of his bus, scanning the countryside for potential danger. Jim felt his strength return as he joined Mick.

"How's Felicia, Mick?"

Mick diverted his eyes from the distant mountain he had been studying and examined the dirt and gravel at his feet. His brow furrowed. "I don't know. Sharon says she's touch-and-go right now. We've got to get her to a place with better conditions. She needs antibiotics and pain killers." His looked again at the distant mountain.

"What is it, Mick? What do you see out there?"

Mick took a folded piece of paper from his shirt pocket and gave Jim a drawing of what looked like several office buildings and other structures surrounded by a fence similar to the one that had enclosed the prison. Scattered about were large radar dishes and radio antennae towers.

"I don't understand. What is this?"

"Mount Weather. Sharon recognized it."

Jim looked again at the picture in his hand. "But she said the place was infested with those damned things, didn't she?"

"Yes, she did. Isabelle did the drawing and gave it to me. I think she wants us to go there."

"You're going to risk all our lives on what an eight-year-old girl thinks we ought to do?"

"Do you have a better idea?" Mick snapped. "If you do, I'd love to hear it." Mick regretted his outburst as soon as the words were out. But he couldn't help but think some unseen force using the small child, was guiding their steps. "I'm sorry. I don't mean to take this out on you."

"It's okay. It's not just you; it's all of us. We're falling apart. But you have to understand that Sharon said everyone there had become walking dead. That's over a hundred creatures. And we don't have any ammo to speak of." He paused thoughtfully. "I know there were military personnel there but I don't know if we can secure any more weapons before they catch on to us."

"Then we'll use rocks and sticks if we have to. I mean to take the place back from them."

Jim laid a comforting hand on Mick's shoulder. "Then that's what we will do."

CHAPTER 64

For the last ten miles, the buses had climbed steadily up the snake-like road, getting closer and closer to the entrance of the semi-secret installation hidden deep within the mountain. There had been no sign of civilization or flesh-eating corpses.

Mick led the way but he was beginning to think he had taken a wrong turn somewhere, despite Sharon's assurance that he hadn't. When the massive grounds came into view, it looked exactly like the picture Izzy had so meticulously drawn. To their surprise, there were no creatures milling about.

Mick brought the bus to a stop near the main entrance gate and Jim pulled up beside him. They sat, unmoving, for several moments. No one attempted to leave the buses. Wary of what they might find, they were not anxious for another fight. Until last autumn they had been regular people, living regular lives. For all they knew, they might be the last survivors of a dying species. They were frightened and tired and running low on hope.

Sharon stared out of the window in disbelief. Of all places, they had come here, the last place she wanted to be. She shuddered at the thought of what lay beneath the mountain.

Jim was the first to get out and look over the grounds. He saw no creatures. Evidently they were quite content to stay underground in their less-than-perfect condition, happy to wander to and fro.

Jim held his AK-47 with the rifle butt resting on his hip, wary of the plan. Mick walked up beside him.

"So far, so good."

"So far."

"What now?"

Jim stared at the buildings before them. There were so many places for the dead to be concealed. Everything had to be searched and it had to be done quickly, before dark.

"We'll start up top. Hell, I don't even know how to get below. We'll need Sharon for that." He turned to face Mick. "I need two more people."

Mick aggressively pulled the bolt back on his rifle to show his readiness. "We'll get Matt to go with us."

"Not you, Mick. If something happens—"

"That's bullshit, Jim. You know as well as I do that if we don't make it here, we're done for. I'm going."

Mick was right. There *was* nowhere else. If they weren't successful here, they were at the end of the line.

"All right. We'll take Matt with us," Jim said. "Everyone else stays in the buses until we're finished. We take it one step at a time. Clear it out, room by room. If we die, three more have to take our place and finish it up. If we run out of ammo, well, I guess we'd better start looking for those rocks you were talking about."

Almost two hours passed before the three men returned to the buses after checking out all of the buildings above ground. Their mood was lighter; they had not fired a shot.

As soon as he reached the bus, Mick sidestepped down the isle through the crowd until he got to Felicia in the back. Dr. Brine still watched over her. The deep frown on his face effectively dampened Mick's spirits.

Felicia lay on the floor in front of the emergency exit, covered with a gray prison blanket, it was all that kept her warm in the thirty-degree temperature. Izzy slept on the seat in front of Felicia.

"How is she, Doc?"

"I've done all I can, Mick. It's in God's hands."

Mick looked at Felicia. The drugs had not worn off yet but they would soon. Hopefully, those hands the good doctor put his trust in were not the same vindictive God who unleashed this hell on earth.

CHAPTER 65

After much coaxing, Sharon stepped out of the bus and looked at the all-too-familiar compound. In her opinion, they were jumping from the frying pan into the fire. Wasn't there a better place to go?

A slight smile suddenly graced her pleasing face as the realization dawned on her that all of her equipment was here. Everything she needed to continue her work was in that God-forsaken hole in the ground. Maybe this was a good thing after all.

"I crawled through the air shafts," she told Mick, pointing to the far end of the complex. "I'll show you, if you're ready."

Mick pocketed his ammunition. It wasn't much but it was all they could spare; some had to be left with Jim and Matt to protect the others. Jim hadn't slept in almost twenty-four hours so it was too dangerous for him to go in this sleep-deprived state. Mick would check out the situation with Sharon and then return to get organized.

As Sharon led the way, Mick kept an eye out for any stragglers that might have wandered topside since their search. His nerves had settled a bit but he was a little nauseated. He was tired of fighting, tired of being responsible for everyone's well being. For his own sanity, something had to change for the better.

Sharon led him down an embankment to the backside of one of the office buildings. The darkened airshaft was positioned in the side of the mound behind some evergreen shrubs. Mick pulled out a flashlight he had taken from the bus. If he'd been better prepared, they'd have taken more supplies. He was thankful for what they did have.

He shined the light down the shaft and saw that it dropped a ways before leveling out. A metal ladder hung on one side.

"All right, Sharon, I'll take it from here. We only have the one light. No sense in you getting into a bad spot, too."

"I'll be fine. Look." She pointed to several tall towers with glass-covered panels at their tops. "Solar power. The emergency lights are on. Besides, you'd never find your way without me."

Sharon saw a disapproving look flash across Mick's face. Before he could argue, she said, "Don't worry. I'm not going to get out of the shaft and neither are you. This is a scouting mission, remember?"

Mick nodded and they crawled inside. There were no emergency lights in the passageway, just a faint glow from the register openings filtering through. Batteries nearly spent, the flashlight barely lit the shaft enough to see.

The first register opening was fifty feet away. Their combined weight on the tin shaft floor made popping noises that echoed throughout the passage as they crouched along. Each time the noise occurred, they stopped and listened, unsure whether they had made the noise or something was ahead of them. A turn in the shaft near the first register prevented them from seeing as far as they would have liked.

The flashlight dimmed even more, making their endeavor more frightening by the second. Every step produced another pop under their feet. Sharon turned to look in the direction from which they had come. She thought she heard a moan but it was too dark to see. Her body stiffened with fear and her fingernails dug into Mick's side, causing him to flinch and turn suddenly.

On reflex, he shined the light in that direction. The corridor was empty and the flashlight dimmed again. Mick slapped the flashlight against his palm several times until it got brighter.

"What's wrong?" Mick asked.

Sharon stared down the shaft. "Nothing," she fibbed. "I stumbled."

"Well, be careful. You're making me jumpy."

When they came to the first register, the unmistakable odor of rot offended their senses. Sharon held her hand over her nose and mouth as Mick looked through and saw a large hall.

"Can you tell where we're at by that hall?"

"Yes. It's the hall leading from the War Room to the main street."

"Street?"

"You haven't seen anything yet, Mick. This place is huge. If we follow this shaft another thirty yards or so, it will lead to an opening that comes out in my lab."

"I don't want to come out in the lab. I want to see what's going on down there. Is there another air return vent that will let me see into that street you're talking about?"

"Yes. Around the corner, about fifty feet."

The flashlight faded; they were in almost total darkness. Mick switched it off and stuck it in his pocket. They turned the corner and saw light from the next opening. Just a few more feet and Mick could get a good look at what stood in their way.

Time warped. Minutes passed like hours. Finally they arrived at the vent above the main street of the underground city. Mick pressed his face against the grates. His lips moved but no words were audible.

Sharon moved closer. From over his shoulder she saw the street below. "They're dead!" she whispered. "They're all dead!"

CHAPTER 66

The floor below was littered with unmoving bodies. Even more confusing, it appeared the massively decayed bodies had been dead for some time.

Mick turned his face from the vent and the rancid smell. "Are you sure they were all zombies?"

"I'm positive, Mick. I saw them with my own eyes, up close and personal. I don't understand it."

"If they're all dead," Mick grinned, "we might be able to go down there." A glimmer of hope twinkled in his eyes. "We might not have to fight it out with them again."

Mick felt as though a great weight had been lifted from him. He didn't know how much more he could stand, how much longer he could cope. He didn't care how or why they were dead. They were dead and that was enough for him.

In no time at all they reached the vent leading into the lab. Upon reaching the opening, they were confronted with a new puzzle; the creature Sharon had studied months ago was still strapped to the table. It was still alive.

They lowered themselves through the hole and down to the floor.

Sharon eyed the creature writhing on the table. "I don't get it. Why have all of the others died while this one continues to live?"

The zombie labored against his restraints, growling like a dog. His rotting teeth snapped and clicked and Sharon took a step backward. "He was sure in a better mood when I left."

Mick looked at the zombie. "He's probably pretty hungry."

"Hunger has nothing to do with it. He doesn't know me anymore. He's just doing what he has to do, instinctively."

Mick covered his nose with one side of his open jacket. "Stinks like a son of a bitch in here."

Sharon grabbed two facemasks from a box on a table and gave one to Mick. "Put it on. It'll help filter out some of the stench. If we're going out there, we'll be glad to have them on."

Mick listened for any sign of movement from the other side of the door. When he was satisfied that he had heard nothing, he pulled back the last bolt locking the door and opened it a crack.

To his relief, the creatures out there were dead. They looked almost natural lying on the floor, as natural as any dead person might look after five months in the grave.

He counted eleven in the hall leading out to the street. His nose wrinkled as the putrid odor penetrated his mask. Turning again to the creature on the table, he withdrew his gun and targeted its head.

Sharon grabbed his arm. "No. I need him for research."

Mick dropped his aim and looked at the creature. There was still the question of the moment; why was it still alive?

They searched the compound. All zombies except the one in the lab had ceased to function. All in all, they counted one hundred and twenty-six rotting bodies, including the three he had almost tripped over when entering the power station.

Mick scanned the panel of controls. The power could be turned on from right here, he thought. The place was very impressive. A dam at one end of the lake supplied power. As the water fell over a sixty-foot cliff, it turned the turbines that ran the generators. The main breaker had simply kicked off, causing everything to shut down.

He pushed the handle up and the motors roared back to life. Seconds later, the lights came on and there was a slight breeze as the air began to circulate. He smiled slightly and leaned his head back in relief.

A quick look around and it would be time to get everyone inside, especially Felicia.

CHAPTER 67

Mick rested his head on the bed next to Felicia. Her breathing was better now but she had not been awake since leaving the prison.

Jim gathered a small group of able-bodied men to help with the task of disposing the corpses that littered the compound before the survivors could properly settle in.

The power outage had rendered the frozen food in the freezers useless but there were plenty of canned and dry goods. There was fresh water and separate quarters, game rooms and a small, fully equipped hospital. It was the Hilton compared to the prison.

Once again their fate was in their own hands.

Mick dozed off and missed Felicia's hand move under the covers. He jerked awake. How long had he been asleep? He looked at Felicia. Her face was expressionless, her eyes still closed. Was she breathing? A lump formed in his throat. "Please God, not her."

She moved again. He watched her blanket. It didn't rise and fall the way it should on a breathing person.

Mick stood. His heart hammered in his chest and his mind fogged.

Then Felicia's eyes fluttered open.

Mick released the breath he'd been holding in a rush of joy. Her eyes were not open with the vacuous stare of the dead. Hers were filled with life and soul.

Felicia smiled weakly and reached out a slender hand. He took it tenderly between his own and kissed it.

"Thank you, God!" Mick's voice cracked with emotion. "I prayed so hard for you to be all right, Felicia, for you to come back to me." He brushed a tear away. "I couldn't have gone on without you."

Felicia moved and winced at the pain in her chest. "Where are we?"

"We're safe."

"Where's Izzy?" She tried to sit upright.

"She's safe, too. She's here, in the next room. It's gonna be fine. You need rest."

Felicia laid her head back on the pillow. "I'm hungry."

CHAPTER 68

There were no more corpses in the bunker below. It began to smell better now that they were gone.

Jim stood close to Amanda and watched the dump truck heavy with corpses round the turn and disappear.

Amanda leaned her head on Jim's shoulder. It was the first time she could remember hearing birds sing since leaving her house that fateful day so many months before. It seemed like another lifetime ago; a life someone else had lived, not her. She felt as though she were observing her life from the outside, disconnected from it.

Jim slipped an arm around Amanda's waist and inhaled the first sweet breath of an early spring like day; thankful they had been directed to this place, this haven, and this refuge.

He wondered if the hand of God had orchestrated their deliverance. It was possible, but if that were the case, then the calamity that had befallen mankind may indeed have been Armageddon. Jim was not a particularly religious man. He preferred to think it was man's own flaws and shortcomings that had brought about his demise.

Sharon walked through the heavy steel doors to the lawn outside. This time there was no Gilbert Brownlow to deal with. His carcass had been loaded onto the truck with the others, lost and forgotten. No grave marker would dignify his life with kind words. No circle of friends would weep. His fate was appropriate; he had become fertilizer for the ground and food for buzzards.

Her research could continue now. The possibility loomed that she would never figure out what had happened but it was all she had left to do. At least she had a new starting point.

Unlike the creature strapped to her examination table, the bodies that had revived inside of the complex never saw the light of day after their resurrection. They stopped functioning shortly thereafter and normal decomposition began to take its toll. If there were a connection there, she would find it.

In any case, they were finally safe from the dreadful ordeal that had overtaken the world. That was something to be happy about. They were safe, for the time being.

Matt stopped the orange dump truck with a government sticker on the door at the edge of an overlook. He walked to the edge of the cliff to view the scenery of the valley below. Griz got out and relieved his bladder near a telephone pole.

Several small towns were scattered across the valley floor. Lilliputian in size from this viewpoint, Matt felt like a giant who could squash them with little effort. He held out his hand, positioning it so that an entire town fit between his thumb and index finger then squeezed them together. Looking down from so high a place, everything appeared insignificant, trivial. He imagined that if he were far enough away from the world, the entire human race would appear much the same way. Not much to look at, no real loss.

An historical marker had been placed close to the edge identifying the view.

CHESTER'S POINT
A scenic view of the Shenandoah Valley
God's Country

Matt turned away from the magnificent view and went to the back of the truck. He removed the pins that held the gate closed. He thought it a shame to defile the beauty of this place with his loathsome cargo but who would care now? Once done, he wouldn't be returning here.

"Come on, Griz. Let's take out the trash and go home."

CHAPTER 69

More than two months had passed since the ragtag group claimed the mountain installation as their new asylum. Most of them had settled in quite nicely into quarters far superior to those at the prison. Others found the transition more difficult. Some despaired over the loss of loved ones in their escape from the prison.

April rain turned the pallid landscape a bright green and helped lift everyone's spirits. The horror that had forced them into their new hideaway was noticeably absent. They had not seen a single ghastly monster.

No one believed that the phenomenon was over, or that it was safe to venture out from their secret habitat. They thought the creatures simply had not found their way to them yet. No one was willing to investigate for fear of leading them back to their safe haven.

Felicia was up and around after two weeks of bed rest. She and Mick took up residence together and informally adopted Izzy, who was still unable to utter a word. That didn't stop her from expressing herself with lovely drawings that covered the walls in their underground three-room apartment.

Jim found the War Room the most interesting because of the hi-tech communication equipment and television monitoring systems. It took some doing but he managed to get a few of the satellite feeds working.

One communications console in particular scanned thousands of radio bands at once.

Each day he and a few others listened to the pink noise that continually buzzed from the speakers, hoping to receive a signal from other survivors, hoping they were not alone in the world. They listened in shifts and they waited.

There were no safety worries in this underground fortress. Heavy steel doors secured each entrance into the subterranean passages leading to the seven-level complex. Shortly after their arrival, Jim had seen to it that every airshaft was reinforced and equipped with video cameras. There wasn't an inch of ground that couldn't be monitored at all times. They had enough supplies to last for years.

Console lights blinked as the video transmission bounced from one satellite to another. Jim cracked his knuckles and rubbed his weary eyes, looking at the clock for the fifth time in as many minutes. Another watch had come to pass without so much as a peep from anyone-anywhere.

He was too tired to care any longer. Tomorrow was another day. Maybe a signal would come in then. One more glance at the clock. It was one-thirty in the morning. He gathered his notes and schematics and stuffed them into a battered manila envelope. He left the War Room, closing the door behind him.

The numbers on the War Room clock changed from 1:39 to 1:40. The radio receivers were still on and the static echoed in the empty room.

"This is Tangier Island, off the coast of Virginia. Does anyone read? This is Tangier Island off the coast of Virginia. Does anyone read me? If anyone can hear me, please answer."

EPILOGUE

The evil finally ended and mankind was again able to come out of hiding to take his place among the living world. Sometimes I think back on it and wonder why. Why in all His wisdom, God didn't find some other way to rid the world of its foul cargo, the infestation of corruption and lawlessness. Did it seem to Him the proper and holy thing to do? Are we that different in mind and spirit that we can't see the righteousness of His actions? Who's to say that the world won't fall into the same condition again, and if it does, will such a calamity be brought upon it again?

According to the Bible, thirty-five hundred years ago a great deluge swept away Godless people to their watery graves. Out of the entire populated world, only seven survived. Think of it; Seven! Except for those seven, were they all corrupt?

At least we fared better this time around. Pockets of survivors were found in every corner of the earth. Many more than we had expected to find. They all inhabit the same regions as they did before the plague but even now new nations arise.

What will this New World be like? Will we finally learn to live together in peace? Or will we fall prey to the same desires that have caused our downfall in the past?

Some prefer to believe that God had nothing to do with it. Some prefer to believe that it was our own selfish deeds that destroyed us. I for one am not sure what to believe but I'm anxious to see if an answer is revealed.

It ended as abruptly and mysteriously as it began, without warning or reason. Some still labor to find a clear answer. I'm quite content to forget it and live my life with love and kindness, compassion and caring, the way I was taught by the people who raised me. They weren't my real parents but they took me in and made me their own and they loved me as though I was their own.

My new mother didn't know my name and I was in no condition to tell her. She named me Isabelle, after her grandmother. After all the thought I have given it, I still can't remember my given name. It doesn't matter. For all intents and purposes, I am Isabelle and always will be.

Maybe there is hope after all. Something is different now, something I can't put my finger on. People have changed. I can see it in their eyes. It's nothing blatantly noticeable. Most people probably haven't even noticed but I have. It's there.

I hope that what we went through never happens again. Until then, I'm going to live. My garden needs tending and it's a beautiful day.

God, it's great to be alive!

THE END